＊ ＊ ＊ ● ＊ ＊ ＊

PRAISE FOR DONNA GRANT'S
BESTSELLING ROMANCE NOVELS

"Grant's ability to quickly convey complicated
backstory makes this jam-packed love story
accessible even to new or periodic readers."
—*Publishers' Weekly*

"Donna Grant has given the paranormal genre
a burst of fresh air..." —*San Francisco Book Review*

"The premise is dramatic and heartbreaking; the characters
are colorful and engaging; the romance is spirited
and seductive." —*The Reading Cafe*

"The central romance, fueled by a hostage drama, plays
out in glorious detail against a backdrop of multiple ongoing
issues in the "Dark Kings" books. This seemingly penultimate
installment creates a nice segue to a climactic end."
—*Library Journal*

"...intense romance amid the growing war
between the Dragons and the Dark Fae is
scorching hot." —*Booklist*

＊ ＊ ＊ ● ＊ ＊ ＊

OTHER BOOKS BY DONNA GRANT

CONTEMPORARY PARANORMAL

DRAGON KINGS® SERIES

Dragon Revealed ~ Dragon Mine ~ Dragon Unbound

Dragon Eternal ~ Dragon Lover ~ Dragon Arisen

REAPER SERIES

Dark Alpha's Claim ~ Dark Alpha's Embrace

Dark Alpha's Demand ~ Books 1-3: Tall Dark Deadly Alpha

Dark Alpha's Lover ~ Dark Alpha's Night

Dark Alpha's Hunger ~ Dark Alpha's Awakening

Dark Alpha's Redemption ~ Dark Alpha's Temptation

Dark Alpha's Caress ~ Dark Alpha's Obsession

Dark Alpha's Need ~ Dark Alpha's Silent Night

Dark Alpha's Passion ~ Dark Alpha's Command

Dark Alpha's Fury

SKYE DRUIDS SERIES

Iron Ember ~ Shoulder the Skye ~ Heart of Glass

DARK KINGS SERIES

Dark Heat ~ Darkest Flame ~ Fire Rising ~ Burning Desire

Hot Blooded ~ Night's Blaze ~ Soul Scorched ~ Dragon King

Passion Ignites ~ Smoldering Hunger ~ Smoke and Fire

Dragon Fever ~ Firestorm ~ Blaze ~ Dragon Burn

Constantine: A History, Parts 1-3 ~ Heat ~ Torched

Dragon Night ~ Dragonfire ~ Dragon Claimed

Ignite ~ Fever ~ Dragon Lost ~ Flame ~ Inferno

A Dragon's Tale (Whisky and Wishes: *A Holiday Novella*,

Heart of Gold: *A Valentine's Novella*, & Of Fire and Flame)

My Fiery Valentine ~ The Dragon King Coloring Book

Dragon King Special Edition Character Coloring Book: Rhi

DARK WARRIORS SERIES

Midnight's Master ~ Midnight's Lover ~ Midnight's Seduction

Midnight's Warrior ~ Midnight's Kiss ~ Midnight's Captive

Midnight's Temptation ~ Midnight's Promise

Midnight's Surrender ~ A Warrior for Christmas

CHIASSON SERIES

Wild Fever ~ Wild Dream ~ Wild Need

Wild Flame ~ Wild Rapture

LARUE SERIES

Moon Kissed ~ Moon Thrall ~ Moon Struck ~ Moon Bound

WICKED TREASURES

Seized by Passion ~ Enticed by Ecstasy ~ Captured by Desire

Books 1-3: Wicked Treasures Box Set

HISTORICAL PARANORMAL

THE KINDRED SERIES

Everkin ~ Eversong ~ Everwylde ~ Everbound

Evernight ~ Everspell

KINDRED: THE FATED SERIES

Rage ~ Ruin ~ Reign

DARK SWORD SERIES

Dangerous Highlander ~ Forbidden Highlander

Wicked Highlander ~ Untamed Highlander

Shadow Highlander ~ Darkest Highlander

ROGUES OF SCOTLAND SERIES

The Craving ~ The Hunger ~ The Tempted ~ The Seduced

Books 1-4: Rogues of Scotland Box Set

THE SHIELDS SERIES

A Dark Guardian ~ A Kind of Magic ~ A Dark Seduction

A Forbidden Temptation ~ A Warrior's Heart

Mystic Trinity (a series connecting novel)

DRUIDS GLEN SERIES

Highland Mist ~ Highland Nights ~ Highland Dawn

Highland Fires ~ Highland Magic

Mystic Trinity (a series connecting novel)

SISTERS OF MAGIC TRILOGY

Shadow Magic ~ Echoes of Magic ~ Dangerous Magic

Books 1-3: Sisters of Magic Box Set

THE ROYAL CHRONICLES NOVELLA SERIES

Prince of Desire ~ Prince of Seduction

Prince of Love ~ Prince of Passion

Books 1-4: The Royal Chronicles Box Set

Mystic Trinity (a series connecting novel)

DARK BEGINNINGS: A FIRST IN SERIES BOXSET

Chiasson Series, Book 1: Wild Fever

LaRue Series, Book 1: Moon Kissed

The Royal Chronicles Series, Book 1: Prince of Desire

MILITARY ROMANCE / ROMANTIC SUSPENSE

SONS OF TEXAS SERIES

The Hero ~ The Protector ~ The Legend

The Defender ~ The Guardian

COWBOY / CONTEMPORARY

HEART OF TEXAS SERIES

The Christmas Cowboy Hero ~ Cowboy, Cross My Heart

My Favorite Cowboy ~ A Cowboy Like You

Looking for a Cowboy ~ A Cowboy Kind of Love

STAND ALONE BOOKS

That Cowboy of Mine

Home for a Cowboy Christmas

Mutual Desire

Forever Mine

Savage Moon

Check out Donna Grant's Online Store at

www.DonnaGrant.com/shop for autographed books,

character themed goodies, and more!

This is a work of fiction. All of the characters, organizations, and events portrayed in this novel are either products of the author's imagination or are used fictitiously.

www.DonnaGrant.com
www.MotherofDragonsBooks.com

SISTERS OF MAGIC

SHADOW MAGIC

DONNA GRANT

NEW YORK TIMES BESTSELLING AUTHOR

Chapter One

Hawthorne Castle
Central England, 1127

*J*ealousy, if left unbridled, could turn a good soul as black as Satan.

And so it was the first time Serena of Hawthorne saw Lord Drogan of Wolfglynn with the beautiful woman on his arm. The jealousy was instant and sharper than any needle that could pierce her skin. Serena shouldn't have noticed.

She was a *bana-bhuidseach*, a witch, cursed and forever alone. Because of what she was, men rarely caught her attention. Except for Drogan.

Her sure-footed gait faltered and then stopped as the crowd in the great hall parted to allow her a view of Drogan for a heartbeat. In that moment, his image became etched in her memory for all time.

People teemed around her, but her gaze locked on Lord Drogan of Wolfglynn. What she saw made her break into a sweat, and her soul stirred for the first time.

Dark, auburn hair, with a slight curl at the ends, fell thick and straight to his broad shoulders. He had a high forehead with gently arching brows over eyes of a rich golden brown. His nose was straight and aristocratic, his mouth wide and full.

He wore a brown leather jerkin over a deep green tunic that did nothing to conceal the rippled muscles in his arms and chest. Her gaze moved lower to his thick legs in tight leather. Boots, worn but well cared for, encased his feet and calves.

Serena caught a glimpse of something shiny at the top of his left boot, suggesting a hidden dirk. The broadsword and dagger strapped to his waist let all know he was a warrior.

She lifted her gaze to find Drogan staring at her. For the briefest of moments, Serena found herself starting toward him. Then someone bumped into her. It was all she needed to break away. She turned her back on Drogan, and on the longing in her heart.

Duty called.

Drogan stood frozen as he scanned the throng for another glimpse of the elusive beauty who had captured his attention. The longer he looked and didn't see her, the more irritated he became.

There had been something about her that was...different from any woman he had been around before, and he had been around plenty.

"Drogan, who are you looking for?" Penelope asked in her usual high-pitched voice.

He almost groaned, but spotted several young ladies looking his way. "No one. I think those women are trying to gain your attention," he said and hurried away.

Penelope was his cousin and, although she had a comely face, her constant whining and complaining would try the patience of a saint. And he was far from being a saint. He hadn't wanted to bring her, but had seen no way out of it.

A loud commotion stirred the massive crowd. People parted as Gerard and his wife, Maris, entered the great hall. Drogan chuckled to see his friend with such a silly grin on his face. But then, Gerard had much to be pleased about. He had found the woman of his heart and now had a beautiful baby daughter.

Aye, Gerard had much to be happy about.

Drogan cast aside his doubts and fears as his friend walked toward him. He clasped Gerard's arm as they greeted each other. It was nice to know Gerard hadn't let his warrior body go to mush, which meant he still trained as hard as he used to.

"I didn't know if you would come," Gerard said as he smoothed his dark hair from his face.

A laugh escaped Drogan. "I would never miss this, old friend. You should have known that."

"Aye," Gerard said with a huge smile. "But as lord of my own domain, I know how burdensome it is to get away, even for a day. How long can you stay?"

"As long as needed."

Gerard seemed to relax. "Good. Aye, very good."

Something in his tone unsettled Drogan as his smile slipped. "Is something amiss?"

"Not at all," Gerard assured him. "It is just that now that we have little Jocelyn, I worry over much. I fear I won't be able to protect her."

Drogan released a breath he hadn't known he'd been holding. His ever-present companion, the darkness that threatened to drown him in its depths, stirred and roared to life. It took every ounce of control for Drogan to ignore it. "I'm sure all fathers feel the way you do."

"It is my greatest wish that you learn very soon."

He laughed with Gerard, but inside Drogan knew it would never be. Too many things had been done, too many memories haunted him, especially one...

"Dark are your thoughts."

The soft, melodic voice shook him to his core. He turned his head to see the elusive beauty glide past him. He could have sworn she had spoken, yet she hadn't looked at him.

Drogan followed her with his gaze. "Who is that?"

"Who?" Gerard asked.

Before Drogan could explain, Maris beckoned them. He trailed Gerard to his wife and infant daughter, though his gaze lingered on the spot where the lady had been a moment ago.

"Drogan, I'm so glad you came," Maris said as she took his hand in greeting.

He looked to his friend's wife with a welcoming smile. Maris wasn't a great beauty, but her light brown hair, gray eyes, and heart-shaped face had turned Gerard's head quick enough.

"I wouldn't have missed it for the king."

Maris gave him a bright smile and led him to the cradle. "This is stunning. You have much talent in those hands of yours, Drogan of Wolfglynn. Too bad they are used for wielding a sword."

"Don't chastise me, my lady. A man must do what he can to survive these times."

Her bright eyes clouded. "Don't remind me."

Drogan hated that he had brought up something so dreadful. He hadn't meant to. Was he becoming as uncouth as his mother always said he would? Had being a knight for the crown done that to him?

A bell rang loud and clear in the great hall. It took only one toll for the masses to quiet. While he stood beside Maris, Drogan took the time to scan the crowd for the woman. She was here. He knew it.

"What lady has you looking for her? Penelope?" Maris

asked.

"Heavens, no," Drogan said. "I left her with a pack of other young women where I hope she stays."

"It was kind of you to bring her."

Drogan shrugged. "I know how it is to be cooped up somewhere you have no wish to be."

"How long until her father returns for her?"

"I'm not sure that he will."

"Oh."

Drogan heard the sadness in Maris' voice. She would know how Penelope felt since the same thing happened to her.

He listened as Gerard talked of the loyalty of his people and the blessings God had given him in Maris and Jocelyn. There was no mention of the hell they had walked through or the sins that stained their souls, nor would there be. Drogan doubted even Maris knew everything. Some things were better left secret for the safety of all involved.

"And we are fortunate enough," Gerard said, "to have someone living within our borders who will add her blessing to my daughter."

Drogan glanced at Gerard, unsure what he meant. He knew Gerard was religious, but shouldn't a priest perform the blessing instead of a nun?

Drogan heard the gasps of awe and turned to find none other than the mysterious beauty coming toward him. Her steps were unhurried and graceful, as if she floated on air.

There was an ethereal glow about her that made him want to reach out and touch her to see if she was real.

The first thing he noticed was her hair. Her head was unadorned, and hair as black as midnight hung to her waist in soft waves. But when she met his gaze and he saw the dark blue of her eyes, he was entranced.

Large, expressive eyes dominated her face. High cheekbones and plump pink lips pulled up in a half-smile, which suggested she knew something others did not, and only added to her delicate loveliness.

He could do little more than stare as she stepped on the dais and walked past him to look into the cradle. His feet moved of their own accord and took him closer to her.

"It is a beautiful cradle, my lord," she said to Gerard.

He smiled. "It was a gift from Lord Drogan of Wolfglynn." He faced Drogan. "Drogan, this is Lady Serena."

Her attention shifted to Drogan. "Please tell your woodworker that he crafted an excellent piece, my lord."

"You already have."

Her eyes widened a fraction. "You did this?"

He nodded once.

She moved back to the cradle and ran her hands over the intricately carved wood. "It is magnificent, my lord. You have a special gift."

He gave her a smile, but wasn't able to say more as she turned to stand beside Maris. Drogan inhaled and caught a whiff of lilac. Instinctively, he knew it came from Serena.

7

Serena. The name suited her. It was just as commanding, elegant, and beautiful as she was.

"So, she's caught your fancy," Gerard whispered as he moved closer.

Drogan shrugged.

"She isn't like other women." The warning in Gerard's words wasn't hard to miss.

"How so?"

"That will be for her to share."

Drogan nodded and shifted his gaze to Serena. She stood next to Maris as they each looked at the sleeping infant. The people in the great hall shuffled about and whispered as they waited.

Serena raised her hands and tilted her head back as she closed her eyes. Drogan saw her lips moving, but couldn't make out the words no matter how hard he strained. Yet, upon looking at Gerard and Maris, they seemed content in what Serena said over the infant.

It was over as quickly as it began. Serena stepped away from the cradle, and the villagers of Hawthorne began to come forward to offer their gifts to the new daughter of their lord.

When Drogan next looked up, Serena had once again disappeared. He began to walk away when Maris took his arm and led him to a chair beside Gerard's. She pushed him into the chair before smiling at her husband as he accepted the gifts.

"You are wasting your time with Serena," Maris said.

Drogan fought the urge to roll his eyes. "What makes you think I'm even interested?"

"You mean besides the fact you have barely taken your eyes off her?" Maris sighed and sat in Gerard's chair. "I want you to be happy, Drogan. Find a wife and make a family at Wolfglynn, but you will find none of those things with Serena."

"I don't want those things," he said. "They are for some, but not me. You should know that."

"Gerard overcame his nightmares, at least enough to accept me in his life. There is no reason you cannot do the same."

Drogan looked into her gray eyes. "Gerard is lucky to have you."

She laughed and cocked her head to the side. "Ah, but you are trying to change the subject." Her smile vanished. "I warn you we will not see Serena hurt. She is special to us, to Hawthorne."

"What is she?" he had to ask.

A slow smile spread across Maris' face. "Something extraordinary."

"So I am not good enough for her," he teased.

"Not so. If I didn't know her like I do, I would try very hard to match the two of you together."

Drogan laughed. "I'm glad for your happiness, Maris, but, as I said, it isn't for everyone." He stood then. "Now, I'm going to find Penelope and make sure she isn't causing a spectacle."

Chapter Two

*S*erena leaned her head back and let the wind enfold her. The chill of the breeze made her wish she had thought to bring her cloak, but she had needed a quick escape from the great hall, from Drogan and his searching brown eyes. She ventured onto the battlements where she knew she could be alone. She loved looking out over Hawthorne and its people from the lofty perch.

She lifted her gaze and stared at the inky sky as the stars twinkled overhead. It was a full moon, and its bright light illuminated everything in its soft glow.

But she had no need of a light to know when Drogan drew near. She sensed him. She lowered her head to look at the land that was Gerard's by birthright, but hers in God's eyes.

"Hello, Lord Drogan," she said without turning around.

He stepped beside her and placed his hands on the stone wall. "How did you know it was me?"

"You have a very unique scent. The sandalwood is very strong, but I also smell traces of pine and a hint of cinnamon." She kept her eyes straight ahead, afraid to look at him.

Afraid of what she might see in his beautiful eyes. But more afraid of what she might do just to have him touch her.

"Do I unsettle you?" he asked quietly. "I have a feeling you don't care for me."

His statement surprised her so much, she swiveled her head to him. She stared at his profile for a moment. "It is the truth. You do unsettle me, but not for the reason you think. You are a good man, my lord."

"You say that as if you know it to be true."

"Because I do know it to be true."

His golden-brown eyes shifted to her. "How do you know that? Because Gerard and Maris said so?"

"Actually, nay. I know it because I feel it." She reached up and placed her hand over his heart. "Here."

As soon as she touched him she knew she'd done the wrong thing. Something strong, something primal moved between them. It was heat, it was passion. And it doomed her.

"What are you?" he whispered, eyes narrowed on her in puzzlement.

Serena quickly dropped her arm and fisted her hand to keep the warmth of him against her as long as possible. "I am a woman."

He snorted. "You are much more than that," he said and turned to look at the land again.

Serena sighed and leaned against the battlement wall. She didn't move away from Drogan, although she should have. Every fiber of her being screamed to run as far away from Drogan as she could. She'd always listened to her conscience. Why would she ignore it now?

But she knew the answer. It was the desire, the need she felt inside Drogan. The longer she stood beside him, the more she sealed her fate.

"I am a *bana-bhuidseach*."

"What is that?" he asked as his gaze swiveled to her.

"It is Gaelic for witch."

For several moments, he stared at her. She returned his look, watching him as he studied her.

"A witch?" he repeated softly.

"Aye. Gerard and Maris, along with the people of Hawthorne, protect me."

"And why would you tell me? I could spread word of what you are," he said, his posture now tense.

For a brief second, she closed her eyes. "You won't do that, Lord Drogan. You care for Gerard and Maris too much to ever bring any type of sadness to their door, and you can tell how much they care for me."

"And that I don't understand," he said, his voice rising on the wind. He stepped away and folded his arms over his chest. When he spoke again, he had regained control. His deep brown eyes were narrowed, suspicious. "I've known Gerard for many years, and never once has he spoken of you. We've shared horrors you cannot imagine. Why would he keep this from me?"

"You are blaming him for the wrong thing. You act as though you are angry because he never told you, when in fact you are angry because you cannot imagine he would believe in something like me."

She didn't have long to wait for his reaction.

His arms dropped to his side as he stepped toward her, his voice low and deadly. "How did you know that? How did you know what I was thinking?"

She inhaled deeply. "I am a witch, my lord. Not in the sense you would think. I am not evil."

"Tell me more then." He spoke softly, but she knew he was close to the edge of reason.

She began this conversation, though for the life of her she didn't know why. She trusted few with the truth of what she was. But, regardless, she would tell Drogan everything. "I come from a line of women blessed with certain abilities."

"Like what?" He leaned his elbow on the wall as he listened.

"I feel things deeper than you. For instance, the wind. Do you feel it?"

"Aye. It is barely touching my skin."

"Is it cold?"

"It is cool enough in this summer heat. Why?"

"To me, it feels like the icy fingers of winter. The heat from the sun may make you sweat, but it can, and sometimes does, blister my skin."

"Does everything affect you thus?"

"Aye."

He nodded as he thought over her words. "Any other abilities?"

"A few," she answered. She knew he had learned enough this night. There was no need to go into the many other things she could do.

Silence filled the air, and she was content with it. Though she liked to be alone on the battlements, she didn't mind him being there. And that frightened her as nothing else could.

"A line of women, you say," he said.

"For many generations it has been so, but we are dying out. There are just a handful of us left in this land."

"Your abilities do not pass onto your children?" he asked, his brow furrowed.

"It only passes onto the females, but that isn't the reason we're dying out."

"What is it then?"

"We were cursed. By one of our own."

Drogan stood in shocked silence as Serena's words penetrated his brain. Cursed? By one of her own? But why? He was about to ask when a guard called out to Serena from the tower entrance.

"Lady Serena, Lord Gerard and Lady Maris wish you to seek them in the solar."

There were so many questions he wanted to ask Serena, but they would have to wait. He should have stayed on the battlements since what Gerard wanted with Serena was none of his concern, but instead, he followed her to the solar with every intention of walking away once she was with Gerard.

"Good evening," Serena bid Drogan as she walked through the door Gerard held open for her.

"Drogan," Gerard said. "Come in."

Curiosity weighed heavily on Drogan. He nodded and walked into the spacious solar to find Maris beside the cradle. He scanned the chamber and found Serena standing under a window, her dark blue gown flooded with moonlight and her pale skin glowing.

Despite what he had heard, he still wanted to know her. He wasn't the type of man to believe in anything she had spoken of, but there was no doubt there was something different about her. And he had known Gerard too long not to believe he also trusted Serena.

"Have you reconsidered?" Gerard asked Serena.

Serena shook her head, her black mane swaying with her. "I have not."

Maris stepped toward her. "I know you gave us your reasons, but it would make me feel so much better. Please, Serena, I beg of you."

Drogan watched as Serena dropped her chin to her chest and closed her eyes.

"We would not ask if it wasn't important," Gerard said.

Drogan didn't move from his spot beside the door. Whatever was going on, he knew it hurt Serena. He watched as she lifted her blue eyes to him, and he saw the brief flash of pain before resignation filled them.

She walked to the cradle, and then turned to address Gerard and Maris. "Do not ever ask this of me again."

After both Gerard and Maris nodded, Serena reached into the cradle and touched Jocelyn's tiny arm. Drogan heard a soft chant, the words in a language he didn't understand. For a moment nothing happened, and then Serena sucked in her breath as her face contorted with pain. Drogan saw her begin to fall and caught her a moment before she hit the stone floor.

He sat there with the most alluring woman he had ever encountered in his arms while his best friend and wife stood over them.

"What happened?" he asked Gerard, not bothering to disguise the anger in his voice. "I've never known you to intentionally harm a woman. She's as cold as ice."

"Give her a moment," was all Gerard said.

The longer Drogan sat there, the more enraged he became. How could Gerard have put Serena through that kind of pain, and then not care that she had passed out? Maybe Gerard wasn't the man Drogan thought he knew.

All thoughts of Gerard faded as Serena stirred in his arms. Her warm breath fanned his neck and she moved her head, her eyes fluttering open to look at him. He was caught, trapped. Ensnared.

And he never wanted to be let go.

"Are you all right?" he asked.

"I will be in a moment." She looked around, her lips pressed into a thin line, and her brow furrowed in confusion. "What am I doing in your arms?"

"I caught you."

A small smile pulled at her lips. "No one else would have dared. Thank you."

He returned her smile, not sure why someone wouldn't have helped her.

"Serena," Gerard started, but Drogan held up his hand.

"Give her a moment." Drogan repeated Gerard's words with acid inflection. "Can't you see she's weak?"

Gerard's eyes flashed with surprise before he nodded.

Drogan helped her into a chair. Once he was sure she was all right, he faced his friend. "Now you may proceed."

Gerard didn't waste any time. "What did you see?"

"Please understand that I only see glimpses." Serena folded her hands in her lap and looked at the floor. "She's going to live a very long life with many children and grandchildren."

"Are you sure?"

She nodded. "Are we finished?"

"Aye," Maris said.

Drogan was at Serena's side as she rose shakily to her feet. He wrapped an arm around her to steady her and said, "I will see you to your chamber."

"It is not necessary. I do not live in the castle."

"Then I will see you to your home."

He thought she might argue with him, so he was surprised when she nodded. "All right."

Drogan waited until they had departed the castle and

reached the bailey before he spoke. "What happened in there?"

She shook her head. "Wait. Not yet."

He held his tongue as they walked down the winding path. He guided her effortlessly in the moonlight until they came to the cottage. It was dark within as she opened the door and stepped inside. The aroma of lilac, barley, and pine assaulted him.

"Stay there while I light the fire," she said and moved away from him.

In moments, a fire blazed in the hearth, and she had lit candles. He scanned the cottage to see several batches of flowers and other herbs hanging from a beam on the ceiling to be dried. Row upon row of jars lined a portion of the wall beside the hearth.

The cottage was small but welcoming. A curtain divided the main room from another chamber, which held a bed. A small table with two chairs stood between him and the hearth. Another chair sat by a window on the opposite side.

"Please sit." She indicated the table. "It is late, and you haven't eaten. Would you like me to prepare you something?"

Drogan shook his head. "Do not trouble yourself. I will eat when I return to the castle."

She walked to the fire and rubbed her hands together for warmth. She still shivered, but she looked much better than she had after she had awakened in his arms.

"I suppose you want to know what Gerard wanted of me," she said.

"Aye. I've never known him to be so adamant about something that would hurt another. It is not like him."

She sighed and faced him. "He wanted me to see Jocelyn's future."

"And can you?"

"If I look deep enough. What he doesn't understand is that I always see the same thing. Death."

Drogan sat back at her words and watched the distaste distort her beautiful face. "Every time?"

She nodded. "It is a part of everyone's life. It doesn't matter if they will die an hour or three score years from now. I always see it."

"Do you see anything else?"

"Sometimes," she admitted. "Though it is very rare."

He narrowed his eyes as he realized what she had done. "You lied to Gerard and Maris."

Serena turned away and ran her hand through her long, black hair, pushing it away from her face. "There was a reason I lied. If I had told them what I saw, I'm not sure what they would have done."

"What did you see?"

She slowly released a breath. "She will die before her fifth year."

"What?" Drogan thundered as he rushed to his feet and came to stand before her. "And you didn't think they deserved to know?"

"As I said, there was a reason."

Serena waited for him to regain his composure before she

continued. At first, she hadn't wanted to tell him what she knew, but then she realized he might be able to help her change Jocelyn's fate.

Once Drogan resumed his seat, she walked to the table and sat in the other chair. She leaned her arms on the table and whispered, "I don't know what, but Gerard has done something, or witnessed something, in his past that will claim not only Jocelyn's life, but also his and Maris'. Things can change to alter someone's fate, which is what I'm hoping for all of them."

"You saw that when you touched Jocelyn?"

She nodded. "The person who kills them is doing it to silence Gerard."

"Why kill Maris and Jocelyn?"

Serena shrugged and sat back. "I don't know. I suppose he assumes Gerard will have told Maris, and the man cannot allow that information to pass on to Jocelyn. Whoever this man is, I sense he is someone of great importance."

She gauged Drogan's reaction, and when he blew out a breath and ran his hands down his face, she was sure he knew what Gerard had done.

"I need your aid," she said. "Gerard thinks of you as a brother, someone he can rely on. You must help me convince him."

"Of what?" Drogan asked his arms outstretched to the side. "What do you want him to do? Leave Hawthorne, his birthplace and rightful home?"

"I would never ask him to leave," she said and rose to her

feet. "But what I would ask is for him to face the fact that there is something in his past that will not leave him alone until he takes care of it. It is the only way he and his family will ever be safe."

Chapter Three

*S*erena didn't let her guard down until Drogan had left her cottage. She slumped in the chair and pressed her hands to her throbbing head. A part of her would never forgive Gerard for making her look into Jocelyn's future.

The horrid images of death and of souls searching for a way into Heaven made her stomach churn viciously. She wished she knew of a way to lead those souls out of this realm to wherever they belonged, but she didn't.

She hurried to brew some herbal water to relieve the ache in her head, but there was nothing that would help the pain in her heart at knowing Gerard and his family would die unless something was done.

And Gerard was very stubborn. She had a feeling Maris knew nothing of the dangerous part of Gerard's past that was catching up to him and, if Serena was correct, she had a suspicion Drogan was also a part of it.

Before she could do anything, she needed to know what Gerard and Drogan had done. It would be easy to rectify. All she had to do was get close enough to Drogan to look into his past. She had never done such a thing before, but maybe it was time to try and see how far she could use her magic.

Somehow, some way, she had to speak to Gerard. Things had to change in order for fate to alter her course.

In truth, she hadn't lied to Gerard and Maris, for she had also seen the outcome should the evil lurking in Gerard's past be thwarted.

The kettle whistled letting Serena know the water boiled. She crushed cinnamon and mint in a cup and poured the steaming water over them. After stirring it well, she took the drink back with her to the table.

She sat and inhaled the heady aroma before taking a sip. It burned her tongue, but it was worth it to get rid of the ache in her head. She needed rest for tomorrow, because it would bring a whole new set of worries.

Drogan strode into the castle to find Gerard and Maris sitting in front of the hearth. He started toward them, but when he heard Gerard laugh, he hesitated. After another moment, Drogan shifted his course.

There had been a great feast after the gifts were presented

to Gerard and Maris, but Drogan had missed it when he walked Serena to her cottage. Now, his stomach growled with hunger as he made his way to the kitchens.

He was lucky enough to run into a servant who promised to bring him a tray. After thanking her, he walked up the stairs to his chamber. He supposed he should check on Penelope, but he had no desire to listen to her whining. He had bigger things on which to concentrate.

No sooner had he reached his chamber than the servant brought his food. He sank heavily into the chair before the hearth and reached for a piece of meat. Exhaustion reigned heavily over him after his long journey with Penelope, the excitement of seeing Gerard after so many months, and then Serena and the grave news she had imparted.

He tore a piece of bread in half as his stomach growled again. His mind went over Serena's words as he bit into the crusty bread.

There was no doubt what she meant by an evil in Gerard's past. It was the same wickedness that haunted Drogan's nightmares. What he couldn't understand was why it should come back to plague the present as well as the future. The evil deeds they had committed in the name of the king was something only four men shared, which meant if the threat didn't come from him or Gerard, it must come from one of the others.

But surely not. Each of them had something to lose if word ever leaked about what had occurred. They all knew this.

Drogan's gut twisted as he thought of anything happening to little Jocelyn. He would speak to Gerard on the morrow. Maybe between them, they could piece together who would dare to come for Gerard. Somehow, Drogan would have to omit what Serena knew, and that she had lied about Jocelyn's future.

He sighed wearily. Would there ever be a time when his life was dull and sane?

"What are you talking about?" Gerard demanded testily as they rode across Hawthorne land.

Drogan briefly squeezed his eyes closed and gripped the reins a little tighter. When he opened them, he found Gerard watching him. "I'm simply asking if anything strange has happened lately."

"Not at all. Why?"

"I worry about you and Maris."

Gerard laughed, but it sounded strained, as he rubbed his stallion's neck. "You shouldn't. You know how handy I am with a sword, my friend."

"Aye, I do. However, I also know there are things in our past that could very well come back to trouble us."

"It is dead and buried, Drogan," Gerard said, his voice low and dangerous as he stared straight ahead. "Leave it alone."

"It is never dead and buried. You need to realize that."

Gerard jerked his mount to a halt and glared at Drogan.

"Is that the reason you give for not marrying? Because of the things you've done in the past? We had no choice, or do you forget that part? It was either do it or die ourselves!"

"I know that," Drogan growled as he drew up his mount. "As for why I haven't taken a wife, it is none of your concern."

"And neither is the safety of my family any of yours." Gerard clicked his horse into a run.

Drogan rubbed his eyes with his thumb and forefinger. The last thing he wanted was to raise Gerard's ire, but it seemed that was the only thing he had accomplished.

"Shite."

He needed to talk to Serena again. Maybe she could tell him how to approach Gerard.

Serena had just finished plaiting her hair when a knock sounded on her door. A little thrill leapt inside her when she opened it to find Drogan.

"You do not look happy." She moved aside so he could enter.

"I tried to speak to Gerard."

She motioned to the chair as she took a seat. "What happened?"

"He thinks what was in the past will stay in the past. He won't listen to reason." He sat and threw his gloves on the table.

"It is going to take some time, but we might have a little in which to turn his way of thinking."

"You said five years."

"Nay, I said she would die before her fifth year. I never said they would all die together."

"God's teeth!" he bellowed as he gained his feet and paced the small room. "Are you telling me it could happen any day?"

She nodded. "It is a miracle that I saw it at all. We have time, but we must act quickly before it is too late."

He reached over and grabbed her arm. "Come," he said and pulled her out of the chair. "We are going to talk to Maris."

Serena sucked in a pained breath at the rough way he took hold of her. Pain consumed her, making her stomach roll, but she didn't pull away. She didn't need to look at her arm to know a huge bruise had already formed.

Drogan released her arm instantly with regret shining in his eyes. "Did I hurt you?"

She sat for a moment and blinked as she took control of the pain. A faint throbbing lingered, nothing like what normally gripped her. She pushed back the long sleeves of her gown to look at her arm. To her amazement, it wasn't bruised. She always bruised. Always.

Her gaze jerked to his to see him frowning.

"Serena? Did I hurt you? It wasn't my intention."

"I know," she managed to say past the knot in her throat. "I'm...I'm all right."

And that's what frightened her the most. For many

years, she had no trouble keeping her heart and body safe from the men at Hawthorne, but now would come the true test.

Drogan.

"Is no one allowed to touch you?"

"It's not that they aren't allowed. It's that I don't wish it. The slightest touch bruises my skin."

More gently than she could have imagined from his large hands, he took her arm and examined her. "How long does it take for the bruise to appear?"

"Usually immediately."

His golden-brown eyes met hers, searching, seeking. "Why is there no bruise?"

Her gaze traveled down to his sun-bronzed hands holding her arm. She could feel the warmth of him seep into her skin. It spread through her body, curling around her, enveloping her. Cloaking her.

Nothing had ever felt so good. And if a simple touch could give her so much pleasure, what would happen if he pulled her against him? If he kissed her? If he claimed her as a man would a woman?

Serena had never wanted to know until that moment. A yearning she'd never felt before, a hunger she couldn't control took her. She'd known the moment she'd seen Drogan that he would be her ultimate test. How foolish she'd been to think she could pass it. Not only would she fail, but she would most likely throw herself, body and soul, into whatever Drogan wanted to give her.

It would mean her death, but the pleasure that tempted her was too heady to resist.

Her mind was in a whirlwind, but she drew in a ragged breath and tried to calm her racing heart. "We must find Maris," she said, seeking any way to change the subject.

She didn't want to talk more about how his touch hadn't hurt her, not until she had thought on it more herself. Or at least found a way to control the way her blood heated just thinking of Drogan.

Drogan nodded and released her arm. The sudden loss of his heat brought a chill, causing her to shiver. Luckily, he didn't notice.

"I'm sure she's in the castle," he said and walked to the door. He held it open for her.

Serena grabbed her cloak, putting it on as she hurried past him and started for the castle. As hard as she tried, she couldn't focus on Maris and Gerard. All she could hear were her mother's dying words.

Guard your heart well, Serena love. Don't be a fool and give it away to a man who will only leave you. We are cursed and dying out, but I would rather see our line fade than have you know the pain I have endured.

Promise me that you will heed my words!

And Serena always had. She had seen firsthand the agony her mother suffered through the years. Serena didn't know what her father looked like since he had left before she was six days old.

It was the curse that had taken him from her mother. A curse no witch could outrun.

Serena didn't lie to herself. She wanted to be normal and have a husband and a family, to be loved and cherished, and to watch her children grow. But it wasn't meant to be. She had accepted her fate long ago.

Then why did her heart quicken when Drogan was around?

"Are you trying to put distance between us?" he asked, a teasing glint in his eyes.

"What would you do if I said aye?"

He shrugged his wide shoulders. "I would want to know the reason."

"You unsettle me," she blurted before she could stop herself.

"Good. Because you unsettle me."

His words halted her steps, and she faced him. "*I* unsettle you?"

"Is that so hard to believe?"

"Aye. Why?"

He took a step toward her. "Because I don't believe in what you are. I don't believe in anything that isn't normal, yet here you are showing me things I never dreamed could occur."

She heard him lower his voice. It had thickened, coaxing her. She turned her head away and inhaled deeply. "I cannot help what I am."

"As I cannot help what I am—a titled lord and knight of the king. Is that why I unsettle you?"

She laughed and shook her head as she looked at him. "Nay. Gerard is the same as you."

"They why is it I am different?"

She opened her mouth to tell him, but promptly changed her mind. He didn't need to know everything about her. She resumed walking. "It is simply that I am not used to men being around me."

One side of his mouth pulled in a grin. "As beautiful as you are, you expect me to believe that?"

"I do."

He gave a snort, but didn't reply. Their talking ceased as they walked through the gatehouse to find people crowded near the stables.

"What is it?" Drogan asked.

"I don't know."

He took her hand and pushed his way through the people, making a path for her. She noticed that he kept a light grip on her hand and people out of her way. They had almost made it to the center of the group when a child darted between her and Drogan. The boy stumbled and fell hard against her leg.

The cry tore from her lips before she could stop it. The crowd silenced as they hastily backed away from her. She bit her lip to take her mind off the pain burning along her leg.

"It is sorry I am, Lady Serena," the lad said as he stood and swiped away the blond hair hanging in his eyes. "I didn't see you. Please don't tell Lord Gerard."

"It was an accident. There's no reason for Gerard to know," she said past the forced smile.

She was thankful Drogan kept a hold of her so she didn't tumble to the ground. With the lessening of the pain, she lifted her face to him. His gaze dropped to his forearm where she had sunk her nails into his skin.

Chapter Four

"Forgive me," Serena whispered and immediately released him.

"Nay," Drogan said and tugged Serena closer to him. "Come, I will protect you."

When they reached the center of the group, they found Gerard kneeling with several of his knights around him.

"Gerard," Drogan called and was relieved to see his friend lift his head and give him a tight smile before Gerard's gaze shifted to Serena.

"Make way for Serena!" Gerard shouted.

The men hastened to clear a path as Drogan and Serena stepped forward.

"What happened?" Drogan asked.

"I...what is the matter with Serena?"

Drogan turned to find Serena's face as white as death.

"Let's get inside the castle," he said and reached for her. He leaned close to her ear. "Can you walk?"

She nodded, and they started toward the castle. They reached the steps when Drogan noticed that Gerard was on the other side of Serena helping her mount the stairs as well.

"I wasn't expecting you and Drogan back so ear—" Maris began until she noticed Serena. Her gaze shifted from one to the other. "What happened?"

"We'll explain once Serena is seated," Drogan said.

"In the solar." Maris ran ahead of them.

Drogan wasn't about to make Serena walk that distance. He swiftly lifted her in his arms. She laid her head on his shoulder and wrapped her slender arms around his neck.

"You should have told me," he chastised her.

Maris pointed to a chair when he walked into the solar. "Set her there."

Once Serena was on the oversized chair, Drogan stepped away so Maris could see to her, but he didn't go far. He stayed near as she explained to Maris what had happened.

Maris raised the hem of Serena's gown to her knee and rolled down her stockings. Drogan didn't get a chance to enjoy the brief view of her shapely leg as his eyes took in what Maris was searching for. He gulped at the huge, black and purple bruise that covered most of Serena's lower leg.

"That lad did this to you?" he asked.

Serena nodded. "It is what I tried to explain at the cottage."

He understood now, but it still was difficult to fathom.

Maris covered Serena's leg then turned to her husband. "And what happened to you?"

Drogan then got his first good look at Gerard. He was dusty and grass clung to his clothes, as if he had rolled down a hill.

"I was attacked."

"Attacked?" Drogan and Maris said in unison.

Gerard nodded. "It was only one man. I was able to stop his assault."

"Not before becoming injured yourself," Serena murmured from the chair.

Gerard faced her. "The point is I got away."

"The point," Serena said as she slowly rose to her feet, "is this is just the beginning."

"What?" Maris asked and took hold of Gerard's hand. "What are you speaking of, Serena?"

Serena clasped her hands together and twirled her thumbs around each other. "I did not tell you everything when I looked into Jocelyn's future."

Gerard's gaze narrowed. "What did you leave out?"

"When I peer into the future, I am shown two paths in which someone's life can journey."

"And you were shown two with Jocelyn?"

Serena nodded to Maris. "I was." She swallowed and dropped her hands. "I chose to tell you of one path"

"The other?" Gerard prompted. "Why did you not speak of it then? I have never heard you say there were two paths."

Drogan watched anger spark in Serena's blue eyes as her

nostrils flared. "If you saw the things that I have seen, you would not ever speak of them. It's because you are family to me that I put my life in jeopardy."

"What?" Drogan asked as he walked to Serena. "What do you mean you put your life in jeopardy? You said nothing of this last eve."

"I think it's time you told us everything," Gerard said.

Serena didn't want to do any such thing, and she wouldn't. All they needed was enough to stay alive. The rest...well, the rest was meant to be.

"All right," she said and turned to the window. She had no desire to see the anguish in Maris' eyes. "The second path I saw for Jocelyn was short. She would die before her fifth year."

She heard Maris gasp, and her own heart clenched. But she had to finish. "It isn't just little Jocelyn who will die, however. Both you and Maris will be killed, Gerard."

"Why?" Gerard asked, his voice tight with emotion.

Serena turned and found Maris enfolded in Gerard's arms, her head on his chest as she cried silent tears.

"It is something in your past. Something you have done that is pushing a man to see it finished."

Her stomach churned when Gerard's face went white, and he glanced at Drogan. It was just as she expected. Drogan was part of it, but she would see that he lived as well.

"If you wish to save your family, you must leave Hawthorne before it's too late." She glanced out the window. "I fear it may already be too late."

Jocelyn chose that moment to let out a wail, and Serena thought it fitting. If she could have done the same, she would have. The future looked bleak for all of them, Drogan included. But she had seen a sliver of hope in Jocelyn's future, and she was going to grasp it with both hands.

"Make your decision, Gerard," Serena said as she walked to the solar door, doing her best to disguise the limp from the injury. "You haven't much time."

"Wait," Maris said just as Serena reached for the door. "What do you suggest we do?"

Before she could respond, Gerard spoke. "You and Jocelyn will leave Hawthorne immediately. I will send as many knights as I can to protect you."

"It will do no good," Serena said before he could go on. "If you do not leave with your wife and child, you all shall die."

"My knights are some of the best in England," Gerard thundered.

But his ranting did not frighten Serena. "This man who is coming for you will kill you, Gerard. And while it will take him years, he will find Maris and kill her also. Though Jocelyn will be small and will know nothing about why her parents were killed, this man will not take any chances. He will kill her as well."

Maris collapsed against her husband in tears. "I just found you, Gerard. We just began our family. I cannot lose either of you now."

"You won't," Drogan said.

Serena slid her gaze to him. She knew he would do whatever it took to keep his friend alive.

Gerard ran his hand down Maris' back. "What do I need to do, Serena?"

"You must leave and take Maris and Jocelyn. Go somewhere safe, somewhere this man can't find you."

"If it's who I think it is, he will find us."

"Who is this man?" Maris asked as she stepped away from her husband. "What haven't you told me? I thought we shared everything."

"There are some things better left buried, my love. It happened long before I met you."

"Then how is it you knew who Serena spoke of?"

Serena stepped toward her friend. "When something is left dead and buried, one knows the evil doesn't truly die. Though Gerard hoped it would never surface, he also knew there was a chance it might."

Maris looked from Serena to Gerard to Drogan, then back to Gerard. "And you didn't trust me enough to share this? After everything we've been through?"

Serena watched Maris pick Jocelyn up and exit the solar. Her friend needed time to digest all that she had been told before she could face it.

"You need to tell her," Serena said to Gerard.

"Nay," he said as he watched his wife walk away. "I might lose her."

"If you don't tell her, you will lose her," Serena warned.

"There should be no secrets between a man and a wife, if there is love between them."

Gerard faced her. "Did you see the secret I have kept from my wife?"

"Nay. I didn't even see the face of the man who is after you, though I sense he is someone of great importance. But he is also someone with great evil in him."

She looked over to find Drogan staring at the floor, his jaw clenched. Whatever secrets Gerard hid were nothing compared to the ones locked within Drogan.

"Make your decision, Gerard. The evil draws nearer." She waited until Drogan glanced at her before she walked from the room.

She had done everything she could. The rest was up to Gerard.

Chapter Five

*D*rogan waited until the door closed behind Serena before he spoke. "You know she's right."

"Aye," Gerard said as he sank into a chair. "I had thought after all these years, it was over."

"So did I," Drogan admitted. He scuffed the toe of his boot on the stone floor. "What fools we were."

"Who do you think it is?"

Drogan shrugged as he raised his eyes to Gerard. "I'm not sure. Both are very powerful men now. I think we should prepare for either of them."

"Or both."

"Serena saw only one, and only one attacked you."

"True, but we are knights, Drogan. Why would you fight alone if there was a chance you could team up?"

"Did you see the man's face? Recognize his movement or anything?"

Gerard shook his head.

Drogan ran his hand through his hair. "You and your family must leave."

"I won't leave my home and run like a coward," Gerard said and jerked to his feet.

"Saving your family isn't being a coward," Drogan stated. He took a deep breath and tried again. "You have what most men envy from a distance. Don't throw it away because of your pride. We will get this bastard, but by our way. Not his."

Gerard nodded. "I want both of them dead. After this, I want to live my life in peace."

"And peace is what you will have, my friend."

"Will you help me get my family safely out of Hawthorne?"

"You should know you don't even have to ask."

Gerard hung his head. "I've never known real fear until I took Maris as my wife, and with the arrival of Jocelyn that anxiety has doubled. I cannot lose them."

"You won't. And I know the safest place for them."

Gerard lifted his head. "Where?"

"Wolfglynn."

"You don't think he'll know that is where I'll go?"

Drogan shrugged. "I'm hoping he thinks exactly that. You and I will be at Wolfglynn, but I'll send Maris and Jocelyn to my uncle's across the sea."

For the first time since they entered the solar, a ghost of a smile played on Gerard's lips. "There isn't anyone who will get past that wily old man."

"Precisely," Drogan said with a smile.

Serena rocked Jocelyn as Gerard and Maris argued. The great hall was all but deserted after the evening meal, because they knew there was something going on between their lord and lady, and because Gerard wanted privacy.

"Would you just listen to me?" Gerard pleaded with Maris.

"Nay. Not until I know the truth of why this man is after you."

"Knowing will not make it any easier for you," Drogan said as he walked to the dais.

"I think I know what's best for my marriage," Maris argued as she glared at Drogan.

Drogan threw up his hands. "Sorry, Gerard. I thought it might help."

Gerard rolled his eyes and reached for Maris who ducked away from him.

"Dammit, woman," he thundered.

Maris narrowed her eyes on her husband. "Don't you dare take that tone with me!"

Serena hid her grin by bending down to kiss Jocelyn's soft head.

"I saw that," Drogan said as he leaned close.

She looked at him from beneath her lashes. "Hush. You're going to make it worse if I start laughing."

"All right!" Gerard shouted. "I'll tell you. Just please sit down so we can discuss this."

"Tell me now," Maris demanded.

Serena rose to her feet and walked between the couple. She faced Maris. "Your daughter needs you, but more importantly than that, your husband needs you. He has promised to tell you. Take comfort in that and let's formulate a plan to get you out of Hawthorne."

When she returned to her seat, she saw admiration shining in Drogan's golden-brown eyes.

"That was very good," he said. "How did you know what to do?"

"I'm a woman. I know how Maris thinks."

He chuckled. "I'm glad someone does."

Gerard sighed as he sat by his wife. "All right. Drogan and I have come up with a plan."

"It had better involve me and Jocelyn accompanying you," Maris said.

"Of course. You, Jocelyn, Drogan, and I will set out for Wolfglynn with forty of my knights."

"Nay," Serena interrupted.

"You think we need more knights?" Drogan asked, his brow knotted in confusion.

Serena shook her head. "Nay, less. As in none."

"Are you daft?" Gerard asked, his tone implying he thought she was.

"Not at all," she said as calmly as she could after being asked if she were insane. "This man will be on the lookout for

46

a large group leaving Hawthorne. You need to leave in such a manner that everyone thinks you are still here."

"A disguise." Drogan nodded his head in agreement and looked to Gerard.

"Exactly. We need to leave at dusk when most of the villagers are in their cottages preparing for the evening meal and bed," Serena continued.

"We?" Drogan asked her.

"Aye, we. I'm going with you. Trust me, you're going to need me."

"Nay," Drogan and Gerard said in unison.

"It's too dangerous," Drogan added.

Maris snorted. "If Serena says we need her, then she comes." She raised her eyes to Gerard. "Right, my lord husband?"

Gerard nodded and looked to Serena. "I'd like it noted that I would rather you stay. You know what will happen if you leave."

"I know," Serena answered. And she did. Death, though none of the others knew that. They were concerned that the world would find out what she was.

"Since that is settled," Gerard said, "I'll finish explaining the plan, unless it isn't safe for us to venture to Wolfglynn."

Serena shifted her gaze to Drogan. "Wolfglynn is where we need to go."

She noticed Drogan's eyes narrow, but her secrets would stay her own. For now.

"Why Wolfglynn?" Maris asked. "If this man knows

Gerard, won't he also know that Gerard and Drogan are like brothers?"

"That's what we're counting on, love," Gerard said.

Drogan nodded to Maris. "We plan to fight him at my home."

Maris closed her eyes for a moment. "Tell me how Wolfglynn is safer than Hawthorne."

"You've never been to Drogan's castle, so you cannot know, but it isn't just where Wolfglynn is located, there's also the matter of Drogan's uncle," Gerard explained.

"Serena?" Maris asked. "Are you sure?"

Serena nodded and smiled. "It is where we need to be."

"But you, Jocelyn, and Serena won't stay there," Gerard said to Maris.

Maris rolled her eyes. "I won't be parted from you."

"We have no other choice until I rid England of the monster who threatens our world," Gerard said.

Serena shifted her gaze to Drogan. "Just where would you send us?"

"To my uncle's across the sea," Drogan answered. "The only way to his castle is by water. If neither Gerard nor I come for you, then my uncle will know what to do."

Serena nodded. "It's a solid plan. Well thought out. When do we leave?"

"Not before a couple of weeks. I have some guests coming," Gerard said.

Serena got to her feet when Jocelyn began to fuss. "Did

you hear nothing I said earlier? You cannot wait. We would have left tonight had I been given the chance."

"Serena—"

"Nay," she said. "This isn't sport, Gerard. It is about the lives of your wife and child and future children. Do not disregard what I have seen."

"We'll leave in two days," Maris said. "That will give us plenty of time to gather what we need."

"And the guests?" Gerard asked. "We might be able to fool the villagers into thinking we're still here, but that ruse will fail in two weeks."

"If everything goes according to plan, you might very well be returned before your guests arrive," Drogan said.

Serena held her tongue. There was no need to speak of what could happen now. Events could change the course of the future. She was betting her life on it.

"Do we tell no one we're leaving?" Gerard asked.

"No one," Serena answered.

"What will they think?"

"We will tell everyone in the morn that Jocelyn has taken ill. You and Maris stay in your chamber with Jocelyn. Drogan and I will make sure everything is ready before we leave. We'll then we'll depart Hawthorne."

"Everyone will think we're with Jocelyn," Maris said. "I like it. I don't have to lie to anyone."

"It will fool them for a couple of days before they investigate," Drogan pointed out.

Serena nodded. "True. However, by then we will be on our way."

Jocelyn began to cry, and Maris rose to her feet. "It is time to feed and put her to bed. I will see you tomorrow evening," she said to Drogan and Serena.

Serena watched her friends as they left the hall. She turned to find Drogan beside her. "You don't want me to go."

"Nay."

"Why?"

"I fear for you. You are as delicate as a flower, Serena."

Her chin lifted a notch. "I won't slow you down. I know how to take care of myself."

A corner of his mouth rose in a grin. "I'm sure you do. We'll have to travel slowly with Jocelyn with us."

"Not too slow," she said and walked to the door only to feel his hand on her elbow.

"Let me walk you home."

"I'm safe here. No one would dare harm me."

He shrugged one thick shoulder. "Humor me."

And even though Serena knew she was tempting herself, she couldn't refuse him.

Chapter Six

rogan knew he should have stayed at the castle, but he couldn't resist being alone with Serena. Despite his wariness of what she was, there was no denying the attraction, the need he felt whenever she was near. He had never felt such a pull towards a woman before. It intrigued him just as much as Serena did.

He hadn't lied when he said he didn't believe in what she was. There had been a few people during his travels that had shown those rare signs of being extraordinary. Maybe it was because he hadn't understood how they could do the things they did, but whatever it was, he hadn't wanted to be near them.

Until Serena.

Drogan told himself it was her beauty and wit, but he knew it was much more than that. She was all that was graceful and serene. Yet, he'd caught a glimpse of desire and yearning in her blue eyes.

"You're quiet," she said as they walked down the path to her cottage.

"I'm thinking of the next few days."

"Are you worried we won't make it to Wolfglynn?"

He shook his head. "I'm more concerned about taking two women and an infant into the wilds of England. Many dangers, not just this man after Gerard, await us."

"You know who this man is."

It wasn't a question, so he saw no need to lie. "I do."

"Good."

They reached her cottage. He wanted to spend more time with her, to learn more about her. More than that, he just wanted to be near her. Racing through his mind were dozens of reasons, but which one would she believe?

"Thank you for walking me," she said. She studied him a moment before she licked her lips. "Do you wish to come in?"

He grinned as she tilted her face up to him, and the moonlight illuminated her. He'd never seen a woman so beautiful, so alluring. He wanted her with a fierceness that bordered on insanity. He'd known her just a few days, but it felt as if she'd been a part of his life for eons.

Drogan fisted his hands to keep from pulling her against him and claiming her lips for a kiss. "I would like that."

He waited until she had lit candles and started a fire before he followed her inside and shut the door. He inhaled the delicious aroma of herbs as he made his way to the table. His gaze followed her as she moved around the kitchen, her eyes darting to him again and again.

The thick braid securing her black mane ran over her shoulder to stop alongside her full breast. His breath quickened as he admired the gentle swell of her curves. His gaze traveled the length of her, noting her small waist, the gentle flare of her hips, and the regal way she held herself. Need, primal and intense, coursed through him like fire in his blood.

He had wanted—and had—many women during his life, but there was something different about Serena, and it wasn't the fact she was a witch.

Drogan tried to swallow and found his mouth dry, which only made him think of her lips, of kissing her, of her sweet mouth moving along his skin. He swore inwardly as his gaze drifted to her mouth.

An image of her lying in his bed, her wealth of midnight hair spread around her as she opened her arms to him, welcoming him while he gently parted her pale thighs. His breathing grew harsh as he imagined skimming his hands along the smooth flesh of her thighs before he thrust inside her again and again. He could almost hear her cries of pleasure, could almost feel the nails she would sink into his back.

The image was so vivid, so real, that it took Drogan a moment to realize where he was. He pressed the heel of his hands against his eyes, and tried in vain to gain some control over the fiery need that was running rampant through him.

"Drogan," Serena whispered near his ear, her hand soft and comforting on his shoulder. "What troubles you?"

He didn't want comforting. He wanted her. In his bed. Beneath him. Screaming his name.

Drogan clenched his jaw and dropped his hands to find her face mere inches from his. He feasted on the clear depths of her eyes. There were as blue as the sea at Wolfglynn, turbulent and bewitching, and watched him as if she could read his thoughts.

As if she could see into his soul.

A soul that was as black as her hair.

Drogan inhaled deeply. "You shouldn't stand close to a man unless you want to be kissed."

She jerked back as if scorched. He hated how that gesture bothered him. Obviously the attraction he thought was between them only went one way.

They stared at each other for several moments in silence, the tension thickening. The spell was shattered when a knock sounded on her door. Drogan sighed and dropped his chin to his chest as Serena opened the door.

A smiling couple entered the cottage, the woman holding something in her arms. The sheer joy on Serena's face left Drogan breathless as she took the tiny bundle. A small, flailing hand let him know she held an infant.

"Sit, Fanny," Serena said and motioned to the chair with her chin. "You shouldn't be out of bed."

Fanny sank into the chair Drogan vacated. She held her stomach and moved hesitantly. "I couldn't wait, milady. We had ta come."

"I would have visited first thing in the morning." Serena never took her eyes off the bundle as she rocked the infant.

After a moment Serena's eyes lifted and met Drogan's. He saw the light shining in her eyes. There was happiness there, but also a sadness that made his chest ache.

"Lord Drogan, this is Fanny and Thomas. They have come to show off their precious new daughter."

Fanny gasped. "How did you know it was a girl, milady?"

Serena smiled and cooed at the baby. "I just do. What is her name?"

"Well," Thomas said anxiously and glanced at his wife. "We were hoping ye'd name her."

Serena went utterly still. Slowly, her head lifted to the couple. It was a great honor and privilege to be asked to name a child, but it was one she didn't want. She looked back at the sleeping child, so innocent and beautiful.

"There are many names that come to mind," she murmured, buying herself some time.

"Please, milady," Fanny begged. "If it weren't for ye, I'd not have her."

Serena glanced up to find Drogan leaning against the wall next to the hearth, studying her with those dark, seductive eyes of his. She wished she could read his thoughts, but that was one gift she didn't have.

"I didn't do anything," she answered.

"But ye did," Fanny said, nodding. She faced Drogan. "For six years, we tried for a child. Finally, I came to Lady Serena and she helped me. Without her, there wouldn't be that lovely babe in her arms." Fanny wiped the tears from her face.

All eyes turned to Serena. She looked at the baby, but not too closely. She had no desire to see the infant's death.

After a moment, she lifted her gaze to Fanny. "What is your favorite name?"

"Mary. After me mother."

Serena smiled and kissed the baby's head. "Hello, Mary. Welcome to Hawthorne." She handed the infant back to her mother. "Now go and get some rest, Fanny. Your daughter needs you."

"Thank ye, milady," Fanny said with tears running freely down her face.

Serena smiled and helped Fanny to stand. "Take care of your family, Thomas."

"Ye know I will, milady," he said as they walked out the door and into the night.

Serena sighed. When she turned away from the door, Drogan was staring at her.

"You do that a lot," she said.

"What?"

"Watch me." She moved the kettle over the fire to boil water.

"It's because you're very interesting." He shoved off the wall with his shoulder and came to stand beside her. "I had no idea you could help a woman conceive."

"I didn't," she confessed. "Fanny and Thomas were trying too hard. I sensed that a child was in their future and just helped her along."

She saw him nod out of the corner of her eye. "Well, whatever you did, they are grateful to you. Are you sure you want to leave Hawthorne?"

"Nay. I never want to leave, but I know that I must."

He took hold of her and urged her to face him. "I don't suppose you'll tell me why?"

"There is nothing to tell. I want to be sure Jocelyn, Maris, and Gerard live. It is as simple as that."

Drogan lips twisted wryly. "There is nothing simple about you, Lady Serena. Methinks there is much you keep secret."

His hands, large and warm, wrapped tenderly around her arms and pulled her toward him so that only breaths separated them. His touch was comforting, soothing, and all too calming for her heart that raced wildly in her chest.

His eyes enthralled her, fascinated her.

Captivated her.

Shadows and secrets lurked behind those golden-brown depths, and she sensed they would eventually destroy him. The thought saddened her. He was a good man, a great knight —one Gerard both trusted and honored.

"Didn't I tell you not to stand too close to a man?" His deep voice was low, barely above a whisper.

It did strange things to her body. She found her eyes lowering to his mouth, and her blood warming with every beat of her heart. Her body shook. Not because he touched her, but because he hadn't touched more of her.

No matter how many times she told herself to put distance between them, Serena couldn't do it. For once, her heart was in control. And it wanted Drogan.

"It was not I who came this close."

A small smile pulled at his lips. "So, I am to blame?"

"It would seem so, my lord."

"Yet, you don't move away."

She cocked her head to the side as her eyes shifted to his wide mouth once more.

He groaned. "Don't do that, Serena."

"Do what?"

"Look at me like that."

Her gaze jerked to his to find his eyes smoldering, ablaze with desire. She ought to step away, but for the life of her, she couldn't. Her heart hammered erratically, both in fear and excitement. If she stayed, she didn't know what would happen.

But she couldn't leave.

Then her mother's words of warning rang through her head. *Guard your heart, Serena.*

An image of her mother, broken in body and spirit, filled her mind. Tears pricked her eyes as she backed out of his grasp. Regret flashed in Drogan's dark eyes, but she must do everything in her power to guard her heart, no matter how tempting Drogan was.

"I would never hurt you," he said as he dropped his arms.

"It isn't that."

After a slight incline of his head, he turned and walked to the door. He paused when he reached it and looked over his shoulder at her. "I would ask that you stay here, Serena."

"I go with Maris and Jocelyn." She waited until he closed the door before she said, "Their lives depend upon it."

Chapter Seven

*D*rogan tried to look away from the frightened hazel gaze, but he couldn't. He had been that terrified once as well. The difference was Drogan had lived through it.

"Please," the boy mouthed.

Drogan had done his assignments without question, without remorse, because he had believed the men traitorous to England and the crown. But he knew this was wrong. The kind of wrong that would see him burn in Hell.

"We can't do this," Cade said.

Drogan looked to Cade and Gerard. Cade was right. Regardless of what threatened them, they couldn't carry out this duty. It had nothing to do with the crown, nothing to do with protecting England.

"We won't do it," Drogan stated.

The evil laugh that followed his statement sent chills racing down his spine. It was then Drogan knew they were about to cross the line they had vowed to never traverse.

Drogan stood on the battlement as the sun rose through the thick clouds. He had slept little as he went over everything they must gather for the journey.

Sword in hand, he headed for the bailey to begin his daily training. The exertion was just what he needed to relieve his mind of a certain black-haired temptress who wanted nothing to do with him.

But after two hours of vigorous activity, Serena still filled his thoughts. It didn't help that she walked among the villagers and people called out her name, distracting him. Thrice, he had nearly been injured because he turned when he heard her name.

How in the name of St. Peter was he supposed to travel with her when he hungered for her so much? He was just a man, after all.

It wasn't until he finished with his bath and returned to his chamber that he began to pack. He had just pulled on his boots when he realized he had forgotten something. Penelope.

He slumped onto his bed and buried his head in his hands. He was *not* bringing her along. He'd have to figure out some way to leave her behind. Maybe she could stay here until he and Gerard had completed their business. It would be the safest place for her.

A light rain began to fall as he looked out the window. Not fit weather for traveling, but he knew Serena would insist upon it.

He'd traveled with kings and queens, servants and knights, but he had never traveled with an infant or a witch. It would definitely be an adventure.

As planned, Gerard and Maris remained in their chamber. Serena waited as long as she could before she ventured to the castle. She had strolled through the village that morning, thinking to keep away from Drogan, but wherever she went, she saw him—standing on the battlements, training with the knights, talking to the people. He was everywhere.

She had sought the safety of her cottage, but that hadn't helped. Though she had busied herself with packing herbs she wouldn't be able to find outside of Hawthorne, the activity did nothing to stop her thoughts from returning to Drogan time and again.

When she could stand it no longer, she ventured to the castle. To her surprise, Drogan was nowhere to be found. She was a little disappointed, but after chiding herself, she realized it was for the best.

"Hello," someone called from behind her.

She turned to find the pretty blonde who had been on Drogan's arm, and jealousy surged through her. "Hello. I'm Serena."

"I know." The girl giggled, the sound high pitched. "I've heard all about you from everyone. I don't think I've ever met anyone as loved as you seem to be."

Serena wondered if the giggles would stop. "You came with Lord Drogan, yes?"

The girl nodded her head so hard Serena feared the girl's wimple would topple off. "I'm Penelope, his cousin."

"Really?" Serena couldn't keep the smile from her lips. Penelope was his cousin, she repeated to herself, grateful that she hadn't made a fool of herself by asking Drogan or Gerard who Penelope was.

Penelope nodded again. "I begged Drogan to let me come, and I didn't stop until he agreed. I can be very persuasive."

Serena chuckled, wondering just how long Penelope had needed to beg before Drogan had given in. "Are you having fun at Hawthorne?"

"Delicious fun," she said, her brown eyes wide with delight. She giggled again and stepped closer. "I hope we don't leave anytime soon."

Serena wondered if Drogan had intentionally forgotten Penelope or intended to leave her at Hawthorne. Either way, no one had said anything about her accompanying them to Wolfglynn. "I don't think you need to worry about that."

"Wonderful," she cried and hurried off without another word.

Serena was exhausted after talking to her. The girl didn't slow down, her excitement suffocating everyone. With a sigh, Serena made her way toward the stairs.

She walked to Gerard and Maris's chamber and knocked. Maris let her in, and she saw Drogan sitting with Gerard talking in hushed tones.

"They are going over last-minute details," Maris said as she shut the door. "I was beginning to wonder if you had changed your mind."

Serena gave her a reassuring smile. "Are you worried?"

"Extremely." Maris twisted her hands, the anxiety showing in the lines about her mouth. "I don't want to take Jocelyn away from her home."

"You'll be back."

Maris nodded, but doubt still clouded her gray eyes.

"You must remain calm," Serena said. "If not, Jocelyn will fuss the entire way. I know you are worried, but Gerard and Drogan will protect you."

"And you," Drogan said as he walked up.

"I can protect myself."

He raised one auburn brow. "The way you protected yourself against the lad who ran into your leg?"

"I know what to do to make the bruise go away quick enough," she retorted.

Gerard laughed and clapped Drogan on the back. "All right, you two. We've got several days together. Are you going to argue like children?"

Serena chose not to answer. "How long will it take for us to reach Wolfglynn?"

"By horse, it's a three-day journey," Drogan answered.

"We won't be traveling on horse."

They all looked at her. "Didn't I make myself clear last night? We cannot bring any attention to us. We must look like peasants and nothing more."

Gerard didn't look convinced.

"Don't you think people will notice if you're dressed in peasant clothing, yet you ride your great stallion, Gerard? We have one chance to make it to Drogan's castle."

"She's right," Drogan said. "No horses. We'll have to go on foot."

Gerard and Maris looked at one another, their gazes filled with fear and doubt. Serena glanced at Drogan. He had seen the exchange, too.

"How about a cart and horse? That way, Maris and Jocelyn could ride," Serena said.

"I'll see what I can do," Gerard said and headed to the door only to be stopped by Drogan.

"Nay," Drogan said. "I'll take care of that. Make sure you have everything you need."

Serena sighed as Drogan left the chamber. She prayed he could locate a cart and horse without arousing too much attention.

Suddenly, she realized they had forgotten his cousin again. "What of Lady Penelope?"

"Drogan has already talked with me about her," Gerard said. "She's going to stay here while we're gone."

"And our absence?"

Gerard smiled. "It will take Penelope a while to notice, I assure you. She's more interested in herself."

Serena knew that to be true.

"I've gotten together some clothes," Maris said as she walked to the bed. "I'm not quite done, but by tomorrow, I will be."

Serena reached for the items Maris had already laid out. "It would be better if I took them to my cottage. People are used to seeing me walk about at odd times. I'll continue to come and collect a little at a time."

Maris' smile was forced and slipped easily. "I'm afraid, Serena."

Serena glanced over her friend's shoulder to Gerard. His face was lined with worry, but there was determination in his eyes. "Don't fret. You have the strongest, bravest knight in England as your husband. No harm will come to you or Jocelyn as long as he is near."

A tearful smile pulled at Maris' lips as she looked at her husband. "He is strong and brave."

Serena left them then, knowing they needed time alone to prepare for the long journey. No one noticed or stopped her to ask why she carried an armload of clothes. Just as she had told Maris, the people of Hawthorne were used to her doing odd things, which worked in their favor.

She shut the door to her cottage and dumped the clothes on her bed. They would have to be refolded and packed away soon. She turned toward the kitchen to find her table lined with various weapons.

Although she had no wish to touch them, her feet took

her to the table to garner a better look. Only one person would have brought these weapons here. Drogan.

She touched a sword that rested on the edge of the table. Its pommel had an intricately etched cross that was beautiful to behold, and the guard was wrapped in soft leather. It was a sword that had seen many battles.

"Do you like it?"

She jerked around at Drogan's voice. "The sword?" At his nod she said, "Aye. It is simple and not as ornately adorned as Gerard's is, yet this sword seems…" she shrugged as she fought to find the right word, "…beautiful."

"Thank you." Drogan picked it up and slid it in his scabbard.

"It's yours?" She was surprised, though she shouldn't have been. The sword suited him.

"Aye. I have a sword something like Gerard's, but I prefer to keep that one to gaze upon."

"Rightly so," she said with a laugh. She couldn't imagine Drogan going into battle with a sword that held a large ruby in the pommel. "I keep asking Gerard what he will do when that huge stone falls out."

"What did he say?"

She rolled her eyes. "He swears it never will."

"Just like Gerard." Drogan chuckled and began to sift through the weapons. "For as long as I've known him, he's carried that sword. I hope you don't mind me storing these here."

"Not at all. I think leaving from here is the best option."

He laid down a crossbow. "I agree."

"I'm surprised Penelope won't mind staying behind."

He barked with laughter. "If she had her way, she would be at court. As I am the king's man, she doesn't understand why I don't spend more time with him."

"Why don't you?"

He shrugged. "I prefer my home, although Penelope doesn't care for Wolfglynn."

"Why ever not?"

He leaned his hip against the table and crossed his arms over his wide chest. "She says it's gloomy."

"Is it?"

He thought about that a moment and shrugged. "I suppose to some it is, but it suits me."

"So, you think of yourself as gloomy, my lord?"

A slow grin stretched his mouth. "At times, aye."

"With the dark thoughts always so near to you, I can understand why."

The grin dropped from his face, and he straightened to his full height. "What dark thoughts?"

"Relax," she said as she walked past him. She hadn't meant to say anything about the darkness. "I don't know your thoughts. I only sense that there is great darkness within you, as if you are troubled by something that won't go away."

Serena glanced over her shoulder to see that he had calmed. She had no idea that her words could affect him so, but his reaction confirmed he was troubled.

Her attention focused on folding the clothes she had taken from the castle, and so she didn't hear Drogan walk to her.

"It is unfair, this advantage you have over me."

His closeness startled her, but she was determined that he not know it. "It is not so much an advantage," she said as she continued her task. "It is merely my sensing of something. Most people could sense things as well if they but opened themselves up to it."

"Let's make it simpler."

She straightened and faced him. "How so?"

"Tell me something about you."

Drogan waited to see what she would say, and if she would, indeed, tell him something. Her black eyebrows rose.

"I have already told you a great deal about me the first night we met."

"True," he said as she leaned against the doorframe. "Still, you know far more about me than I know of you."

"All right," she said after a moment. "When I was a little girl, I used to pretend I was a lady of a great castle."

Now that was something he hadn't expected to hear. "Truly? I think that is something most little girls dream about."

"Maybe so," she said and turned back to the clothes. "Then something happens in their lives to change that."

Drogan knew better than to ask what she meant by that. He had managed to get her to speak a little about herself, and there would be no more this day.

He slipped back into the kitchen and began choosing

weapons that could be stored with the clothing. When he returned to her bed she was waiting for him. He handed her the weapons and watched as she expertly slid them between the layers of fabric so they wouldn't be seen.

"This will work," she said.

"Of course it will."

She shook her head at him. "I'm talking about everything. It'll all work out fine. As long as Jocelyn, Maris, and Gerard stay together and reach Wolfglynn."

"Are you keeping something from me?" he asked. Something in her words triggered his suspicions, a gut feeling that there was more than she had told them.

Her blue eyes stared back at him. She looked fragile and innocent, but he knew appearances could be deceiving. "Everyone holds secrets."

"Not everyone, it seems," he said as he watched her begin to gather her clothes. "Gerard told Maris his secret last night."

"As he should have," she said. "Nothing should be kept secret between a man and a wife. What they share brings them closer."

"Do you know?" He had to know if the dark secret he and Gerard shared yet remained hidden from her. Quite frankly, he hoped it did, because he didn't want her to find out about their deeds. She saw him as a man of honor now, but if she ever discovered the truth, there would be fear and revulsion in her beautiful blue eyes.

"Nay. I have no need to be privy to that information."

Relief surged through him. It was silly, really. He didn't

know this woman—nay, witch—yet it mattered what she thought of him. Strange, since he had never cared what people thought before. The only ones whose opinions concerned him were Gerard and Cade.

The three of them had been inseparable and shared everything. They might not share the same blood, but they had called themselves brothers.

Now, one had turned.

"Those dark thoughts are claiming you once more."

Drogan raised his gaze to her. "Darkness is part of my life. I tried once to chase it away, but I learned the hard way that it will always be there."

With a huge burden now weighing on him, he gave Serena a nod and left.

He still had much to do. Both he and Serena had to collect food separately. It needed to be enough to sustain four people for the week or more it would take to reach Wolfglynn.

"If only we had the damn horses," he muttered as he walked past the stables.

Chapter Eight

*D*rogan wiped his hair from his face and gave a final glance around. Everything was in place.

The cart was hidden not far from Serena's cottage, and he was grateful that she lived apart from others. It was also fortunate for their little group that several traders had stopped at the castle the day before. With so many villagers and visitors coming and going through the castle gates, no one would think twice about another cart leaving.

"I see you have the cart," Serena said as she walked up.

"I borrowed it from Fanny and Thomas."

"Good," she said with a nod of her head. "They will keep that to themselves. I also hear you loaned them your horse."

Drogan shifted, uncomfortable with her penetrating blue eyes directed at him. "Aye. Since I was taking his, it seemed only fair to lend him mine in case he needed it."

"It was very kind of you. Thank you."

"Is everything ready?"

"I think so. I have packed all the food you brought. Between yesterday and this morning, I've gotten just about everything else packed as well."

He liked the way her black locks shown almost blue-black in the sun. "I'll load everything into the cart once it's dark and hook up the horse. Have you talked to Maris and Gerard about how they will leave the castle?"

"That will be the easy part. It is getting to Wolfglynn that I'm concerned about."

"Gerard and I will get you there. That I vow."

He watched as she walked to the castle. The shrill cry of a falcon drew his attention skyward. The massive bird circled overhead as the sun lowered in the horizon.

It wouldn't be long now.

"All right," Serena said as she slipped inside the master chamber where Maris and Gerard waited. "Are you ready?"

Maris pulled her tattered cloak tighter and nodded. Serena gathered Jocelyn in her arms as Gerard, scarcely recognizable in his peasant attire, walked past her.

"Remember, behind my cottage. One by one."

Maris left first, and then Gerard. Serena counted to fifty, then added another twenty before she too left the chamber. They were all to take separate exits from the castle so no one would identify them.

Just as she turned the corner from the chamber, someone knocked on the door and called for Maris or Gerard. There was no answer, and Serena waited to see what would happen.

After a few moments, the servant departed.

Serena sighed with relief and hurried from the castle. As soon as she reached her cottage Gerard took Jocelyn from her and handed the infant to Maris, who hunkered down in the cart.

"The ride will be rough," Drogan said as he finished hooking up the horse, "but we'll do the best we can."

Drogan had arranged a covering for the cart to keep the sun off Jocelyn. His thoughtfulness surprised Serena. But then again, there was much that surprised her about him, including the attraction she couldn't deny. No matter how hard she tried.

"That was very kind of you to think of Maris and Jocelyn."

"And you," he said.

She stared at him, unable to believe he had thought of her. No one ever did. Everyone assumed she could take care of herself. And she could, but it was nice to have someone else think of her for a change.

"Ready?" Gerard asked.

Serena gave Maris a reassuring smile before Gerard pulled the flap down and tied it. "Ready."

Drogan gave them a little wave and headed down the path. They had agreed to leave Hawthorne separately. Drogan would go first and make sure no one was in the woods waiting for them.

He would then send a signal and Gerard would walk the horse and cart to meet Drogan. Serena would be last, for she would know if anyone noticed the lord and lady of Hawthorne were missing.

She gave Gerard a nod and walked to her cottage to retrieve her bag. She wouldn't be going down the well-traveled road to meet with the rest. She had another route to take.

A whistle from Gerard let her know Drogan had sent his signal, and Gerard was leaving Hawthorne. Serena hurried to take one last look at her cottage and spotted the silver medallion hanging on a peg near the hearth. It was the last thing her mother had given her, but Serena never touched it. It had belonged to her father.

At one time the intricate carvings in the fine metal had mesmerized her, but with every passing day that her father hadn't returned, that fascination had turned to despair. Even so, she couldn't leave it behind. She dropped the medallion into her bag before she blew out the last candle and stepped out of the only home she had ever known.

She caught a brief glimpse of Gerard as the cart disappeared around a curve in the path. Her eyes scanned the rows of cottages and the castle for any signs that someone had recognized him.

After several moments where no one raised an alarm, Serena made her way through the village toward the castle. Few people were outside because most were eating or getting ready to bed down for the night.

The castle was quiet as she walked past, the occupants unaware that the lord and his lady had departed. She found the postern door in the castle wall and slipped out of the bailey. Her feet fell lightly on the ground as she hurried to her destination. The moon was bright and shed its light upon the grave markers.

Set apart from the small group of graves was a simple cross next to a large oak tree. Serena made her way to the cross and knelt beside it.

"I'm leaving, Mother. I know you think I should stay, but I go to save my friends. I shan't be returning, but you already know that."

She looked up at the moon and blinked away her tears. "I kept my heart safe, just as I promised. I have not suffered the pain of losing my husband as you did."

Nor the joy of holding my child in my arms.

"It won't be long until I join you, Mother. Wait for me." Serena leaned over and kissed the cross before she got to her feet and started toward the forest.

To her surprise, leaving Hawthorne wasn't as hard as she had imagined it would be. She adjusted the bag on her shoulder and quickened her steps.

"Where is she?" she heard Drogan say as she neared.

"She had something she had to do," Maris said.

Serena stepped into the small clearing where her friends waited and looked at Drogan. "I'm here now. Are we ready?"

He nodded and grabbed hold of the horse's reins. Serena smiled at Maris as she walked beside the small cart.

"Are you all right?" she asked her friend.

Maris nodded and kissed Jocelyn's small head. "We'll be fine."

Gerard moved to talk to Maris, and Serena didn't want to interfere. She had a choice: she could lag behind the cart, or she could move ahead and close the gap between her and Drogan. Though her heart cautioned against it, she moved forward until she was even with Drogan. For several long moments, neither said anything.

There was contentment in the quiet, an easiness she had never felt before. She didn't feel the need to think of something to say. She could simply walk beside him and enjoy the quiet of the night.

"I thought you had changed your mind," he said after a length.

She glanced at him. He stared straight ahead at the path.

"I told you I was coming. I don't go back on my word. There was something I had to do first."

He nodded but didn't say more. It troubled her that he would think she had gone back on her word to her friends. They continued in silence once more. Serena could hear Maris giggle at something Gerard said, and the happy sound pulled at her soul in a way it never had before.

Serena looked back at her friends. Though Maris rode in the cart and Gerard walked beside it, their heads were close together as they talked and shared a smile while Maris held their daughter.

Drogan saw Serena looking over her shoulder and followed her gaze. "They make a lovely family."

"They do," she agreed and faced the road again. "Too bad more people can't have that type of relationship."

"What kind did your parents have?" He knew as soon as the question left his lips that it was the wrong one to ask.

Serena's body jerked. It was slight, but still he saw it.

"I don't remember."

He wisely kept his mouth shut, although he was dying to know why she couldn't remember her parents' relationship. One of them must have died when she was very young. Such misfortunes were hardly rare. But he doubted she would tell him. He'd have to ask Gerard, and he wasn't even sure Gerard would tell him.

It galled Drogan how tight-lipped his friend was about Serena, though he understood why. What Drogan didn't comprehend was why, once Serena told him what she was, Gerard didn't open up more. To the contrary, his friend became more secretive where Serena was concerned.

And why? Drogan wasn't the type of man to involve himself with a lady he had no intention of marrying.

The fact that he wanted to know all there was about Serena bothered him more than he cared to admit. Late at night, when dreams or nightmares plagued people, he would lie awake and wonder about her.

Whenever he asked himself why, he would think of something else. For too long, he had kept his dark secrets safe. He couldn't chance becoming close to anyone and someone finding out.

Ever.

The moon was high when they decided to stop and rest. Drogan had tried to push thoughts of Serena out of his mind, but it proved difficult with her walking just on the other side of the horse.

He unhitched the horse, for activity always helped him keep his mind away from thoughts that troubled him, and this one certainly did.

"Need some help?" Gerard asked.

Drogan shook his head as he led the horse to a tree and tied him so he could reach the grass and the bucket of water. "See to your wife and daughter."

"Serena is taking care of them. Are you all right, my friend?"

Drogan jerked his head up to glare at his friend. "I'm fine."

"Nay, you're not. You haven't been since—"

"Don't," Drogan growled. He stepped back and took a deep breath. "Don't say it. We swore to never speak of it again, yet that is all we have done since I've arrived."

"And I'm glad you did arrive." Gerard ran his hand through his dark blond hair and sighed. "I didn't want to tell Maris. I did everything I could to prevent her from knowing, but I can tell you I feel much better for sharing it with her."

"I'm glad for you." Drogan didn't look up as he finished readying the harness for the morning.

A hand on his shoulder halted his movements. When he turned, Gerard's face was inches away, his black eyes piercing. "The darkness will claim you, Drogan."

He didn't answer, just waited until Gerard shrugged and walked away.

"It is too late, my friend," Drogan whispered. "It already has."

Chapter Nine

*I*f Drogan found it hard to sleep in the castle knowing Serena was close, it was nothing compared to having her within a few feet of him.

In truth, it was pure torture.

He knew every breath she took, every movement she made until he was delirious with it. The urge to be next to her, the overwhelming hunger to touch her was driving him daft. Never had he felt such need, such...yearning for another woman.

Although she was beautiful and the most enchanting woman he had ever met, he knew better than to want someone he couldn't have.

Despite that, he was curious about her. Maybe he was interested because Gerard and Maris were so secretive about her. Maybe he was intrigued because she was mysterious. Or maybe she caught his eye because she was a witch. Whatever the reason, he had to know more about her.

He rolled onto his side and closed his eyes, fighting for sleep. Instead, Serena filled his mind as images of what he desired most took over.

Long black hair floated around her and her blue eyes sparkled with laughter. A creamy expanse of skin appeared as her gown slipped off her shoulder. She beckoned him with her hand, and he eagerly went to her. He didn't stop her as she pulled him against her soft curves.

Her eyes darkened as she stared at him, and he wondered what her lips would taste like. He was leaning down to find out when a wail jerked Drogan from his fanciful dream.

When he opened his eyes, Serena stared at him from across the fire. For several moments they lay still, studying each other as Jocelyn whimpered. He wondered if Serena knew his thoughts, if her magic as a witch could go that far? Just thinking about her made his blood heat and his cock swell.

She was the first to look away, but Drogan couldn't stop the thoughts from running through his mind, couldn't stop the images of laying Serena down and slowly kissing every inch of her lovely body.

Try as he might, Drogan couldn't get his body to relax. His imagination hadn't helped him, and in fact, had made things worse. He was fully aroused and needed release, something he knew wouldn't happen until he reached Wolfglynn and could find a woman.

He rose and went to Gerard who stood guard. "I'll relieve you," Drogan said as he leaned against a tree.

"Can't sleep?" Gerard asked.

Drogan shook his head. "Go be with your family. I'll finish out the night."

He was thankful Gerard didn't push further. With a long sigh, Drogan settled in for the night.

When Serena next opened her eyes, the sky was gray. Mist hung heavy around her and rain would most likely fall before midday.

She slowly sat up and covered her mouth while she yawned before she stood and stretched some of the soreness from her back and neck. After she rolled the blanket she had slept on and placed it in the cart, she reached for her bag and rummaged until she found her comb.

Comb in hand, she went to their water supply and dipped a finger inside.

"What are you doing?" Drogan asked. "It's water."

"I know." She cupped her hands and reached into a bucket. After she splashed her face with water and dried off, she looked at him. "I have to be careful to make sure the water isn't too hot or too cold."

His forehead creased as he looked at the water. "How do you manage to live, with all the precautions you must take?"

"Everyone takes precautions," she said. "It is just my way of life. People adapt."

"Don't you ever get angry?"

The question surprised her. No one had ever asked it before. "Often, when I was younger. Once I realized it couldn't be changed, I learned to live with it."

He reached inside the bucket and splashed his own face. When he was done, she handed him the towel. "Why do you care so much?"

He shrugged and tossed the towel into the cart. "I'm curious."

"About me? Why? Because I'm a *bana-bhuidseach*?"

He shook his head. "Because you are you, and I've never met anyone like you. I don't get curious about people, Serena. I learned long ago most people are all the same."

He walked to the horse and spoke softly to it before he walked the big animal to the cart.

"He's telling the truth."

She spun around to find Gerard behind her. "You heard all of that?"

"Just the last part. I've known Drogan a very long time, Serena. He's a man I trust with my life, with my family's lives. He's a brother in every sense of the word, but he learned at a very early age that the world was not a good place. I've seen women throw themselves at him, yet he has turned them away."

"Why? Does he not wish to marry?"

"Nay, he doesn't, though I hope to change his mind." He

shifted his gaze to Drogan. "He's seen the worst of people, of life. I know you've sensed the darkness within him. It nearly claimed *me*, and I'm afraid it has already claimed him." His gaze returned to her. "To hear him say he is curious about you puts a smile on my face, because Drogan doesn't get curious about anything."

"I'm glad you managed to chase away the darkness." She started to turn away when his hand stopped her. She looked over her shoulder at him, at his troubled black eyes.

"I know what position this puts you in, but I beg you. Do not refuse him."

Gerard didn't give her time to answer before he walked off, but his words rang in her head like a bell. She couldn't understand how Gerard could ask this of her. He knew the risk, yet still he dared to ask.

She gripped the side of the cart as her mind swam with anger and regret. Even though Gerard and Maris were the closest thing to a family she had, she could not, would not do what he requested. The cost was too high.

Serena unbraided her hair and combed it while she thought over what Drogan and Gerard had said. She hurriedly tied a ribbon at the base of her neck to hold her hair back when Maris handed her some bread and cheese.

She ate alone, watching Gerard, Maris, and Drogan talk about the trip, making sure they had planned everything. It wasn't long before Gerard helped Maris into the cart, signaling it was time to depart.

"There's enough room for you," Maris said.

Serena shook her head. "I think I'll walk for awhile." She didn't miss the look shared by Maris and Gerard, but she wasn't in the mood to talk about anything, especially when the talk was about Drogan.

He occupied too much of her thoughts, anyway.

Not just thoughts, but dreams as well.

It hadn't come as a surprise to have Drogan in her dreams. There she could pretend she was normal, with a normal life. She could pretend that there was no harm in flirting or offering her heart to such a man.

There she could let the dream play out so she could see what life might be like with Drogan. With children.

With love.

How Serena hated herself for even giving in that much. She had no control over her dreams, but the fact she enjoyed them so much made her realize how perilous the attraction she'd denied was. If she gave in, if she allowed herself...

She couldn't even finish the thought.

Serena was careful not to walk too close to the cart or too near to Drogan as he led the horse. She kept to the other side away from everyone and made sure her eyes stayed focused ahead of her, no matter how many times she caught Drogan looking at her from the corner of her eyes. The more distance she kept between them the better.

It wasn't until they stopped to rest the horses and eat a quick bite for lunch that she was forced to talk.

"You've been quiet," Maris said.

Serena shrugged and reached for Jocelyn. "I've a lot on my mind."

"Gerard told me what he asked of you."

Hesitantly, Serena raised her eyes to Maris. "Did he?"

"I told him that he should know better. He recalls better than you how your mother suffered." She bowed her head as she played with the skirt of her gown. When Maris lifted her gaze, they were full of sadness. "He told me many stories of your mother and her beauty. He says you are much like her."

Serena rocked Jocelyn as she listened to Maris. Not many people talked of Serena's mother because they knew the pain it caused her. She blinked away her tears and pushed down memories that threatened to rise.

"I've no wish to see you end up like your mother, Serena."

Serena swallowed and turned away before the tears spilled. It was nice to know Maris was on her side, but it didn't solve anything. Not when Gerard had his heart set on something, and he most certainly did now. Serena wasn't a fool. She knew how much Gerard thought of Drogan. If necessary, he would die for Drogan.

For many years, she'd heard stories of Drogan and the escapades he and Gerard had. Several times, Gerard had asked Drogan to visit, but Drogan had a castle and land of his own that required his attention, and when he wasn't at Wolfglynn, he was with the king.

And then he had finally come. From the moment Serena laid eyes on him and felt the sharp stab of arousal, she had known her heart was in danger.

She walked Jocelyn, ever mindful of where Drogan was. It was a good thing Maris and Gerard were traveling with them. Otherwise, she didn't know if she could keep her distance from him.

Drogan stole a look at Serena as she held Jocelyn. He knew something bothered her. She had been quiet and reserved since they'd begun traveling that morning. From the way Gerard and Maris cast glances at her and whispered, he knew it was something important.

He also knew Maris didn't agree with whatever Gerard wanted.

"I see you looking at Serena," Gerard said as he sat down beside Drogan to eat.

Drogan groaned. "Keep your sword in its scabbard, Gerard. I'm looking to make sure she didn't walk off. These woods are dangerous, especially if we're being followed."

"I don't care that you're looking at her. Frankly, it relieves me."

Drogan rubbed the back of his neck. "Tell me what has changed. At Hawthorne you warned me to stay away from her, and now you act as though you would see us together."

Gerard shrugged, but didn't look up from his food. "Who knows?"

There was something going on. Of that Drogan was sure. Gerard had never been very good at hiding his intentions, and if Drogan waited long enough, he would discover what they were. "I'm going to make sure we aren't being followed," he said as he stood.

He stepped into the woods and glanced back to see Serena staring at nothing in particular, as if something weighed heavily on her mind. Her eyes looked troubled, weary...sad. How he wished he could help her somehow.

With a deep sigh, he began his search of the forest. What he found didn't improve his mood. Someone followed, though they were staying far enough back not to be seen.

Drogan continued up the trail where they would be traveling. It wouldn't be long before they left the woods and lost the shelter of the trees. Being in plain sight, unable to hide, wasn't something he wanted to do with two women and an infant.

"What is it?" Gerard asked as he stopped beside Drogan.

"We're being followed."

Gerard tensed, and his hand reached for the hilt of his sword. "How far back?"

"Far enough that I cannot tell who it is. It is as if they are waiting on something."

"And that is?"

"This," Drogan said and pointed to the path. "The trees will be gone."

"Leaving them in plain sight of us."

Drogan shook his head. "True, but we'll be easy targets, moving as slow as we are."

Gerard cursed. "I don't want Maris to know. There's no reason to frighten her until it's time."

"Agreed."

"What do you want to do?"

"I'll tell you what I think we shouldn't do, and that's venture out into the open." Drogan looked to his friend, awaiting his response, since this decision affected his wife and child.

Gerard glanced into the woods around them. "If we leave the path, it will slow us even more. I cannot chance it."

"All right," Drogan said and returned to the cart. He knew he could not dissuade his friend from staying on the path, but he could do whatever possible to ensure their safety.

Serena had just handed Jocelyn to Maris when Drogan found her. "I need your help with the horse."

She didn't say a word as she followed him to the animal.

Drogan lifted the front hoof of the horse and pretended to show Serena something so Maris wouldn't be alerted. When Serena leaned down next to him, he whispered, "I'm going to watch the back of the cart and the path from now on. Can you lead the horse or drive the cart?"

"Of course. What's wrong?"

"We all knew it would be dangerous leaving Hawthorne."

"Aye. But this seems specific."

"Just a precaution." As she turned to go, he stopped her with a hand on her arm. "Stay alert," he warned.

"I sense anxiety from you," she said.

He shifted his feet as she saw Gerard speaking to Maris. "I would rather you not mention this to Maris."

"I won't. She has enough to worry over right now."

"Do you have a weapon?"

She shook her head, her black hair moving against the light blue of her gown.

"There's a dagger beneath the seat in the cart. Use it if you have to."

She looked down, and he followed her gaze to his hand on her arm. He immediately released her and took a step away. For a heartbeat, his eyes drank in her beauty amid the splendor of the dense trees before he turned to go.

"Be careful," he heard her say, and he had the oddest feeling in his chest. As if his heart moved.

Chapter Ten

*S*erena watched Drogan until he disappeared into the trees. The unease she sensed in him was strong. He was worried. But about what?

Whatever it was, he hadn't wanted her or Maris to know.

She moved to the cart to find Gerard checking his weapons. Aye, without a doubt, something troubled the men. They were careful not to let it show, though, and it surprised and pleased her that Drogan had told her as much as he had. It hadn't been much, but it was more than Gerard had told Maris.

Serena went to the horse and took hold of the bridle. The road before her stretched endlessly, holding all sorts of danger she hadn't been aware of with Drogan by her side. Now, she faced it alone.

"I won't be too far ahead of you," Gerard whispered as he walked past her.

She tried to respond, but her mouth was dry. Many times she had heard the young lasses of Hawthorne beg for some kind of adventure, but she was more content to have her routine and the safety of her home.

Now she had neither.

She clicked to the horse and got him moving. She found it difficult to stay calm with the horse's reins jingling, the creaking of the cart, and the wheels turning on the dirt road. Despite her eyes taking in everything, she was a bundle of nerves.

When Gerard went over the rise ahead of them, she felt alone. When she finally crested it, Gerard was even farther away than before.

Beyond the edge of the forest, a barren landscape spread out before her. Her fear grew tenfold. She had an inkling that leaving the safety of the trees was what worried both Gerard and Drogan.

She glanced over her shoulder, hoping to spot Drogan, but saw nothing except more trees. With her teeth worrying her bottom lip, she trudged forward.

When she emerged from the shaded wood and into the sunlight, a shiver ran through her.

Evil fast approached them.

She tried to make the horse move faster, but the animal was old, and had only had one pace—walk. Several times, she almost reached for the dagger Drogan had told her about but somehow managed to keep her hands locked around the reins instead.

Two hours later, her shoulders ached from the apprehension that had festered in her, so much so, that she could barely turn her head. Her face and neck sizzled from the exposure to the sun, which she normally took such pains to hide from. Maris and Jocelyn had slept, never knowing the fear that enfolded Serena.

Gerard continued ahead of them, stopping every now and again to study the ground. She knew he had found something of interest when he halted and waited for them.

"Something wrong?" she asked when she finally reached him.

He shook his head. "There are carts traveling ahead of us and a small village not far up the road. We might get lucky and make it there before nightfall."

"I hope so."

"Any sign of Drogan?"

She looked behind them. "Nay."

"He'll be fine. If anyone can take care of himself, it's Drogan. I'm going to go check on my family."

A few moments later, Gerard walked ahead of her, letting her know it was time to get moving again. The cart creaked as it began to roll once more, Jocelyn cried and Maris shifted inside the cart. Even with the flaps down, Serena knew Maris was feeding Jocelyn.

Serena forced her mind away from her aching shoulders and stinging flesh to the night ahead, when she could rest her throbbing feet and apply some healing herbs to her skin. All she could think about was moving forward. Always forward.

When she next looked up, the sun was sinking in the sky and Drogan stood at her side.

"Serena," he said and laid a gentle hand on her arm to halt her.

Even though his touch was light, her skin felt as though it were on fire. She cried out and pulled away from him.

He moved until he stood in front of her. "What happened to your skin?"

"The sun," she said and leaned against the horse.

"Why didn't you do something to protect yourself?" he all but shouted. "You saw we were leaving the woods."

"I know." She was more ashamed of herself than she had been in years. "I was so worried about keeping Maris and Jocelyn safe, I didn't think about it."

"Surely it crossed your mind when your skin began to sting."

She glanced up at him to see his jaw clenched. "You know it did."

"So tell me why you didn't stop."

She stood as straight as she could and raised her chin. "Because their lives are more important than mine. I didn't want to take the chance of stopping and giving anyone time to catch up with us."

To her surprise, Drogan took a step back and stared at her. "I've never known a woman who could astound me like you're able to."

"If that's a compliment, it's a poor one," she snapped,

wanting to sit down and rest. She had never been so exhausted in her entire life.

"Do you have something to put on your skin?"

"Aye."

He shifted closer to her. "I'd pick you up myself and set you in the cart, but I'm afraid I'll cause you more pain."

Despite her aches and her stinging skin, she smiled. "How much farther until we stop?"

"We aren't far from the next village. I wanted to reach it if we can."

"Then I will manage until then." She got the horse moving again.

Just two steps later, she wished she had let him help her into the cart. She had never known she had a stubborn streak, and she found she didn't like it at all. Thankfully, they reached the small village before she collapsed, but it was a close thing.

Gerard and Drogan had decided against going into the village, determining they should stay on the outskirts, hidden from the main road. All Serena wanted to do was lay down and sleep. Instead, Drogan insisted she eat and see to her skin.

She wanted to tell him to leave her alone, but that took too much effort. And then she had no argument at all when he brought her bag to her. The herbs she needed to treat her skin were inside.

After she rummaged through the bag, she found what she needed and began to grind the herbs in a bowl. Once that was done she poured a little water onto the herbs until it made a paste, and then smoothed it onto her skin.

She knew how she looked—not to mention how she smelled—but she didn't care. The cooling effect of the aloe mixed in the herbs relieved the sting. She lay back on her blanket, thinking to rest a moment, but sleep immediately claimed her.

Drogan watched Serena grind the herbs and smooth the mixture on her skin. A small smile tugged at her lips, letting him know the mixture soothed away her pain. He just hoped her burn would be gone by morning and that she remembered to properly cover herself the next day.

He couldn't explain the anger that had overtaken him when he'd seen what the sun had done to her. Her beautiful, creamy skin was red and blotchy, and if he wasn't mistaken, some blisters were forming. Exhaustion had taken its toll on her body. He wished the journey was easier, but they were just getting started and had barely managed to cover the necessary distance in the first day.

At least they had reached the village. Whoever followed them was hanging back on purpose. Drogan just wished he knew who trailed them. Knowing the enemy made the fight easier.

"She's asleep," Maris said as she sat between him and Gerard. "She didn't even wait to eat."

"She's worn out from the day," Drogan answered and glanced at Serena.

Maris looked at him, then Gerard. "Both of you look tired as well. Is everything all right?"

Drogan almost laughed as Gerard groaned.

"It was just a long day," Drogan answered.

Maris nodded in agreement. "There's enough food in the cart to make it a few more nights before we need to hunt."

"Serena and I got all we could. I don't know how she managed to obtain so much, but it was twice as much as I did," Drogan said.

"She's quite amazing."

Drogan found himself looking at Serena once more. She was amazing. He'd never met another woman like her and, if he was honest with himself, he never would. He had no idea women like Serena even existed. Witches, yes, but she was so much more than that.

She was putting her life in peril to see her friends to safety. Drogan knew of no other woman who would even think of doing that, yet Serena didn't hesitate in volunteering to go.

"You seem deep in thought," Maris said.

Drogan glanced at Gerard before he looked to Maris. "Not really."

Maris chuckled and reached over to make sure little Jocelyn was covered in the nearby cradle. "As good a liar as you are, Drogan, even I can see past that one."

"I'm thinking about the day ahead," he lied again.

"And gazing at Serena while you do it?"

Gerard flashed a smile at him, and Drogan groaned. "I'm worried about her and you and Jocelyn, Maris. This is a long, dangerous journey, and I want to see that we all reach Wolfglynn alive."

"Good," Maris said as she stood, the smile gone from her face. "Remember that whenever you look at Serena. She is meant for no one, Drogan. No one."

"Why?"

Maris sighed and looked over her shoulder at Serena. "It's the curse. Don't make her suffer as her mother did."

Maris would tell him no more, so he faced Gerard. "What does she mean?"

Gerard shrugged and stared at him.

"Did you know Serena's mother?"

"Aye," Gerard answered after a deep breath.

Drogan raked his fingers through his hair. "You want us together?"

"I do."

"Even if it brings her pain?"

"I do."

Drogan snorted and slowly gained his feet. "I don't understand you. Why would you want to cause her pain?"

"Because she might help you."

Drogan dropped his chin to his chest and laughed. "Ah, Gerard. There is nothing that can help me." He looked at his friend. "Leave me be. I'm content where I am."

He spun on his heel and stalked toward the village. When he spotted the well, he grabbed a water skin and went to retrieve some water. While he filled the skin, he noticed how cool the water was. Much too cold for Serena.

As he retraced his steps to the camp, he spotted five wagons lined just inside the village. A woman wrapped in a blanket stood watching him. The shadows allowed him nothing but her outline, but her presence disturbed him.

When he returned to the camp and poured the water into a bowl to heat over the fire, he noticed Maris studying him. He sighed and said, "I just want to make sure Serena can use the water. It is too cold coming out of the well."

For several moments, Maris said nothing. "You surprise me, Drogan, and few people do that."

He shook his head since he had no idea what she meant. He was looking out for the welfare of the women as he had been raised to do.

An image of his mother and father flashed in his mind. It had been a long time since he'd thought about them. His father had been a hard man who knew only one thing—how to use a sword. He had passed that skill to Drogan.

His mother had been quiet and meek, ruthlessly ruled by Drogan's father.

When Drogan had seen Gerard and Maris together, he realized not everyone had a relationship like his parents.

Too bad such joy wasn't meant for him.

Chapter Eleven

*S*erena's stomach wouldn't let her sleep. As much as she fought to ignore her hunger, it roused her out of her slumber. She opened her eyes to see the stars shining above her. The moon in all its glory hung in the sky, shedding its light on all.

The smell of food made her stomach growl. It was no use, she would have to rise and eat before she would find sleep again. She rolled onto her side and sat up. Maris and Gerard slept together nearby with Jocelyn cuddled in Maris' arms. It was a beautiful picture, and Serena couldn't help but stare at them.

An owl hooted in the distance, drawing her attention back to what plagued her. She rose on her knees and reached for the meat roasting on the fire. The heat scorched her fingers a bit, but it was worth it to taste the wonderful flavor.

"Is it too hot?"

She started at the voice. Drogan sat not far to her right.

"It is a little warm, but I can manage. How long did I sleep?"

"A few hours."

She nodded as she sat and went back to eating, mindful that she was being watched. It was then she noticed the bowl of water placed by her mat. She reached over and felt the water and found the temperature perfect.

Her gaze found him. "Did you do this?"

His nod was brief.

"Thank you."

He shrugged. "The well water was cold, even to my fingers."

A little ripple of joy rushed through her. He thought enough about her not only to get her water, but also to heat it so it wouldn't hurt her.

After she finished with the meat, she rinsed the paste from her skin. In the few hours it had been on, it had almost healed the blistering.

"You work magic with those herbs."

She smiled. "Not really. I just know what to use when."

"Did you learn that from your mother?"

"Aye. My mother was very knowledgeable about such things."

Suddenly, she felt a great rush of energy surround her. She climbed to her feet and peered into the darkness, seeking the source, needing to know what would pull at her in such a fantastic way.

The energy was powerful, and she didn't sense any type of evil or malice in it. It called to her, beckoned her. Summoned her.

"What is it?" Drogan asked as he unsheathed his sword.

"I don't know," she whispered.

Then Serena saw her. She walked into the light of the camp wrapped in a dark blanket, her blonde hair falling to her hips in waves of gold. The woman was so beautiful she could have no rival.

They stared at each other for long moments until the woman's lips spread into a smile. "I thought I sensed you."

Serena cocked her head to the side and stared as it dawned on her who this woman was. "You are *bana-bhuidseach*?"

"I am. It has been too many years since I last encountered one of our kind."

Serena swallowed, her chest aching at the truth of the woman's words. "I haven't seen anyone since my mother died."

"There are few of us left, I think." The beautiful woman looked around the camp until her gaze came to rest on something.

Serena followed the other woman's gaze to see Drogan holding his sword. She was about to tell him to put it away when the woman spoke.

"My name is Adrianna." She walked slowly to Drogan. He stood still as Adrianna circled him and then returned to Serena.

"I am Serena of Hawthorne."

"We need to talk," Adrianna said and walked away from the camp.

Serena moved to follow her, when Drogan's hand on her arm stopped her.

"Don't go far," he urged. "I'll be here if you need me."

She touched his hand. "It is the first time since my mother I have come across one of my own kind. Trust me. I am safe with her."

"I hope so."

Reluctantly, Serena pulled out of Drogan's grasp. She followed Adrianna to a spot near the edge of the village. Adrianna faced the wagons, the blanket still wrapped around her.

"There is darkness that threatens to take hold of him."

Serena sighed. "I know. I've sensed it."

Adrianna looked at her then. "You know of our curse?"

"I do. It crushed my mother."

"Yet, you would tempt yourself by being near him?"

"I have no choice. A great evil pursues my friends, and I must see them to safety."

"The couple that sleeps?"

Serena nodded. "I have seen their deaths and a way for them to live."

Adrianna sighed and looked away. "Then you must do as you have seen."

Serena closed her eyes and savored the companionship of one of her own, although she knew it would end soon.

"The journey ahead of you is treacherous," Adrianna said softly.

Serena opened her eyes and drew in a shaky breath. Then she spoke the words she had shared with no one. "It will be my death."

Adrianna's gaze snapped to her. "You've seen this?"

"It is the only way to keep my friends alive, and it's imperative they stay that way."

"Ah," Adrianna said and hung her head. "Our life isn't an easy road is it?"

Just then a group of men walked to the wagons, and one of them waved to Adrianna. They were clothed in vibrant colors, their hair dark and long. *Roma.*

"You travel with them?"

Adrianna nodded and smiled. "Aye."

"Is one of the men yours?"

The smile fell from Adrianna's lips. "I tried to keep my heart safe, but I was unsuccessful. It is rather frightening how swift love can claim us."

Serena's stomach clenched in fear and sorrow. "At least you have your child."

"I lost him two months after his birth from a fever."

Tears filled Serena's eyes. "I am so sorry, Adrianna. No one should have to suffer thus."

Adrianna lifted a corner of the blanket and dabbed at her eyes. "We must live with what is given to us." She looked at Serena. "Sleep well, Serena of Hawthorne."

When Serena returned to camp, Drogan was waiting for her.

"Are you all right?"

She nodded and slid beneath her blanket. "It's strange that I should meet up with a *bana-bhuidseach* when there are so few of us."

"I'm sorry that you can't stay and visit with her longer."

She stared at Drogan. "It was enough to have the few moments I did." She rolled on her side and tugged the blanket tighter as sleep pulled her under.

Cade's bright blue gaze stared hard at Drogan. "You know what he plans?" he whispered.

Drogan nodded and turned. He couldn't continue to look into Cade's eyes so filled with accusation and disgust.

"We must do something," Cade said, his voice rising.

"There's nothing we can do." Gerard ran a hand through his hair. "We have our orders."

Cade cursed and paced the small chamber they shared. "We've done enough already for him. For years we've been in the king's service, doing as he and his lords have commanded, never questioning what they asked. We must question this now."

Drogan rose to his feet and stepped in front of Cade. "If we do, we die."

"I won't be able to live with myself if we do this, Drogan," Cade stated, his eyes carrying the weight of his words.

For the first time since Drogan had met Cade, he saw fear and doubt in his friend's gaze.

"We will get through this," Drogan vowed.

The dream shifted as screams sounded around him. Over and over. Blood was everywhere. Coating him until he thought it would stain his skin.

And Cade...Cade was no longer Cade.

Drogan opened his eyes to find Gerard leaning over him. Gerard gave him one last shove before he straightened.

"All quiet?" Drogan asked as he pushed the nightmare from his mind. He couldn't allow himself to visit that memory, of that dreadful day that had altered all of them in some way.

"Aye." Gerard walked to Maris.

The sky was still dark, but it wouldn't be long before the sun peeked over the horizon. They needed to get moving. Drogan got to his feet and washed before he rolled the blankets and tucked them in the cart. He was going to wake Serena when he found her brushing her hair as she sat on the back edge of the cart.

"Feel better?"

She grinned. "Much."

"We have another long day ahead of us."

She nodded and finished braiding her hair before she jumped to the ground. He was fastening the horse to the cart when he heard Maris gasp. When he spun around, Adrianna stood by the fire.

"You are all in great danger," Adrianna said and looked around the camp until her gaze rested on Serena. "The evil that races after you will catch you before this day is over."

Drogan clenched his hands as Gerard held a trembling, white-faced Maris in his arms.

"They could have caught us yesterday, but didn't," Drogan said.

Adrianna's gaze shifted to him. She was beautiful, he'd give her that, but she seemed almost cold. Her blue eyes held none of the warmth of Serena's.

"I know what I saw." She turned back to Serena. "If you wish to carry out what you have to do, then you must heed my words."

"What do you suggest?" Serena asked.

"You must split up."

"Nay," Gerard said.

Serena went to him. "Gerard, please. She's like me. Listen to her."

Once Gerard understood what Adrianna was, his entire attitude changed. Drogan had a feeling he was being left out, shown only enough to ease his curiosity and keep him from asking too many questions.

"My people are leaving this morning as well," Adrianna said. She pointed to Gerard and Maris. "You two and the baby need to come with us. We'll be able to conceal you in one of our wagons. One of the Roma will take your cart and head in a different direction."

Drogan saw the hesitation in Gerard's eyes. His friend looked to him, but Drogan didn't have an answer. It was apparent Serena believed this woman, and that was almost enough to convince Drogan.

"Drogan will take you to Wolfglynn," Adrianna said.

Drogan looked at Serena, not believing she would have told this woman where they were headed.

"I didn't tell her," Serena told him, as if reading his mind.

Adrianna took a step closer. "After I talked to Serena last night, I went to my wagon and saw what threatens you. Serena is right in wanting to keep your family alive," she told Gerard.

"And what about Serena and Drogan?" Maris asked, her voice shaking.

Drogan's brow furrowed as he saw the look Adrianna cast at him before she turned her pale blue eyes to Serena. "They must continue on together." She took Serena's hands in hers. "I tried to see another way, but there isn't one."

Drogan knew he had done foul deeds in the name of the king in his past, but he could keep Serena safe. Unless that wasn't in question. Had Adrianna seen something else that caused her pain at leaving him alone with Serena? He looked closer at Serena and Adrianna and saw a brief lock of sorrow cross Adrianna's face.

It was obvious the two shared a secret, something even

Gerard and Maris knew nothing about. And whatever it was, it wasn't good.

"You haven't long to decide," Adrianna said and looked pointedly at Drogan. "I'll be at my wagon when you do."

With that, she was gone.

Drogan inhaled a deep breath while everyone watched him. He looked to Gerard first. "What do you think?"

Gerard shook his head and turned to Maris. "I don't know. If we can believe her, it might be something we should think about, though I'd rather us stay together."

Serena couldn't accept that they didn't believe Adrianna. "What does she have to say to prove herself? I sense her worry and fear. She is risking herself as well as her people to help us."

"True," Gerard said. "You trust her? After meeting her just last night?"

Serena bit her tongue and prayed for patience. "You have known me all my life, Gerard. Have I ever led you wrong?"

"Nay."

"And I most certainly wouldn't do it now with your life and your family's lives in danger."

When he didn't answer, she turned to Maris who had bent down to pick up a crying Jocelyn. "Maris?"

"I'm afraid," she said. "I've been afraid since I first found out that Gerard was in danger, and we had to leave our home. I don't know what to do, but if you trust her...then so shall I."

Serena reached over and hugged Maris. "I believe she will

bring you safely to Wolfglynn. She wouldn't split us up if it didn't somehow hinder the evil behind us."

"It will confuse him," Drogan admitted. "He won't be sure which way you went."

"Most likely he will come after you," Gerard said.

Serena looked over her shoulder at Drogan. He nodded. "I hope he'll do just that."

"We'll be fine," Serena told Gerard and Maris. "Hurry and make your decision, for the Roma leave soon."

In less than thirty minutes, they had broken camp and come to a decision.

Maris hugged Serena tightly. "Hold onto your heart."

"I will," Serena promised as she pulled out of the embrace and reached over to kiss Jocelyn. "I will see you soon, angel," she whispered to the child.

"Serena," Gerard said.

"Just keep them safe. We'll see you in no time." She stepped back as Gerard and Drogan exchanged a few words in private.

"I'm sorry I could not find another way," Adrianna said as she walked up.

Serena shrugged. "I'm strong enough to deny him."

Adrianna stared at her.

"I am," Serena insisted.

"I hope so. Be careful, Serena."

She walked to Drogan's side as Gerard led the cart after the Roma. As much as she tried to deny it, she knew the real adventure was about to begin.

Chapter Twelve

"We better get moving." Drogan lifted Serena's bag onto his shoulder. He wished they could have bought some horses, but it was too risky to acquire them in the same town where they parted from Gerard and Maris. It would have to wait for another town or home they encountered.

"Which way are we going?" Serena asked.

He glanced at her. Her braided black hair hung over her left shoulder, and she held her back stiff and straight, as if she faced the horrors of the world.

"I won't let you come to harm."

Her startling, vivid blue eyes shifted to him. "I know, or I would never have agreed to Adrianna's suggestion. Gerard trusts you with his life as well as the lives of his family. I also trust you."

Her faith stunned him. He gave her a slight nod of his

head and pointed to the forest in the far distance. It was densely wooded, giving them plenty of places to hide if need be. "I think it wise to stay off the roads."

"I agree. The fewer people who see us, the better."

He smiled at her thinking. "Precisely."

"Well, I suppose we ought to be on our way."

He held out a hand to stop her. "It'll be a bit before we reach the woods. You must cover your skin."

"Long sleeves will take care of my arms."

"And the rest?"

With a quirk of her brow, she reached into her bag where it hung from his shoulder and dug inside. She pulled out a few items and smiled. "Gloves for my hands and a hat to help cover my face."

After she had donned the garments, he nodded. "Ready?"

"Aye," she said and reached for her bag.

"I'll carry it."

Her smile was that of a mother talking to a slow child. "You are carrying yours. There is no need to tote mine as well. The least I can do is carry my own."

Drogan consented. "Only if you promise to let me know if it becomes a burden."

"Agreed," she said. She took the bag and settled it on her shoulder before she fell into step beside him.

He kept the pace steady, but it was much quicker than they had the previous day. He imagined they'd cover almost twice as much ground as he'd foreseen.

His thoughts turned to their group being parted. "Did you know we would have to split from Gerard?"

She shook her head as she walked amid the tall grass. "It wasn't something I saw before we left, but I'm sure had I looked last night, I would have seen as Adrianna did."

"You mean something changed?" It was disturbing to even think along the lines his mind was traveling.

"Aye. Either something we did or something the people following us did was different from my original vision. It happens frequently. I should have tried to look last night when we reached the village."

"You were exhausted. You can't expect to do everything."

She halted and looked at him. "It is my duty to keep Gerard and his family alive. I take that seriously."

He stopped beside her. "It is also my duty, and so is keeping you alive. I take *that* seriously." He knew there was more than she let on, but he allowed her to keep her secrets since he had plenty of his own that nothing could get him to share.

She hung her head for a moment and sighed. "I'm sorry, Drogan. I didn't mean to sound curt. It is only that this is very important to me."

"I understand." And he did. It was just as important to him that he find which evil was after Gerard and end it. It was past time for that evil to die.

She gave him a small smile and began walking. He let her stay a ways in front of him so she wouldn't see him turning to look behind them.

After a few moments, she ran across a long limb about the size of her wrist. She looked over her shoulder at him and grinned. "Ha. A walking stick. Just what I needed."

He found himself chuckling at her enthusiasm. "You've never been away from Hawthorne, have you?"

"Nay. My mother was born and raised there, as was her mother and her mother before her. I love Hawthorne and never had a desire to leave."

"It is something your people do, staying in one village for that long?"

She laughed then, the sound floating around him like butterflies. *Butterflies?* Good Lord, what was coming over him?

"Tell me, Drogan. Is it something your people do, living in the same castle generation after generation?"

He pressed his lips together. "All right. I get your meaning."

"I may be a witch, but I am still a woman."

That was for sure, Drogan thought. *All woman.* He cleared his throat and pulled his gaze away from the gentle sway of her hips. For a moment, he had the strongest urge to lay her down in the thick grass and make love to her.

He closed his eyes, begging his body to cool down and focus on arriving at Wolfglynn. But his body, it seemed, liked being in a constant state of arousal, especially now that he was alone with Serena.

By the time they stopped to rest, Drogan needed to dunk himself in cold water. Badly. His thoughts centered on having

Serena naked in his arms, her soft moans begging him for more.

There had been times in his past when he had craved a woman, but not to the extent or depth of his hunger for Serena. He watched her furtively as she removed the man's hat from her head. The sun had disappeared behind the large, ominous clouds rolling their way.

"It looks like rain," she said as she stared at the clouds.

He dragged his gaze from her and looked to the sky. "That it does. I doubt we will be dry much longer."

But somehow, the clouds and the rain stayed to the east of them, giving them a reprieve. Drogan said a brief prayer of thanks as they trudged across the countryside. He worried that straying off the main road would be too difficult for Serena, but she proved remarkably adept, something rare in the ladies he knew—or most women for that matter.

His admiration for her grew with each step she took. He expected they would need to take many breaks, but after the short one they took before noon, they didn't stop again until it was time to eat.

Even then, she rested her feet, ate her food, and was then ready to proceed. At this rate, they might just make it to Wolfglynn in a matter of days.

There was no doubt being alone with Drogan put Serena on edge, but only because she knew what was deep in her wanton soul. She kept ahead of him to avoid being too near. But even those few steps didn't stop her from feeling his presence, of knowing his tall, muscular body was behind her.

Of feeling the bonds of her attraction growing, thickening with every step.

There was no denying the pull he had on her. She fought to keep her eyes straight ahead and not look at him. She desired to talk to him just to give her a reason to look deep into his golden-brown eyes.

None of what she did seemed to bother Drogan, for which she was most grateful. They kept a comfortable silence as they plodded across the land, and she both dreaded and looked forward to the coming of the night.

There was real fear in her when she thought of the nights they would spend together. Alone. She had no doubt he would never touch her unless she wanted him to, and that was the real folly for she did crave his touch.

Desperately.

Light and warm, his caress was something she rarely, if ever, experienced when someone touched her, which made her wonder what it would feel like to be kissed by him. To walk into his arms and lay her head on his chest. To have his arms wrap around her and hold her for the night.

Ah, a kiss. It was something she had never experienced. She had witnessed it enough times, and Maris certainly looked as though she enjoyed it. Serena had heard the sighs of the girls, had seen the way they smiled after a kiss.

She was missing something extraordinary, she was sure of it. But did she dare to chance her heart for one kiss?

The answer was a loud, and very resounding, yes in her mind.

To feel normal for just one moment in time. She'd never allowed herself to even dream of the possibility, but now with the attraction that took over her entire thoughts, she could think of little else.

"Do you need rest?" Drogan asked as they passed a huge boulder protruding from the ground.

She stopped after stepping over several rocks and leaned against the boulder. "Aye, it would be most appreciated."

"You should have told me you were weary."

Serena chuckled and glanced at him. "Drogan, I've been tired since I woke this morning. Nothing will change that, nor will griping about it. We must travel and travel fast."

The way he gazed at her, with such heat and intensity, made her stomach flutter and chills race over her skin. Their gazes locked, and for half a heartbeat, Serena thought he might come to her, touch her. But he remained three paces away.

"You are a very rare woman, Lady Serena."

"In more ways than one," she added.

"Tell me about the curse."

She accepted the water skin he handed her and drank deeply. After she wiped her mouth and handed the skin back to him, she thought over his request.

"Speaking of my people and their ways isn't something I

usually do."

"I know," he said after he took a drink himself. "I'm curious to learn more about you and your people. What happens when your people die out? Don't you want the knowledge that magic existed to live on?"

She sighed and fingered the hat she had kept in her hand in case the sun returned. Somehow Drogan had the ability to make her look at a situation in a completely different light. There was no denying her people were dying out. How much longer did they have before no more witches existed?

Serena didn't believe it was too far into the future.

"The curse has been around for centuries. Once upon a time, the *bana-bhuidseachs* were many upon this land."

"Were they always here?"

She shook her head. "We came from a distant land full of sand and great monuments that reached to the sky."

"What brought your people here?"

"I don't know. That part of our history has never been told as far as I know. If there was a reason, it was lost through time and the telling of our history. I suspect they wanted to see more of the world," she said and rose to her feet. "Come. I will tell you more as we walk."

She reached for her bag, but Drogan was quicker and slung it on his shoulder. With a grin, she gripped her walking stick and started forward.

"As our history puts it," she continued, "the *bana-bhuidseach* were happy and prosperous here for a time. Until Helen."

"Who was this Helen?"

"The one who caused the curse. It is said no woman before or since has ever held such beauty. It is said her beauty caused the flowers to cry."

He snorted. "I've seen beauty before, Serena, but only once have I gazed upon a woman who might make flowers cry."

The jealousy within her roared to life, and despite her attempts, she couldn't keep the sarcasm from her voice when she asked, "Really? And who would that be?"

"You."

Her feet refused to move after she heard him. When he turned to look at her, she could only stare. "There is no need to flatter me."

"In case you haven't noticed, I'm not a man who says anything he doesn't mean."

Joy blossomed and spread through her body like liquid gold. She had kept away from men for a reason, but she had heard and witnessed flirting and the flattery of men. Never had she thought any would be directed at her.

It was an odd, beautiful feeling she would hold within her for the rest of her days. "You think me pretty?"

"Aye. Even a blind man could see your beauty."

She licked her lips as a smile pulled at her mouth. "Words worthy of poetry, my lord. I didn't expect that from a hardened knight."

He chuckled and shifted his feet. "I don't claim to write

poetry or gilded phrases to bring a woman to her knees. I believe in honesty. It's how I've tried to live my life."

"And an admirable job you have done." She wondered at the shadow that flitted across his eyes at her words, but she chose not to speak of it.

She continued walking, thinking of her ancestors and how one of her kind might have kept a man like Drogan at bay. Was it even possible? Did she want to try?

And that's what terrified her. She wasn't sure she wanted to push Drogan away. It wasn't just because of his fine body or flattery. It was the man, the hardened, soul-weary man who walked beside her that threatened all she had of herself.

It would be so terribly easy to give in to the need, the desire that prodded her.

"Will you finish your story? I'm eager to hear the end."

"Of course. Where was I? Oh, Helen. Helen knew she was the most beautiful woman to walk the earth, and every man and boy around flocked to her side, begging her to become their bride. This was at a time when my people lived together."

"Many of you?"

"Aye, from the accountings, they say we were larger than most cities you come across. I would wager to guess that we were greater in number than the people of London."

Drogan whistled.

"I know," she said. "There were a few outsiders, non-*bana-bhuidseach*, and they didn't care what we were."

"Strange how times change."

She nodded. "There was a young lad who was in love with Helen. He wanted her desperately and managed to win her favor."

"Until."

She grinned when she saw his expectant look. "How did you know there was an 'until'?"

"There always is." One side of his mouth tilted in a smile.

"A man came to the village. He was a man of the king with great wealth and a title to accompany it. Helen liked what she saw and abandoned the young lad for the titled lord and the wealth she would have as his wife. The young man was so devastated that he threw himself into the river and drowned."

Drogan grunted. Leave it to a woman to cause some type of disaster, he thought to himself. "I take it this is when the curse was given."

"Oh, aye. The young man's mother was one of the elders. She was so grief-stricken and bereft that instead of cursing Helen, she cursed our entire people."

"And what was the curse?" Curiosity had driven him to ask about it in the first place, but now he had to know what it entailed.

He waited patiently while Serena glanced at him, as if deciding whether or not to divulge the secret. Just as he was about to give up on discovering the answer, he heard her soft sigh.

The sound of a horse neighing jerked him around. "Run," he said and took hold of her hand.

Chapter Thirteen

*D*rogan looked for a place to hide, but all there was for cover was the tall grass. All he could hope was that the horses were few and didn't trample him and Serena beneath their hooves.

They ran as far as they could with Drogan looking over his shoulder every few moments. When he caught sight of a horse, he yelled for Serena to drop to the ground.

He covered her with his body, putting his arms around her head to help protect her. She trembled beneath him, and he wished they had been able to find some sort of shelter in which to hide. The grass afforded them little protection, but at least it was something.

They were lucky enough that the riders skirted them and continued on. Drogan lifted his head and watched as the last rider passed them.

"They're gone," he said.

"Were they looking for us?"

"I don't think so."

He looked down to find Serena looking over her shoulder at him, her face mere breaths from his. Her soft bottom hugged his rod, bringing instant, hot awareness to him. His body roared painfully to life, and no matter how many times he told himself to roll off her, he couldn't.

He'd wanted to do nothing but touch her since they'd departed that morning on their own. Just one touch, but he hadn't dared. Now that he was on top of her, all he could think about was her delectable, kissable lips.

His blood pounded as he gazed into her blue eyes. He thought he might have seen longing in her gaze. His head lowered slowly, hesitantly. Just as he was about to touch his mouth to hers, she turned away.

"I'm glad they're gone," she said, her voice breathless and soft as a whisper.

Drogan quickly moved off her and got to his feet. "Aye."

While he pretended to adjust his weapons, she stood and brushed the dirt from her gown and looked around nervously.

"I suppose we should move on?"

He straightened his shoulders and nodded, his yearning for her stronger than before now that he'd felt the length of her body against him. "Night will be falling soon, and I don't think we'll be lucky enough to find shelter or woods."

"Which means?"

"No fire."

"Oh," she said and walked ahead of him. "At least we have some food Gerard and Maris shared with us."

Once again, Drogan allowed her to stay in front of him. He needed time to cool his aching body before they stopped for the night, and he had no wish for her to see him aroused as he was. And if he got close to her again, he wasn't sure if he could keep a leash on his desire.

He wanted her that badly. The more he told himself to stay away, the more he craved her.

Drogan reached out and let the end of her braid touch his fingers. If he couldn't touch her as he wanted, he'd touch her when he could. It wouldn't be enough, not ever enough. He feared even if he did make love to her not even then would his desire be quenched. She affected him that deeply.

He'd never known a woman could do that to a man. Was it her magic? Or the woman herself? Her beauty was unmatched, but then again so was her bravery and cunning.

It wasn't until he began to wonder what strong, noble sons they could have together that he pushed all thought of her from his mind. Or he tried.

No words were shared as the sun continued its descent until only red and gold streaks were left in the sky. He paused and looked around. As he had feared, they hadn't reached the woods or any safety.

"It's one night in the open," Serena said. "We'll make do."

He marveled at her attitude. "Are you always like this when faced with such obstacles?"

She shrugged one shoulder. "I suppose. How else would you have me be?"

"Most women I've known would moan and groan and cry about how unfair it all is."

"How strange. Maris isn't like that, and I don't know any of the women at Hawthorne who are like that either."

Drogan laughed. "You never know how a person will react until something doesn't go their way. The ladies at court would cause a stir if their linens weren't turned down correctly on their beds."

"I think those women are spoiled."

"I think you're right."

She laughed softly and raised her face heavenward.

"What is it?" he asked, suddenly alert.

"Don't you feel it?"

He looked around, expecting to feel...something. "Nay."

"It's the wind."

His gaze went to her, and he stared, transfixed. Just the slightest movement of her hair let him know that indeed the wind blew. The rapture on her face was beautiful to behold, and he would do just about anything to see her gaze at him with such an expression. Though he wasn't sure he could ever bring such joy to a woman.

It was disconcerting and brought the darkness that much closer to him. Who would have known that being in the company of a witch would make him almost wish the darkness would leave?

Unable to watch the pleasure enfold her, Drogan turned

away. He adjusted the bags he carried and looked in the direction the horses had taken. They traveled on the same course.

"You didn't feel it?" Serena asked softly again.

Drogan shook his head, refusing to look at her.

"It is one of the rare times the weather doesn't pain me in some way." She took a deep breath and squared her shoulders. "I'm sorry if I kept you waiting."

"Take what enjoyment you can, for there is little of it in this world," he said and began walking.

He heard her sigh. "Such cynicism. Do you derive no enjoyment from this life at all?"

Drogan laughed dryly. "Enjoyment," he murmured as he knelt and studied the horse tracks. "I used to pray that I would find some small measure of happiness in my life, but I soon learned that men such as me don't get that kind of contentment."

"Maybe you're wrong," she said and placed her hand on his shoulder.

Drogan's body stilled. Heat from her touch went through his jerkin and shirt to his skin, and then sank deeper. He looked at the hand, and then slowly stood to face her. Her hand fell away, and he immediately missed her touch. Once more he found himself falling into the blue of her eyes.

He wondered what she was thinking, if she had wanted to touch him as much as he had been trying to devise ways to touch her. The longer he stared, the more he felt himself opening up to her. He feared she might sense the darkness, might see it. He could have stood there all night staring at her. But the reminder of their mission flared in his mind.

"There were six of them."

Her brow furrowed. "What?"

"Six horses. Riding fast. They happen to be on the same course as we." He turned and looked into the distance. "We should be safe traveling off the main roads, and that group of men are moving faster than us."

When he glanced back at her, he was grateful to see that she would delve no further into his feelings and the darkness that reined within him. For her to see it would mean she would discover his sin. And that simply couldn't happen. It was his alone to carry.

Never to share.

They moved faster now. He took the lead but shortened his stride so Serena could keep up. Never once did she complain. He half wanted her to. He wasn't sure how to deal with a woman who didn't grumble and whine the entire time he was with her, which was why he made acquaintances of the more common women. The ladies of royalty and nobility grated on his nerves with their incessant carping. He had anticipated the same from Serena and got something wholly different.

Night descended before Drogan decided to stop. He had seen a giant oak in the distance and had pressed on until they reached it. He handed Serena her bag and dug through his for the food. By the time he had gotten out what they would need, she sat on a blanket she had laid next to the tree and waited for him.

"It's all we have," he said as he handed her the bread and cheese. "Maybe tomorrow night we'll be able to light a fire, and I'll hunt."

"This is perfect," she said and reached for the food. "If it's safer without a fire, then you will not hear me complain."

He nodded and sat down to lean against the tree next to her. The heavens were ablaze with stars. He loved to study them and watch the moon as it changed nightly. It was a peculiarity of his nature that he hid from everyone, including Gerard.

"Is someone still following us?" Serena asked.

"I'm not sure. I would have to leave you alone while I checked, and I'd rather not. I think we need to keep moving as fast as we can to reach Wolfglynn."

She sat there for a moment chewing her food. "Do you think we confused them by splitting up? I would rather have them following us than Gerard and Maris."

"I, as well, but I have no idea if it worked or not."

She shifted her face toward him. "Would you have fallen for it?"

"It's difficult to say. I would like to believe that I wouldn't, but then again, I don't really know unless I'm in that situation."

"Do you think we'll reach Wolfglynn before the Roma?"

He heard the worry in her voice and wished he could take it away. "It's my plan. We covered more distance than I had planned. If we keep going as we did today, then we might very well reach my home in a matter of days."

She looked at him then. "But you told us without a horse it would take us nearly a week to get there."

"That's when we were traveling with the cart on the roads. We can cover a lot more distance by staying off the well-traveled paths. It keeps us from coming across towns, but it also keeps us hidden. I figure we can reach Wolfglynn in two to three days."

"And if we had a horse?"

"Even quicker."

She murmured something he didn't catch, and then louder said, "Tell me about your home."

Her request startled him. "It's a wild place far to the north. It's gets very cold there. My mother hated it, and few women who have ever visited have enjoyed it."

"Is that why you don't have a wife?"

He looked at his hands as he tore a piece of the bread. "It's one of many. Some men are destined to have families. Like Gerard. Then, there are men like me."

"Men like you?" she asked.

He looked at her and smiled. "I'm more suited to my solitary life at Wolfglynn."

"Why was it named Wolfglynn?"

"We have wolves. Not as many as we used to, but they are still there. It's on the coast where the land drops off to rugged cliffs and the dark blue waters of the sea."

"I've never seen the sea. Is it beautiful?"

He shrugged though she wasn't looking at him. "I think so. You can smell the salt thick in the air, and the wind is always blowing."

"And the castle?"

Drogan smiled in spite of himself. He loved his home immensely, even though it held bad memories of his parents. "It is a huge stone mass built near the cliffs, but I think it's perfect."

"I can tell," she said and smiled. "I can't wait to see it. I'm sure I will love it just as much as you."

For some reason, he wanted her to see it and to know what she thought. Strange that. He rarely invited anyone to Wolfglynn. It was his haven to regroup and relax after weeks at court.

"Good night," she said and turned over to burrow under her blanket.

"Good night." He watched her for several moments before he leaned his head back and closed his eyes.

Serena stretched her sore back the next morning and winced. She saw Drogan's questioning look as she climbed to her feet.

"I must have slept on a root."

"They can be a menace."

She rolled her eyes at his flippant tone. She often woke in a pleasant mood, but not sleeping well due to the root and what had occurred yesterday left her not quite herself.

When Drogan had landed on top of her, all she could think about was the feel of his hard, very male body on hers. She had thought he would kiss her, but she had worried that she would do it wrong and turned away. Now, she wished she had stayed still to see what he would have done.

She pushed up her sleeves to splash some water on her arms and face when she noticed her arms.

"What's wrong?" Drogan asked as he passed by her.

"There's nothing there."

He peered over her shoulder. "Nay, just your arm. Were you looking for something?"

"Bruises," she said and looked over her shoulder at him. "From yesterday when you fell on me."

His forehead creased. "I tried not to land hard."

"Nay," she said and got to her feet to face him. "You didn't fall hard, but hard enough that I would normally have bruises."

He took her arm and turned it one way then another. "No bruises." He raised his gaze to her. "What does that mean?"

"I have no idea." She stared down at his large, calloused hands engulfing her small arm. Heat radiated up through her body, and she grew acutely aware of him.

When she raised her face, she noticed just how close they were to each other, and it had been her doing. He hadn't moved, but she had stepped toward him when she had stood. He trained his gaze on her, waiting to see what she would do.

She should back away, but her feet wouldn't listen. Indeed,

they told her to move closer. She found it difficult to look anywhere but into the golden eyes that beckoned her.

There was no denying the darkness that surrounded him, but she sensed it hadn't penetrated him fully yet. Maybe that's what drew her to him, the darkness. Whatever it was, she knew she was going to have a very difficult time keeping her heart safe.

But the reasons for that were becoming more and more difficult to remember the longer she was with Drogan.

Chapter Fourteen

he day passed in a blur for Serena. The sun stayed
hidden behind the ever-present clouds, and rain
threatened to drench them, yet didn't. They stopped and ate,
but she couldn't remember what she put into her mouth. And
there was little talk between them.

She would like to think it was because she sensed
something urging Drogan faster, but mostly it was because
she was weary down to her toes.

By the time they stopped for the night, all she wanted was
a bath and a warm bed. Instead, she got cool water to splash
on her face and the hard ground to sleep on. Her only comfort
was that they had reached another forest, and the shelter of
the trees afforded them a small fire.

"I'll be within screaming distance," Drogan told her as he
picked up his bow and arrow.

She waved him off. "I'll be fine. Just go. I'm starving."

He gave her a quick nod and disappeared into the trees. Serena leaned close to the small fire to warm her hands. It was summer, but the nights still chilled her. She wondered what it would be like to be regular, to experience the snow without having to worry about freezing to death, to lift her face to the sun without having to worry that she would blister, or to sink into a nice hot bath instead of lukewarm water.

She blew out a long sigh as she arranged her blankets and sat cross-legged to unbraid and comb her hair.

In no time at all, Drogan returned and began to clean the rabbit he had captured. While he positioned it over the fire to cook, she watched him earnestly. He moved as though he had done this chore thousands of times and could do it in his sleep.

"How long were you in the king's service?" she asked.

"Almost ten years."

"That's a long time."

He shrugged and sat back, looking across the fire at her. "One does what the king demands."

"You didn't like being in his service?"

"You could say life at court doesn't suit me."

She smiled, recalling the times Gerard would rant about court. "Gerard, either."

"Some people live for it, but I just wished to return to Wolfglynn. It's the only place I belong."

"Did you get to know King Henry well?"

"Very," he said with a nod. "I liked him. It was the other men that made my hackles rise."

"It's one of those men who is after Gerard, isn't it?" she asked, watching him closely.

His gaze lifted to hers, and he stared hard. "Ask no more questions regarding that, Serena, for I will tell you nothing."

"I don't believe you or Gerard could have done anything that would make someone turn their backs on you. Maris still loves Gerard after he told her."

"Aye," Drogan said as he rose. "Maybe so, but, you won't gain that information from me."

She let it drop though she longed to dig deeper. Usually her curiosity wasn't this ferocious, but for some reason, she had to know what drove Drogan and why the darkness wanted to claim him.

As he returned to the fire, something dove right at Drogan. She didn't have time to call out a warning before it reached him. She watched as he ducked and fell to his knees, letting out a string of curses.

"Shite. What was that?" he asked as he rose up on his elbow.

Serena tried hard not to laugh, but her mirth wouldn't be tamped down. Soon, she was doubled over at the image of his eyes growing round when he saw something coming at his head.

"I'm delighted you find this amusing, my lady. I was attacked," he said as he got to his feet.

His affronted attitude made her laugh harder.

"Serena," he said, his voice low and threatening.

She pointed over her shoulder as she wiped the tears of

laughter from her eyes and rose to her feet. "It was only Nicodemus."

"Nicka...what?"

"The owl, Drogan."

He stared past her. "You have a pet owl?" he asked incredulously.

"Nay," she said and turned to face the owl. "He just showed up at my cottage window one night several years ago and kept coming. I figured if I was going to have a nightly visitor, he needed a name."

She heard Drogan snort as he moved around behind her. Laughter threatened again, but she was careful to hide her smile.

"Nice to see you, Nicodemus," she whispered to the bird. She saw Drogan scowling at the owl.

"Does he always attack people?"

"Nay. It's the first time I've seen him do that, although he has been gone for a few months now. He's quite friendly."

"Sure he is," Drogan grumbled as he rotated the rabbit over the fire. "Food is almost ready."

Serena returned to her blanket, barely masking the smile from her lips. She waited until he pulled away some of the meat and handed it to her before she spoke again. "Hmm. It smells wonderful."

He grunted what she assumed was a thank you. It was rather humorous to see that he was put out by the untimely arrival of Nicodemus. Somehow, Drogan's discomfort made him seem more normal.

Before, he had kept every emotion under tight control, and this let her get a glimpse of how he truly was. It was nice, if she did say so herself.

"You needn't frown so," she said as she bit into the meat. "Nicodemus won't bother you again."

"So you say," Drogan retorted as he sat back and began to eat.

"This is good," she said after several more bites.

A small smile pulled at his lips. "It's just because you're hungry and tired."

Serena shrugged. "It doesn't matter why. It's the best food I think I've eaten."

"Now I know you're exhausted."

She laughed, and Nicodemus gave a loud hoot. When she raised her gaze to Drogan, he eyed the owl with menace.

They finished their meal in silence and afterwards, Serena felt her eyes grow heavy. She covered herself with the blanket and lay down, intending to watch Drogan sharpen his dagger.

Drogan buried the bones of the rabbit and stepped into the darkness of the trees where he would rest and keep watch over Serena.

The owl still perched on a branch not far from Serena. He wondered if the owl would follow them all the way to Wolfglynn. At least he didn't have to feed him.

Drogan settled against a tree and leaned his head back. He

wasn't sure how long he had been there before he heard her cry out, but he was awake immediately.

He rushed to Serena's side at the same time she jerked upright. "What is it?"

"I don't know," she said and put a shaky hand to her forehead. "It was an awful dream."

"Everyone has dreams."

"There was something different about this one," she said and turned haunted blue eyes to him.

Trepidation grew as icy fingers of understanding gripped him. "How so?"

"I saw Gerard and Maris. They never made it to Wolfglynn."

"Did you see what happened to them?"

She shook her head. "I cannot remember."

Drogan sat back on his heels and looked at the glowing embers of the fire. "Do you have dreams like this often?"

"I've only had one or two before, but this one was much more intense than any I have ever had."

That wasn't what he wanted to hear. "Is there any way you can find out anything about Gerard and Maris?"

"I can try." She shifted until she was sitting on her knees.

She placed her palms on her thighs and closed her eyes. She made no noise, and for a moment, he thought she might have drifted off to sleep. Until her eyes flew open as she gasped and fell sideways.

Drogan caught her in his arms. As he held her against his

chest, his face pressed against the side of her head, he could feel her trembling. "What did you see?"

"The evil knows you're helping Gerard. He's coming to kill you."

"I assumed as much. What about Gerard and Maris?"

"They're still safe. Unless he catches you. We must reach Wolfglynn soon." She closed her eyes and sighed, her voice drifting to nothing.

And with that, he was left holding a beautiful, sleeping witch. Drogan leaned back until he was lying on the ground, cradling her head on his chest as he stared at the stars above him.

It was rather ironic that he had stayed away from the female nobility, yet whom did he find in his arms? It also bothered him that he enjoyed holding her. She fit perfectly against him, and if not for their dangerous mission, he could almost find himself wanting to court her.

Almost.

Big, dark eyes gazed up at Drogan, imploring him silently for help. He gripped his sword and prayed for God to intervene, to stop the madness. But it seemed God was too busy that day to hear the prayers of someone like Drogan.

Across from him Gerard looked ill at ease, and Drogan wondered if any of them would be able to carry out the orders.

"Now," Nigel's voice boomed near Drogan.

How Drogan wanted to plunge his sword into the bastard's gut, but to do so would mean certain death. Drogan's mind raced for some plan to get them out of this situation, but came up with nothing.

Nigel kicked his horse until the animal nudged Drogan's arm. "Do you forget your oath to the king, Lord Drogan?"

"Nay," Drogan said after finally finding his voice.

"Then do it," Nigel demanded.

Drogan glanced at Cade and Gerard and nodded. They had to carry out their orders. Or Die.

It was a choice none of them had ever hoped to find they had to make.

Drogan awoke with a start, his body shaking from the memories being dredged up. He shivered and held Serena tighter, needing her warmth and goodness to keep the darkness at bay for just a moment longer while he was so vulnerable.

He didn't know why her presence pushed the darkness away, only that it did. It was enough for him. The dreams pulled up long-buried memories he'd hoped to forget. Memories he knew would haunt him until his dying breath.

Serena awakened gradually, as if she were drifting through a fog. She recalled her horrible nightmare, then her search for

Gerard and Maris and finding the great evil that threatened Drogan.

Time was of the essence now.

It was about that moment she realized her cheek rested on a very masculine chest. A strong arm was wrapped around her, and her arm was thrown across Drogan's wide chest while one of her legs was tucked between his.

She tried to move her leg only to raise her gaze to see Drogan staring at her. Her breath caught in her throat at the heat radiating from his eyes. There was a primal look about him, and God forgive her, it excited her.

Nothing could have moved her away from him at that moment. When his other arm came around to pull her closer, she didn't object. He held her snuggly against him, body to body. Had she wanted to run, she knew he would have let her.

But she wanted to know what was next.

She tried to swallow yet her mouth was parched. Instead, she licked her dry lips and bit back a groan when Drogan's gaze lowered to her mouth.

Her breath was ragged as it filled her lungs, and her heart pounded in her ears. She clutched his thick shoulders in an attempt to steady herself, but it seemed to spur him further.

When he moved his head closer to hers, she tingled with anticipation. She looked away from his golden-brown gaze to his wide, full mouth and wanted him with an intensity that frightened her.

Aye, she yearned for him like the flowers yearned for spring.

They were breaths apart as she waited—and hoped—for her first kiss. His lips finally touched hers, soft but insistent. He nibbled, kissed, sucked and tasted her lips until she was breathless and dizzy.

Needy.

His hands roamed over her back, pulling her closer, tighter.

The kiss was everything she had hoped for and more. Then he slipped his tongue in her mouth.

A burning need overcame her as she opened herself to him. Afraid he would stop, she wrapped her arms around his neck. The pleasure coursing through her was hot and thick, and she begged for more.

She was surprised and afraid of her reaction to him, but there was no going back now. Her body had been awakened.

And it wanted more.

Chapter Fifteen

a moan of frustration tore from Serena's throat as Drogan pulled away. She tentatively touched her lips and gazed up at him in wonder. For those few precious moments she'd felt desired and beautiful. She'd felt...passion and bliss.

And she wanted more.

Serena forgot about the need pounding within her and looked at Drogan. He seemed as though he was fighting something within himself, and it would take just a nudge to push him over the edge. His jaw was clenched tight, and his fingers gripped her almost painfully.

If she didn't see how much he was struggling not to pull her to him again she'd have jerked away from him. But if she thought there was need within herself, the raw, stark hunger she saw in Drogan's golden eyes made her heart skip a beat.

"I'm sorry," he said thickly, though by the look in his eyes, she didn't think he regretted any of it.

And frankly, neither did she.

"I've never been kissed before," she said and wondered at how breathless she sounded. "I never knew it could be so...good."

He groaned and dropped his head back on the ground, an arm thrown over his eyes. "Don't tempt me, Serena. You will regret it later."

Regret? Not after she'd gotten such a delicious taste of him. "I don't regret the kiss."

He lifted his arm to look at her. "Neither do I. I've wanted to do that since the first time I saw you at Hawthorne."

She smiled at him and pushed herself up so that she was sitting. There were many things she wanted to say, but didn't know how. No man had paid her the attention Drogan had, and though she desperately wanted another kiss, she didn't know how to ask him for it. Instead, she busied herself with getting ready for the day. By the time they set out, not another word had been spoken about their fiery, amazing kiss.

It was near midday when Drogan finally looked at her. "There's a river up ahead. We'll follow it to Wolfglynn."

A bath was all Serena could think about once he'd mentioned the river. She had washed all she could with the little water they had, but to soak and scrub the dirt and grime from her would be wonderful.

"Do you think we'll have time for me to bathe?"

Drogan bit the inside of his mouth at the mental image of

Serena bathing in the moonlight. His body roared painfully, demanding he take her in his arms again, and he shifted his aching cock to relieve the pressure.

"If we cover enough ground today," he managed to say.

The memory of their kiss would forever be embedded in his mind. She had been sweet to the taste and passionate to the touch. It had taken everything he'd had not to cup her full breasts or pull her against his throbbing rod, but somehow he'd managed to hold that last shred of control. And how he regretted it.

The utter passion he'd witnessed in her blue depths had made him crave her all the more. There was just something so special and unique about Serena that made him want to keep her in his arms forever.

He'd half expected her to slap his face or pull away when he'd leaned down for the kiss. What he hadn't expected was for her arms to wrap around him or for her to respond with such hunger. She'd wanted the kiss as much as he. That thought alone brought him to his knees.

He watched her as they stopped at noon. Her thick, black hair was once again braided to fall over her left shoulder and hung alongside her breast. There was a small smile about her mouth, as if she had some secret she kept.

Maris was going to kill him when she found out what he had done.

"We must go. Now," Serena suddenly said, the smile gone. She jumped to her feet, her lips pressed together.

He looked around. "What is it?"

"I sense the evil, Drogan. It's moving quickly towards us. It is almost as if he knows where we are going."

Drogan didn't ask more. He leapt to his feet before grabbing their bags and Serena's hand. With his grip tight on her hand, he ran as fast as she could keep up with her skirts lifted in her free hand. He heard the gurgle of water the same time Serena tripped and fell. He kept his hold on her, which stopped her from tumbling away from him. In an instant, he was by her side, their bags discarded at his feet.

"Are you hurt?"

She lifted her palm to show him several tiny cuts that crisscrossed her palm and fingers. He cursed and looked over his shoulder.

"The river I spoke of is ahead."

"I'll be fine," she said and climbed to her feet.

Drogan could tell she had given everything she had already. There would be no more running this day. He looked around the trees, trying to recall if there was anywhere they could hide.

"Drogan, I'm all right."

"Nay, you're not," he said and faced her. "We won't get any farther today before he finds us. We need to hide."

She shook her head so hard her braid flipped over her back. "We must keep moving. He cannot catch you."

He took her shoulders in his hands and leaned down until he was nose to nose with her. "He won't, Serena."

She gave a brief nod, and he reached for the bags. "Come," he said and held out his palm to her.

With her injured hand tucked against her, she took his. He gave her a reassuring smile and set out at a quick walk. In no time at all, they reached the river.

"Should we cross it?"

"Nay," he said and looked up to the trees. "But we will hide."

He glanced at Serena to see her mouth drop open. "Are you daft? I cannot climb a tree in these skirts," she said and took a step back.

"You can, and you will." He squeezed her hand reassuringly. "It is the only way."

She sighed, her gaze still doubtful. "All right."

He looked down at her skirts and knew they somehow had to get out of the way.

She noticed his gaze and bent over. "I used to tie my skirts when I was a little girl to play in the water."

He watched as she lifted the back hem between her legs and tied it so that it looked as though she wore pants that stopped at the knees. Drogan swallowed hard as he stared at her shapely calves through her stockings.

"Drogan?"

He jerked his gaze to hers and refused to look down again. Of course, that was rather difficult once he lifted her against the huge oak and helped her place her legs on the first limb. His hand grazed her leg as he showed her how to put her feet on the tree. And once, when her feet slipped, her bottom landed right in his hands.

It was a rather nice behind, he had to admit. One he

would like to further explore. Drogan pushed such thoughts away and climbed with her to make sure she got high enough to be concealed.

A short time later, he had her secured in the oak. "Stay here and don't make a sound."

"It might be hours before they come."

"True," he said and reached into the bags for a water skin and food.

She took it and frowned. "Where are you going?"

He pointed back the way they had come. "Back there a bit. I want to see him when he first comes."

"Won't he know to look in the trees?"

"That depends."

"On what?"

On who it is. "If he's smart enough. Don't worry, he won't find you."

"I hope you're right."

He gave her a bright smile. "I'm always right."

Then to his surprise, she reached toward him and cupped his face before placing her lips on his for a quick kiss that ignited his senses and set his blood afire all over again. "Be careful, Drogan of Wolfglynn."

All he could manage was a nod before he climbed down. Once on the ground, he looked back up at her. She was well hidden in the foliage, though she had a good view of her surroundings. She would be safe.

She had to be safe.

He hurried off to find himself a tree. He found just what

he was looking for not far from Serena. When he was in place he looked over and found her watching him.

Now, there was naught to do but wait.

They waited until dusk before Drogan heard the neighing of a horse. All day, he'd had a nagging feeling he was being watched, but the only person who would be looking at him was Serena, and she had been asleep for several hours.

It could be the damned owl, though he hadn't seen it that morning.

He slid his sword free of the scabbard and made sure his bow and arrows were within easy reach as he anxiously waited for the rider to show himself.

Drogan perched on the sturdy limb and leaned out as the horse came into view. He nearly cursed aloud when he realized he couldn't tell who it was. The rider wore full armor, as if he wanted to be hidden. There were no colors or emblem on the shield, another sign that this knight wanted to keep his identity a secret.

Bastard.

Drogan watched as the knight looked at the ground and their footprints. He wondered if the fool would fall for his trick. When the knight turned his mount around, Drogan knew he had won a victory, small though it was. It would give them a little time to reach Wolfglynn.

They needed to find a horse. And fast.

He climbed higher and watched as the knight kicked his horse into a run to follow the fake trail he had made. In a flash, Drogan grabbed his weapons and jumped from the tree. By the time he reached Serena, she had descended down a few limbs.

"Is he gone?" she asked.

"Aye. For now. We must travel through the night."

She nodded and climbed down the way Drogan had shown her. "Did you see who it was?"

He shook his head. "Not this time."

When she was again on the ground, he noticed she had wrapped her hand using a part of her shift as a bandage. "Ready?"

She smiled. "Very. I'm weary of traveling."

He chuckled and started to follow the river. They had hiked for half an hour when he heard the growl.

"What was that?" Serena asked in a whisper.

Drogan pushed her behind him and faced the woods. "Something I had hoped we wouldn't encounter."

"And what might that be?" she asked, her voice shaky from fear.

"A wolf."

She laughed, the sound laced with hysteria. "Of course. Are you sure?"

"I would know that sound anywhere." He backed her up as he readied his bow and arrow.

He notched his bow when the first wolf emerged from the

woods. As he pulled back on the string to fire the arrow, Serena gasped then screamed.

One look over his shoulder and he saw she had fallen into the river. The water flowed faster than normal, and her pained expression as she broke the water's surface told him it was much too cold for her.

He looked at the wolf and knew he had one option. He jumped into the river and swam after Serena while holding onto his bow and arrow. She had managed to cling to a low-lying limb and that allowed him to catch up to her.

He had just enough time to put away his arrow and sling his bow over his shoulder before her strength gave out and she let go of the limb. He caught her and put his arm under her legs as he found the bottom and climbed out of the river.

He wondered how he would warm her when he spotted something through the trees. His feet carried them through the foliage until he was able to see the outline of a small cottage. It was the only place within leagues of his castle, and he prayed the owner wasn't home so he wouldn't have to answer any questions.

"Hello," he called out as he neared. No one answered, and he soon saw that it was abandoned.

He kicked the door open and peered inside. It was clean, which meant whoever lived here hadn't been gone too long. He went to the bed and laid Serena down. Her lips were blue, and her teeth chattered.

As quickly as he could, he peeled off her clothes and

covered her with several blankets. He was thankful whoever lived here had left some, since their own were wet from their swim.

He found wood near the hearth, lit a fire, and arranged her clothes so they would dry. When he went back to her, she shook so badly the covers kept falling off of her.

"Well, there's only one thing to do," Drogan mumbled before he kicked off his boots, shed his clothes and climbed in beside her.

He pulled Serena against his chest and sucked in a breath at the icy feel of her skin. She clung to him as if he was the one thing keeping her alive, and he began to fear he just might be.

The water had been cool to him, but he could imagine how it felt to Serena. He rubbed his hands up and down her arms, trying to warm her any way he could. With his legs, he tucked hers between his and gritted his teeth at the feel of her feet. They were like the lakes after a winter freeze.

He smoothed her wet hair out of her face and moved her thick braid so it no longer rested against her bare skin. A smile pulled at his lips when he imagined what she would do if she realized she was naked against him.

This was the only occasion that he could recall where he held a naked woman in his arms without making love to her. Though he would like nothing better.

Serena's lithe body snuggled against him, seeking his warmth, and he eagerly shared it with her. The fire crackled, and thoughts of the evil that chased them were the farthest thing from his mind as he closed his eyes and rested his chin on the top of her head.

Chapter Sixteen

*S*erena moved closer to the heat calling her. Her skin hurt from her fall mixed with the icy cold of the water. Gradually, her mind dull from her trauma, she recalled strong arms wrapping around her and carrying her from the frigid waters.

Drogan.

She had no doubt he was the one who had her.

Something tickled her nose, and she moved her head to get away from the annoying nuisance. Muscles flexed and shifted beneath her head and along her body. She stilled and opened her eyes and spotted the rise and fall of a chest—a naked chest—full of rippling sinew and a sprinkling of dark curly hair.

The idea of being in Drogan's arms, of being held and comforted made her throat close up with emotion. Images flashed in her mind of the kiss they'd shared. Heat settled low in her stomach, building until she ground her hips against Drogan. In that instant, past the pleasure her small movement had given her, she realized she was naked.

She squeezed her eyes closed and wondered what she had ever done to Fate to be tempted to throw all caution to the wind as her body urged her to do. What frightened Serena the most wasn't what Drogan might do, but what she wished he *would* do.

The kiss they had shared had awakened something within her, something dark that stirred her to the very depths of her soul. The fact that she and Drogan were lying in a bed naked seemed to push one thought into her mind—experiencing more of the wonderful pleasure he gave her.

She knew all too well that if she wasn't careful, her heart could be shattered and she would be left raising a child on her own. The thought of having a child pleased her more than she would allow herself to think about, but losing the man who she had given her heart just might kill her as it had done her mother.

"How do you feel?"

She jerked at the deep baritone of his voice, thick from sleep. "Not as bad as I could."

"Are you warm enough?"

She noticed he kept absolutely still, only lifting his head to look at her. His gaze, however, showed her how their position and nakedness was affecting him. The heat of his eyes made the blood rush through her ears drowning out everything but the erratic beat of her heart.

"Aye. My skin tingles a bit, but that will go away as the chill leaves me."

He caressed her back with the barest of touches, but it only made her want more of him. The want, the need she had for him only seemed to grow no matter what she did. How could she guard against such an assault?

"You scared the Hell out of me when you fell. What happened?"

"I don't know," she said with a little shrug. She knew she should turn away from him, but she was comfortable and his heat felt so good. "I was backing up to give you room when the ground gave way. The next thing I knew I was in the water."

"I don't know how you did it, but you were smart enough to hang onto a limb. It's the only way I was able to catch up to you in that fast current."

There was a smile in his voice, and she could only imagine how she looked to him. "I'm glad you found me."

Then she made the worst mistake. She raised her head to look at him. Once their eyes met, his golden-brown ones filled with a hunger that made her stomach flip, molten heat raced through her body to pool between her legs.

She recalled his soft, insistent lips giving her her first kiss. Her body moved against his for the second time. He groaned low in his throat and turned on his side to face her. "Stop now, Serena, because I have a thin hold on my control. I'm not sure how much longer I can keep it restrained."

She knew she ought to move away, but for the life of her,

she couldn't. She wanted this as she had never wanted anything in her life. It was as if her future depended on knowing this man as only a woman could.

"I don't want to stop," she said and ran a finger down his cheek, covered in several days' growth of beard.

"Do you know what you're saying?"

"I do. I've been trying to fight it, but I don't want to fight it anymore. I want to feel the pleasure of your kiss again, to have you touch me. With you, Drogan...with you I'm not a witch. I'm a woman. I don't want to think about tomorrow. I just want this."

He said no more as his head lowered and his lips claimed hers fiercely, violently. It was a kiss meant to frighten, but all it did was fan the flames already growing within her. His demanding, insistent kiss kindled a passion that threatened to burn her from the inside out.

The kiss changed and morphed when she met his passion instead of pulling away. His lips softened. They beckoned her to give him all she had, and it never entered her mind to refuse him. He was a force she couldn't stand against, and she didn't want to.

She wanted all that he had, all that he was. And for better or worse, she wanted him to make love to her.

Sensual and carnal. Serena never knew a kiss could be so many things. Just a tilt of Drogan's head, a sweep of his tongue inside her mouth, or his arms pulling her close could affect their kiss.

Their bodies touched from their feet to their shoulders,

and still it wasn't enough for her. She clung to Drogan even as his large hands urged her tighter against him. His hand rest on her hip and held her as he ground against her.

A low moan, one full of longing and passion, fell from her lips when she felt his hardness. He was so hot, so hard against her, and she found she wanted to touch him, to explore the length of his rod with her fingers.

She reached down and wrapped her hand around his thickness. He moaned as his cock jerked in her hand. She ran her thumb over the velvety smoothness of his head before she fisted him again and explored his length.

He didn't give her much time to study the silky smoothness of his arousal before his hand cupped her breast.

Serena's breath left her in a whoosh as he fondled her breast. When his fingers found her nipple and began to slowly run his thumb back and forth over the tiny nub, desire shot through her. The more his hands moved over her breasts and his lips kissed hers, the more the need grew until she was mindless from it.

When Drogan moved atop her she gasped at the wonderful feel of his body stretched on top of her, of the amazing way it felt to have his weight on her. He balanced on his elbows, placed on either side of her head as he gazed at her.

His expression was unreadable, and though she wished to know what he was thinking, it seemed words deserted her. He was giving her a chance to turn him away, but for her, there was no turning back now. The desire was too strong. Her body needed release, and there was only one person who could give it to her.

Serena ran her hands up the bulging muscles of his arms to his wide shoulders. She kept her eyes locked with his as her fingers threaded with his still-damp hair. And then she lifted her hips to rub against him.

His eyes closed for a moment, a low groan tore from his lips. He whispered her name, which sent chills racing over her skin. That simple movement had sealed her fate, but Serena had never been so sure of anything before.

She didn't stop him when Drogan nudged her legs apart with his knee. When she felt his hot arousal lying near the sensitive flesh of her sex, her hips rose against him again, seeking more of him. The sensations pulsing through her caused her to do it again and again, each time the pleasure building, tightening inside her.

And each time, Drogan's rod came closer and closer to her most intimate place. When the tip of him slipped inside of her, she cried out with pleasure and clung to him. He moved up and over her, sending himself deeper, stretching her, filling her. His hardness and heat was inside her, and a thrill rushed through her.

He sank deep within her, and she gasped with excitement and pleasure. Her entire body shook with desire. Through that haze she knew what would come next—the breaking of her maidenhead—but it didn't frighten her. All she wanted was to continue feeling the strange, exhilarating sensations coursing through her.

She sighed when Drogan's lips claimed hers again. His kiss was one meant to mark her as his. It was deep and soul-branding, leaving her breathless and aching for more. Her body softened against him, accepting all that he was.

At that moment, he buried himself to the root.

Serena arched her back as pleasure mixed with pain, but the discomfort quickly fled, leaving her with a burning need only one man could quench.

It was as if Drogan knew what she needed as he began to move within her. Slowly at first, and then gaining speed each time he plunged inside her. With every thrust, her body climbed higher and higher, the need coiling and leading her down a path she eagerly sought. She never wanted the pleasure to end.

She opened her eyes to find him leaning over her, braced on his hands, staring down at her. His muscles flexed as his body strained and shifted. Beneath her hands she felt the sinew, she felt the tension in him building. He continued to thrust within her, but shifted his weight and brought one hand to where their bodies joined. His fingers parted her woman's lips and rubbed his thumb in small circles on a hidden gem, barely touching her.

Serena barely had time to react to the exquisite pleasure before her world shattered. Unending pleasure washed over her and touched every inch of her body. Even while her body convulsed around Drogan's cock he continued to move within her, faster and deeper than before.

Each time he filled her it prolonged her orgasm until

another ripped through her before the first finished. The scream locked in her throat, her body stiffening from the sheer bliss that brought her higher and higher. White lights exploded behind her eyelids while warmth spread through her limbs.

As the last tremor left her she became aware of Drogan's harsh breathing, of the way his body pounded into hers. She opened her eyes and watched, transfixed, as he stiffened, his head dropped back, and he issued a low moan. She held onto him as his body jerked when his climax claimed him, his seed filling her.

She shifted her hips, causing him to groan and move deeper in her. He lowered his head to her forehead and sighed.

They spoke no words as he pulled out of her and rolled onto his back, bringing her with him. She rested her head on his chest, which was becoming her favorite spot, and drifted off to sleep. A smile on her face, and more contented than she ever thought possible.

Drogan tried to even out his ragged breathing as Serena slept. He was ashamed of himself for taking advantage of her. But, at the same time, he couldn't believe he had just experienced lovemaking so intense and pure that it left him feeling more relaxed than he ever had.

The darkness that was always near seemed farther away

now. But he didn't dwell on that. His body was fully sated, yet he wanted her again. Now.

Just as he was imagining how he would make love to her the next time, his memory caught and held something. A man had been by the river when Serena had fallen in.

Drogan had caught a glimpse of him, hidden by foliage, as he jumped in after Serena. The sudden recollection made Drogan realize he had been concentrating too much on Serena and not on his surroundings, which could have deadly consequences for them both.

From the lack of light seeping in through a crack in the wood that shuttered the window, he could tell it was still night. The fire had all but burned out, leaving the small cottage in almost total darkness.

Serena sighed and snuggled against him, rubbing her full breasts along his side. Just the feel of her smooth skin had him hard and aching. He was afraid that now that he had a taste of her, he would never get enough.

When the first light of dawn crept over the horizon, Drogan eased out of the covers and dressed. He felt Serena's clothes and was thankful they were near dry.

He walked to the door and was about to unhook the latch when he heard something outside. It sounded like horses. He reached for his weapons and tried to peer through the crack in the shutters, but couldn't see anything.

As quiet as a wraith, he eased open the door and slipped out into the shadows. He waited patiently, keeping as still as the shadows themselves until he caught a glimpse of something moving toward the cottage. He readied his bow and squinted to get a better view of who it was. They drew near enough that Drogan could see the outline of one man and three horses, but where were the other men?

When the man got within twenty paces of the cottage, Drogan readied the arrow and called out, "Stop where you are."

The man instantly pulled back on the reins of the horse, causing the animal to toss his head in aggravation.

"Who's there?" the man asked.

"Where are the other men?" Drogan demanded instead.

The man looked around. "What other men?"

"The ones who own those horses."

The man looked at the horses and laughed. "These horses are mine, son, and you're in my home. Care to explain?"

Drogan walked from the shadow, his bow still notched and ready to fire. He kept his arrow trained on the man. With his duties, Drogan hadn't gotten to know all of his tenants as he should. "How do I know you're not lying?"

"You don't," the man said and leaned forward, his full head of white hair sticking up everywhere. "Why don't you lower that bow and tell me what you're doing in my home?"

Drogan thought over the old man's words and realized, if necessary, he could easily take him down. Drogan lowered the bow. "My friend had an accident. I needed your cottage to get her warm."

"Her," the old man repeated before he dismounted. "Is she hurt badly?"

"Nay. She fell in the river and needed a night to rest."

The old man tied the horses to a tree near a small shed and walked toward Drogan, a pronounced limp in his left leg. "My name's Thaddeus."

"Drogan."

Thaddeus halted suddenly and rubbed his whiskered chin. "Drogan? Now, that's not a common name. The only Drogan I know is lord of Wolfglynn."

As the old man peered at him, Drogan kept silent. The less this man knew, the better.

"Well," Thaddeus said after a moment. "Let's get inside and get some food cooking. I'm starving."

Drogan realized he hadn't eaten since their hasty meal at noon yesterday. He had given the food to Serena. His stomach growled as he hurried to reach the door first.

"Can you give me a moment with my friend?"

Thaddeus' brows furrowed, but then he nodded. "Of course. I'll put the horses away."

Chapter Seventeen

*D*rogan waited until Thaddeus disappeared into the shed with the horses before he stepped into the cottage. As he shut the door behind him, Drogan feasted his eyes on Serena sleeping contentedly. He hated to wake her, but there was nothing else for it.

He sat on the edge of the bed and touched her shoulder. She rolled towards him and gave him a sleepy smile.

"You're already dressed?" she asked and stretched her arms over her head.

Drogan silently cursed as he watched her full breasts peek from the covers and her nipples harden under his gaze. He had dreamed of making love to her first thing this morning.

"Drogan?" she asked, worry in her voice, as she sat up, keeping the covers against her chest. "Is something wrong?"

He raised his eyes to hers. "The owner of the cottage has returned. He's putting his horses away."

"Owner? He?" she repeated. She blinked and moved a strand of hair that had gotten caught in her eyelashes. "Then I had better dress."

Drogan moved as she scrambled out of the bed, the covers still held against her. As much as he wanted to watch her, he turned and walked to the door.

"I'll be outside waiting."

As soon as the door closed behind Drogan, Serena let the cover fall. She spotted a bowl of water near the bed and cleaned herself. Her clothes were dry, except for a few damp spots. Once she was dressed, she unbraided her hair and searched inside her bag for her comb.

She gasped and fell to her knees as she looked at the contents. Many of her precious herbs were ruined, herbs she didn't know if she would find outside of Hawthorne.

One by one, she took out the contents of her bag and placed everything on the floor. The jars she'd packed hadn't broken and neither had their seals, so at least she still had some of the herbs. But would they be enough?

She didn't know how long she had sat there, but suddenly Drogan was beside her, his golden eyes questioning. She shrugged, trying to find the words.

"I should have been more careful." She nodded toward the herbs. "They're ruined."

He pushed her hair behind her ear. "We will look for more."

She tried to smile, but the weight of what was lost to her was too great. These were herbs she needed if she were wounded and bleeding, but there was no need to worry Drogan with that. It was her concern only. He had other matters to deal with, matters that were much more important.

"It'll be all right, Serena. I promise. I will find what you need."

The sincerity shining in his eyes nearly brought her to tears. She cupped his cheek and forced to smile. "Thank you."

Someone cleared a throat behind her, and she turned to find an elderly man with thick tufts of white hair and a full, white beard.

"Is anyone hungry?" he asked.

She and Drogan exchanged glances before they replied, "Aye."

While Drogan set about picking up the ruined herbs, she brushed her hair and decided to braid it again. It was the most effective way of keeping it out of her face, and she hated wearing the veil and wimple that was in style.

When she was finished, she sat by Drogan at the small table. "May I help with something?" she asked the man.

"The name is Thaddeus, milady, and you just sit right there. This will be done soon."

The food was ready within a matter of moments. When Thaddeus sat on the other side of her, she smiled and said, "My name is Serena."

"A right beautiful name, milady."

She frowned. "Why do you keep calling me 'my lady'?"

He stopped his food midway to his mouth. "Because you are."

She turned to Drogan, but with the slightest shake of his head he told her to leave it. Which was fine with her, for she would much rather eat. And eat they did, until nothing was left. She hadn't realized how hungry she was until she'd smelled the food.

"How much for two of your horses?" Drogan asked.

Thaddeus leaned back in his chair and regarded Drogan. "I just bought those mares."

"I'll pay you amply for them as well has have them returned to you once we reach our destination."

"I don't suppose you'd tell me that destination?"

Serena glanced at Drogan, but he just sat there stonily, refusing to answer Thaddeus.

"I see," Thaddeus said. "You two must be in an awful hurry to travel through the woods instead of staying on the main road."

Again, Drogan said nothing. Serena grew uncomfortable. She just wished Thaddeus would give them an answer on the horses so they could get moving. They had wasted valuable time eating.

"All right. Take two of the horses," Thaddeus said.

Serena rose from the table. "Thank you very much."

He smiled, showing some missing teeth. "Glad I could make you happy."

She gathered up their belongings while Drogan paid Thaddeus and readied the two horses. When she walked outside, Drogan was waiting for her.

"Ready?" he asked.

"Very."

He took the bags and helped her atop the horse before he returned her bag. In one smooth movement, he mounted his mare, and they waved to Thaddeus before riding off.

They hadn't gone far before she nudged her mare beside Drogan. "How do you know Thaddeus won't tell anyone we've been here?"

"I don't," Drogan said. "But I paid him enough coin for the horses and his silence that I hope he will keep our visit to himself."

"Did he know who you were?"

"He suspected, but I never told him."

"That might be to our advantage."

He lifted a shoulder. "We can but hope."

With the horses, they covered twice as much more ground, which helped to make up for the time they lost by her falling in the river. Serena didn't miss the many times Drogan looked over his shoulder.

They stopped rarely, just long enough to rest the horses and eat. They didn't speak of what had occurred between them, which was probably a good thing because she didn't know what to say. Serena still couldn't believe what she had done, but she didn't wish to take it back. It had been a special night, one she would remember always.

It was while they watered the horses that she found Drogan watching her. She looked at him, waiting for what he would say.

"How are you?"

She smiled and patted her mare's neck. "Much better now that my poor feet get a rest."

"That's not what I meant."

She frowned until it dawned on her he was asking about her lost maidenhead. She looked away from him to the sparkling water of the river. "I'm fine."

He moved so fast, she didn't have time to react when he pulled her against him and covered her mouth with his. The kiss was consuming and passionate. The desire rekindled in an instant, leaving her panting and yearning for more. When he ended the kiss, she had to hold onto him to keep steady. She raised her eyes to see a satisfied smile on his face.

"What was that for?"

"I've wanted to do that since you woke this morning, but there hasn't been time."

She didn't miss the little lines of worry around his mouth despite his smile. "I don't regret what we did. I hope you know that."

He looked away from her and played with the end of her braid. "Are you sure?"

"Absolutely."

When he still didn't look at her, she reached up and moved his head until he did. "It was more than I had ever dreamed, Drogan."

Still he didn't move. She didn't know what to do other than wrap her arms around him and lay her head on his chest. His arms came around her to hold her against him. She smiled and briefly closed her eyes, content in the small time they had together.

Their peace didn't last long as one of their horses jerked her head up and snorted. In a flash, Drogan had Serena back on her mare, and they were galloping away.

A little later, he slowed the mares to a walk and pulled up until Serena reached him.

"If we're lucky, we'll reach Wolfglynn by tonight."

She couldn't wait. She had enjoyed her time with Drogan, but the constant worry had brought tremendous stress.

Once they and Gerard's family were inside the stone walls of Wolfglynn, she would feel better. They had made it this far; they would make it the rest of the way.

At least that's what she told herself.

Drogan couldn't wait to reach his home. He never felt more comfortable than when he was within the massive stone walls of his castle.

His gaze found its way to Serena again and again, assuring him she wasn't in pain and was holding up. She rode elegantly, just as she did everything else. There was no denying she was a lady. It was no wonder Thaddeus had known what kind of woman she was.

"Stop it," she said after he had glanced at her again.

"I'm not doing anything."

She rolled her beautiful blue eyes. "You keep looking at me as if you expect me to fall off this horse."

Drogan fought to keep the smile from showing. "You're an excellent horsewoman."

"Then why are you staring?"

He looked away from her intense eyes and gazed between his horse's ears. He found he wanted to tell her how beautiful she was, how courageous he thought she was. How utterly unique he found her as a woman. And how he wanted more time with her.

He could imagine what her reaction would be.

"Drogan?"

He closed his eyes and sighed. He needed to think. "My mare is younger than yours. I'm just making sure yours doesn't need to rest."

"Oh."

Was that disappointment he heard in her voice? It couldn't be. Though they hadn't spoken more about his taking her maidenhead, he suspected that she had let her guard down last eve, but he doubted she would do so again.

All because of a curse.

A curse he still didn't understand. Obviously, it had something to do with a man and a woman, but how exactly?

"You told me about the beginning of the curse. Will you tell me what the curse is about?"

He waited for her to refuse, but she blew the hair out of her face.

"I'm not sure if the matron wanted to curse just the girl or all of the women. The curse was for the girl's husband to leave her after she had a child, but in the end it's what happens to every one of us who give our hearts to a man."

"All of you?"

She nodded and continued to look straight ahead. "It is why our line is dying. Most women would rather go through life alone than to suffer the unspeakable torture of losing the men they love, to be left alone in the world."

"Is that what happened to your father?"

"Aye. He left five days after I was born. I've never seen him, and I have no wish to find him."

Drogan had imagined all sorts of things, but this hadn't been one of them. "I'm sorry."

"It wasn't your doing."

"You already have a tough enough life, but adding a curse that has spanned centuries must make things more difficult."

"We survive."

They rode for a bit in silence, his mind trying to grasp the concept of the curse. "Has the curse ever been broken?"

"Nay. It'll continue until there is no more of us."

"Well, you said yourself you haven't seen any more of your kind before Adrianna. What if one of them had broken the curse?"

She glanced at him as if he had lost his mind. "If that were the case, the word would spread fast. Many have sought ways to break the curse. They've used magic, but every time the curse remains."

"But what if?" he insisted.

"I cannot rule it out. Although, through these many centuries, that has never happened."

"That you know of," he added.

She sighed loudly. "I get your point, Drogan. Anything is possible, but I look at what is before me, and that is the numbers of my kind dwindling to nothing."

He didn't bother to tell her that they could just be in hiding. "Humor me," he said and gave her a smile.

"All right," she agreed reluctantly.

"What if there was a way to break the curse?"

She shrugged. "If the curse had ever been broken, then it would be for that woman alone since it still affects the other *bana-bhuidseach*."

That's what he had thought, but he wanted her to say it. He couldn't understand his need to get her to think along the same lines as him, he just knew it was important. He didn't press her further. She needed to let what had transpired between them settle into her brain.

The nagging sensation that they were being watched consumed him. He looked around, but didn't find anything that would alert him. Someone was there, yet the growing darkness could hide any number of horrors. Apprehension settled uncomfortably in the pit of his stomach, and he gripped the pommel of his sword to quell the feeling.

Something told him to look once more over his shoulder,

and when he did, he could have sworn he saw someone. He quickly pulled up on his mare's reins and turned the horse around.

"What is it?" Serena whispered.

At least she had enough sense not to shout, Drogan thought. He held up a hand to tell her to wait as he peered into the dense forest. Several minutes passed with the only movement being that of the horses' tails, but nothing stirred.

Drogan swore under his breath and pulled the mare back around. Serena waited for him to tell her what had prompted him to turn around.

"I guess I'm just seeing things."

She gave him a reassuring smile. "I've been doing the same thing since we left Hawthorne."

Fear snaked down his spine. "What?"

"It's nothing," she said.

"Please tell me."

"It is just a feeling that we've been watched. I thought I saw something after I fell into the river, but I was in such fear, I know it was just a figment of my imagination."

Maybe, but Drogan doubted it. Strange that they had both thought to have seen someone at the same place. Just then, they crested a small hill, and Serena gasped as she got her first look at Wolfglynn.

He smiled and took a deep breath.

He was home.

Chapter Eighteen

*S*erena couldn't believe the beauty she beheld. This surely was a hidden sanctuary that was shown just to a precious few.

"Now I know why you have no desire to leave," she said.

The orange orb of the sun sank into a sky of pale blue, grand purples, and the barest hint of pink, shedding its fading light onto the great castle of Wolfglynn. And great it was. Serena estimated it to be twice the size of Hawthorne, and that was saying something.

Out of the corner of her eye, she saw Drogan watching her, but she didn't care. She wanted to keep her first glimpse of Wolfglynn with its grand towers, numbering too many for her to hazard a guess, forever etched in her memory. A wall of stone surrounded the entire castle, connecting to a massive gatehouse with two watchtowers.

She couldn't wait to get inside to explore the beautiful

structure. Her hands flexed on the reins as she next studied the forest that ran the length of the west side of the castle.

It was then she smelled it. Sea salt. She leaned her head back and felt the breeze of the sea.

"You feel the sea wind, don't you?" Drogan asked.

"Oh, aye. It is wonderful. I cannot wait to see it."

"And you will," he promised. "But first, we must get to Wolfglynn."

With that, he clicked to his mare and set her off at a hardy gallop. Not to be outdone, Serena whistled to her mare. She and the horse were both eager to arrive at their destination and neither could get there fast enough.

Her mare, that Drogan had thought slow and old, soon caught him. She and Drogan exchanged smiles as they left the forest and road for the great gatehouse. When they reached the road that led to Wolfglynn, he slowed and gave a strange whistle that must have been a signal to the men, for they immediately opened the mammoth gates.

Excitement bubbled within Serena as she rode behind Drogan and entered the bailey of Wolfglynn. It was like Hawthorne's, only bigger. The heavy stone curtain wall was crowned with battlements that had the characteristic square tooth pattern of merlons and crenels. The curtain wall was further strengthened by the many towers.

She halted beside Drogan, who dismounted to greet his knights. It was easy to see that his people respected and loved him by their show of warmth at his arrival. The knights also seemed relieved to find him hale and hearty.

When he turned his golden-brown eyes to her, a shiver ran down her spine. His expression was bold and possessive. She could hear whispers around her as people wondered if she was his bride.

She slid into Drogan's waiting arms from atop her horse. He set her on the ground, and she inhaled the strange scent of sea salt again. Her eyes closed, and she had the odd feeling that she had come home. Her eyes jerked open to find Drogan staring at her.

"We made it."

She smiled at his happy tone. "Aye, we did."

"And," he added with a corner of his mouth lifted in a smile. "I held to my oath to keep you safe."

Her smile widened, and she heard the whispers begin again. That's when she looked down to see his hands still around her waist. She stepped out of his arms to put space between them. She looked at the huge gate, now closed and found herself needing to know about Gerard and Maris.

"What is it?" Drogan asked as he walked to stand beside her.

"I'm troubled about Gerard and Maris." She shifted her gaze to him again. "When do you expect them here?"

He shrugged and ran a hand through his dark auburn hair. "It depends on many things. We managed to travel fast across country, and then we were able to acquire the horses."

"And they're still traveling by road."

"Aye."

To calm herself, Serena clasped her hands together and

twirled her thumbs around each other. The motion always soothed her.

"I'll send out riders," Drogan said. "But first, let me show you to your chamber."

The thought of a bed and a bath melted Serena's bones. She eagerly turned with Drogan toward the castle to find their path blocked by a group of people, mostly women.

Serena had never seen so many comely women in her life. It was hard to imagine Drogan not marrying with so many willing females nearby. He seemed oblivious to the women who nearly fell over themselves to get to him as he pulled Serena around them, but Serena couldn't ignore the narrowed eyes and continued whispers.

The grandeur that met her when Drogan opened the castle doors staggered her. The great hall was immense, filled with row upon row of tables. The dais sat in front of a wainscoted and painted area. Red lines, to represent masonry block, were painted on the whitewashed stone, and each block was decorated with an ornate flower.

A few wall hangings of painted wool were hung strategically in the great hall to check drafts. Rushlights were scattered throughout the hall, some on vertical spikes with a three-legged base, while others were held in a loop and supported from brackets on the walls. She also glimpsed a few oil lamps that provided better light in a shallow bowl on a stand near the dais.

The fireplace was arched and set into a wall on the far side of the great hall where a set of swords crossed over an ancient shield hung on the wall. Overlooking the hall were several balconies, and she could see hallways leading to chambers.

"Words desert me, Drogan," she said as her eyes continued to feast on the brilliance.

"So, you like it?"

She heard the question in his voice and turned to look at him. "Oh, aye. Very much."

He smiled slowly then. "Me, too." It was evident by the pride in his eyes that he loved his home.

She followed him up the stairs to the chambers. More rushlights hung on the wall to overcome the darkness.

"My chamber is at the end of the hall," Drogan said as he stopped in front of a door. "Just in case you need me."

Serena hadn't wanted that information. It would be hard enough to avoid him as it was, and now that she knew where he slept... She nodded, and he opened the chamber door. Deep blue curtains framed a great bed with a heavy wooden frame and soft mattress she couldn't wait to lie upon.

A bench rested in front of the bed and two chests lined one wall, interspersed with perches or wooden pegs on which to hang clothes.

She walked into the chamber, sat on the bench, and sighed as a servant entered and spoke to Drogan.

"Are you hungry?" he asked.

"Starving," Serena admitted.

He chuckled and nodded to the servant who hurried away. "I'll have water prepared for a bath before you eat, if you'd like."

"Sounds heavenly."

Drogan knew of only one thing that heavenly, and that was Serena herself. Despite the dirt and grime from their journey, her hair escaping from her braid, and her gown soiled beyond repair, she was still the most gorgeous thing he had ever laid eyes on.

He made himself leave her, shutting her door behind him. He paused and leaned against it with a sigh. The wisest move was to keep her as far from him as possible, but instead, he had moved her close to him. Possibly too close.

His hands flexed, and he rotated his head to work out the kinks in his neck. He knew the talk making its way around the castle. Everyone wanted to know the identity of the woman accompanying their lord. He wasn't sure why he hadn't introduced her, except perhaps that he wanted to keep her to himself a little longer.

He walked to his chamber and opened the door. His bed, shuttered by dark red curtains, beckoned him, but there was still much he had to do. He unbuckled his sword and placed it on his table before returning to the great hall.

After ordering baths for himself and Serena, giving careful instructions as to how warm to make the water for her, he went to the bailey where a knight led their horses to a stable boy.

"Thomas," Drogan called to his knight as he walked up. "I need you and one other man to return these horses in the morning. Do not wear armor. You'll find the cottage if you follow the river southwest."

"Aye, my lord," Thomas said and led the horses to the stables where they would be brushed and fed.

Drogan scanned the bailey for the one man he needed. He found Grayson leaning casually against the curtain wall, but Drogan knew Grayson was anything but relaxed. He made his way toward his commander, and Grayson pushed away from the wall.

"My lord. You had a safe trip?"

Drogan wasn't fooled by the cool demeanor. He had seen Grayson's silver eyes blaze with anger and resentment many times, though he never directed his displeasure at Drogan.

"I did. How were things here?"

"Normal. No problems. Your uncle came yesterday, saying he knew you would have need of him."

Strange, Drogan thought. How would his uncle know of the danger they were in? "Good. I have something I need you to do. It's most urgent."

"Name it."

"Take two men and leave tonight. Follow the road west. You will come upon a band of Roma where a dear friend of mine is hiding with his wife and child."

"Will they know we're coming?"

"Nay, but knowing Gerard, he'll be on the lookout for something."

"Gerard of Hawthorne?" Grayson asked.

"That's right. You recall what he looks like?"

Grayson nodded. "I'll see it done, my lord, and return them posthaste to Wolfglynn."

"Grayson," Drogan called out as the knight began to walk away. "Make sure no one knows you are knights. No armor or spurs, and keep your weapons concealed as best you can."

The knight nodded once and walked away. Drogan leaned one arm on the curtain wall and dropped his head. He should go in search of Gerard himself. It was the least he owed his friend. He hurried to catch Grayson.

"Don't leave until I get back. I'm coming with you."

"My lord? You've just returned, and with a lady. Shouldn't you stay?"

Drogan shook his head. "Nay. My place is looking for my friend."

He could tell Grayson didn't agree, but he didn't argue more as he went to gather the other knights. A wolf's cry shattered the night, and Drogan closed his eyes at the sound. He had always loved to hear their call, for it echoed in his own soul somehow.

As he headed back to the castle, a silhouetted figure in a high window caught his eye. Serena. They stared at each other for several moments before she turned away. Since their night together, his insides had been torn apart, because he knew he couldn't have her. Ever.

And he hated it.

So many years, he had been careful about with who he shared his bed, and the one time he gave in to the yearnings of his body and a call from his dark soul, he found himself lost in blue eyes. And he feared there could be no return.

Serena wasn't for him. He knew that. The darkness was

too much a part of him to allow something that wonderful, sacred, and beautiful near him. It would destroy her, and he couldn't have that.

It was best if he forgot their night together and focused on the task at hand—killing the evil.

Chapter Nineteen

*S*erena stayed in the water until it began to chill her, and then she scrubbed her body twice and washed her hair three times. When she emerged, she felt like her old self again.

The servants had brought her bag, but none of her clothes were inside. She made do with the piece of linen to wrap around her after she had dried off. Then, she went to the bed and combed the tangles from her hair.

It wasn't long after that there was a soft knock, and a girl not much younger than Serena entered. She had long golden hair that hung in curls at her waist. Her eyes were clear as the morning sky and offered warmth and friendship in their depths.

"My name is Claire, milady," she said.

"Hello. I'm Serena."

"A lovely name." Claire walked to the bed with clothes

across her arms. "Your gowns are being washed, but Lord Drogan asked that I find something for you to wear until yours are ready." She laid a gown of soft green across the bed.

The beautiful gown was several decades out of fashion, but had been well cared for.

"Thank you, Claire."

The servant smiled. "The fit should be close. The gown belonged to Lord Drogan's mother."

A knot lodged in Serena's throat. She ran her hand along the fine material. "It'll do fine."

With Claire's help, Serena donned the gown. The length was a trifle short, but otherwise quite good, and it would do until the morrow.

Once Claire left, Serena curled up on the bench with her feet tucked beneath her. She continued to comb her hair and thought of Drogan. He occupied her thoughts most of the day, and she feared he might occupy much more if she wasn't careful. She pushed him out of her mind and concentrated on Gerard and Maris.

Drogan knocked for a second time on Serena's door, but received no answer. He tried the latch and found it unlocked.

"Serena," he called as he opened the door.

He found her on the bench in front of the bed, her head back and her eyes closed. Not wishing to disturb her, he sat on a stool and waited. Her hair was still damp, as was his. They both had spent a long time at their baths to wash away the grime.

His mother's gown looked good on her, despite it being out of fashion.

A few moments later, she opened her eyes and looked at him. "I saw them."

"Gerard and Maris?"

She nodded. "They seem to be all right. Tired and scared, but unhurt."

"That's good. Do you feel better?"

"A little. However, I won't be fine until they're here."

"I'm leaving with three of my best knights to go find them."

"What?" she asked and rose to her feet. "You can't."

"It's my duty."

She shook her head. "You must stay."

"Give me one good reason."

"All right," she said and sat back down. She reached for him and shuddered. "You know I hate doing this, but it's the only way to make you stay since you won't take my word."

"Don't," he said, but it was too late.

Serena opened herself quickly as she delved into Drogan's future. She saw him many years in the future with gray hair and children all around him. It made her smile to know he would be happy and she was still on the right course.

But it wasn't what she needed to see. She focused on what would happen that night. It took her a little longer, but she found it and looked at both paths.

She jerked her hand away from him as she opened her eyes and took a steadying breath.

"You shouldn't have," Drogan bit out anger and worry deepening his voice.

"I didn't let myself see your death. I couldn't..."

"What did you see?"

She glanced away from him. "I understand your need to go after Gerard and Maris. I, too, wish that I could go after them, but it's futile. The evil watches you. If you leave, not only will you die, but the evil will also kill Gerard and his family."

There was a long silence before Drogan spoke. "And if I don't go?"

She faced him. "Then there is yet a chance that everything we've planned will work, and isn't that what we all want? To live?"

Drogan wasn't happy. Serena made valid points, but not going after Gerard didn't sit well with him.

"All right," he said and sighed. "I'll tell Grayson to leave without me."

The smile she gave him was worth the fear that had stabbed him at her looking at his death.

"Thank you, Drogan."

He looked away and cleared his throat. "Are you ready to eat?"

She nodded. A few moments later, servants brought food along with a small table which they placed near Serena. Once the food had been laid out, Drogan moved his stool to the table and sat. The aroma made his mouth water. Both he and Serena reached for the food and filled their trenchers.

It was a short time later, once all of the food was eaten, that they sat back contented. He noticed Serena's eyes grow heavy. He needed to put her to bed, but he wasn't sure he could leave her when he did. His body demanded another taste of her, to feel her skin against his.

To hear her cries of pleasure.

"I'll see you in the morning." He stood and left without giving her time to say anything.

He didn't breathe again until he was in his own chamber. His body raged with need for the black-haired siren who called to him. With a savage curse, he pushed off the door and stalked to his bed, yanking off his tunic and tossing it on the bench before his bed. He fell back onto the bed and covered his eyes with one of his arms, praying that sleep found him quickly.

Serena wondered at the abruptness in which Drogan left her, but she knew it was for the best that he'd gone. She shifted on the bench, hoping to quell the need pulsing within her. It didn't work.

She slid off the bench and took one more drink of the hearty wine before she climbed into bed. It looked inviting, and she was exhausted. But would sleep come? After being in Drogan's arms, the big bed seemed emptier than ever before.

Every moment of their lovemaking replayed in Serena's head. The passion, the tenderness...the fire.

Her body pulsed with need, and only one man could fulfill that need.

She jumped from the bed and out of her chamber before she lost her nerve.

Drogan had closed all but one of the curtains around his bed, hoping that would help him sleep, but it hadn't. He had given up and propped himself against the headboard with his pillows. One foot was braced on the floor, while his other leg was bent with his foot on the bed. His arm rested on his raised knee as he thought over the many evil deeds he had done.

He didn't know how much of the darkness had closed in on him, or how long he had dwelled within it, until he heard his door creak as it opened. Instantly, he reached down and grasped his sword.

As the person walked toward his bed, he caught a faint glimpse through his bed curtains. The pommel of his sword fit comfortably in his hand as his fingers squeezed it in anticipation of some unknown terror.

And then his heart stopped in his chest as Serena stood at the foot of his bed. He lowered his sword and sat up, putting both legs on the floor as she walked toward him.

Her hair flowed freely, the moonlight illuminating its blackness with a bluish glow as the tresses cascaded over her shoulders and down her back. He tried to swallow, but it lodged in his throat as she raised her skirts and straddled him.

His body ignited at the feel of her in his arms again. No words were spoken as she wrapped her arms around his neck and lowered her head to kiss him.

The taste of her soft, sweet lips was like the sweetest wine, and the more he tasted, the more he wanted. His hands cradled her face as he plundered her mouth. Her breasts pressed against his chest and all he could think about was feeling the weight of them in his hands again. A more lithe, curvaceous body had never roamed the earth, he was sure.

To his surprise, she moved his hand from her face and lowered it to her leg while she lifted the hem of her skirts to her thigh. He broke the kiss and looked at her. Could she know what she was doing?

"Serena," he whispered, but she covered his mouth with her finger.

She shook her head to quiet any more words and gave him a bright smile. Drogan wasn't about to turn away this gift, not when he wanted it so desperately.

It took just a few movements to remove her gown so he could feast his eyes on her exquisite body. Her breasts were full, her waist narrow and her skin as smooth as the finest silk. His mouth watered, and he licked his lips before she brought her mouth to his.

Her hands moved between them until she covered his aching rod. He moaned into her mouth as her hand gave him a gentle squeeze. It was torment to have her touching him, but he wasn't able to pull her away, either. He let her have her way as she eased him out of his breeches.

He sprang free, and she rose up on her knees, putting her breasts level with his mouth. His lips found one pert nipple and suckled until her nails raked his back and her breath came in strangled gasps.

Then, ever so slowly, he lowered her onto his cock. She was tight and so wet, and he slid into her as if he was made for her. When he was buried to the root, she moaned as her head dropped back and her hair grazed his knees.

He held onto her waist as he began to pump his hips. More gasps and moans issued from her plump lips, driving him wild with a need he only felt for her.

She raised her head, her blue eyes half opened as the pleasure consumed her. He loved to watch the way she bit her bottom lip when her desire became intense and her moans and gasps became soft cries.

A groan broke from his throat as Serena began to lift her hips and slide down on him. He gripped her hips harder as he helped to move her faster.

And, as never before, he opened himself up fully. Had she asked for all his secrets right then, he would have gladly told her. Even the ever-present darkness knew better than to stray too close.

Her tempo increased, and he reached up to pinch her nipples, smiling when she moaned low in her throat. He was close to his climax, but there was no way he was going without her.

Just as he moved his hand between their bodies, her breath hitched and her hips move faster. In a matter of moments, she clenched around him, her head thrown back, and her mouth open on a silent scream.

Drogan continued to thrust within her, dragging out her climax as long as he could until his own orgasm took him. He wrapped his arms around her and brought her against him as he spilled his seed deep inside her.

When he was spent, he kissed Serena's neck and leaned back with her cradled against his chest. He had no wish to separate their bodies. It seemed right to have her lying on him, her cheek against his heart and her hair falling over him like a dark blanket.

A wolf howled in the distance, and Drogan felt like doing the same. If things could stay just as they were, he might have a chance at a normal life.

But reality had a way of intruding.

Chapter Twenty

*S*erena came awake to the feel of Drogan's mouth on her shoulder. He had shaved, and she much preferred kissing him without the whiskers that scraped her face.

She smiled and stretched as he leaned over her. "It is still night?"

He nodded. "I should return you to your chamber before someone notices you aren't there."

In truth, she wanted to stay with him, but she knew he was right. She sighed and rose, letting the cover drop to expose her breasts. A smile pulled at her lips when she heard him groan. She had never held this kind of power over a man, and she found it thrilling.

"Do you see something you want?" she teased.

He growled and jerked her against him as he claimed her lips in a kiss that made her knees buckle. By the time he raised his head, she was panting and the delicious ache between her legs had begun again.

"We haven't time," he said as he kissed her neck.

"Then you should have awakened me earlier. And you needn't *return* me. I can see myself to my chamber."

He chuckled and raised his head, his expression now serious. "Why did you come to me?"

"I thought that was obvious." She had hoped she wouldn't bring it up, because she didn't wish to think about the real reason she had ventured into his chamber, but she knew she had to face it sooner or later. And by the look on Drogan's face, it was going to be sooner.

She licked her lips and shrugged at his expectant gaze. His long, auburn hair was tousled and curling near his lip.

"Aren't you afraid of the curse?"

She briefly looked away before she found his dark gaze. "I used to be, but when I'm with you, it doesn't seem to matter anymore."

"And if you become heavy with child?"

His voice was deceptively calm, but she knew him better than that. She needed to tread carefully and word her answer just right or else she would be facing much more than his unwavering gaze.

"If I do, then I will be sure to tell you as well as thanking God for the gift." Her thumbs circled each other in an attempt to calm herself. "I will not try to bind you to me, Drogan. What we are sharing is wonderful, and I don't want to miss out on it."

She didn't resist when he raised her chin until she was once more looking into his eyes.

"I have no wish to deny what's between us, either."

She didn't know why she had thought he might offer her marriage, but she was disappointed when he didn't. She told herself it was irrational and foolish. She was merely a woman to warm his bed, but she would make the most of this joy that was sure to be short lived.

Nor would she agree to the marriage if he did offer. It would be much worse to be married and have him leave than to be his lover without the promise of forever. At least, she had some place to return to. Hawthorne was a wonderful place, even if it didn't compare to the beauty and grandeur of Wolfglynn.

She slid from the bed and hurried to dress. Drogan had said no more and, since her mind was jumbled with other things, she was most grateful. As she was about to walk to the door, he caught her arm and turned her toward him where he sat on the bed. For several heartbeats, he looked at her as if he wanted to say something but couldn't find the words.

She put a smile on her face and leaned down to give him a brief kiss on the lips. "Don't worry. All will be fine."

He allowed her to leave, and somehow she managed to make it back to her chamber before the tears came. It was foolish to cry, she knew that, but still she wept. If only she wasn't a *bana-bhuidseach*, then she might have a chance to have Drogan as hers.

And to her astonishment, she found herself praying she

might indeed have conceived a child, for then she wouldn't be alone anymore. She swore that she wouldn't act as her mother had, because she knew nothing could stop Drogan from leaving her if she did have a child.

It was her life, and she would make the best of it.

Drogan watched Serena leave. He clenched his hands in anger for not offering right then and there to marry her, but he couldn't. It wasn't because he feared some foolish curse. Nay, his fear went much deeper.

He could not, and would not, subject a lady to the darkness that surrounded him. It had taken everything he had to keep it away all these years, yet each day it grew closer and closer until one day it would overtake him. Serena deserved better.

With a savage oath, he sat up and buried his head in his hands at the cruelty of it all. He had found a woman he wanted and needed, but he couldn't have her. Irony was a bitch.

He laughed hoarsely and fell back on his pillow. What he could do was give Serena as much pleasure as she was willing to take until she left. It would never be enough for him, but at least he would have that little piece of time where she had been his.

Sleep most definitely wouldn't come now he realized as he rose from the bed and tugged on his tunic. He fastened his breeches and pulled on his boots before grabbing for his sword and stalking from his chamber. He didn't slow until he reached the battlements and breathed in the fresh air. The sea churned as the waves crashed against the cliffs.

He leaned against the crenel and waited out the night, the wildness of the sea and the forest echoing his own fierceness and desolation.

Serena awoke the next morning to find her eyes puffy from her tears. It was just what she deserved, she told herself, as she rose from the bed. She rummaged through her bag and found a mixture she dabbed beneath her eyes to reduce the swelling.

But there was no herb or remedy that would help heal the torment within, and she didn't want one. For the first time in her life, she was truly living and experiencing things she had only heard about.

A soft knock sounded on the door, and then Claire stepped inside. "I didn't know if you would be awake or not, milady."

Serena smiled as she brushed her hair. "I usually rise early."

"Did you sleep well?"

Serena nodded and turned to find Clair placing her gowns on the bed. She hadn't had room enough to pack but a few things, and now one of those gowns was ruined.

However, she had been wise enough to pack her veil and wimple.

"Which shall you wear today?" Claire asked.

Serena chose the soft yellow gown. She allowed Claire to help her dress, though she ordinarily did this on her own. Claire seemed to want to help, and Serena didn't have the heart to send her away.

Once the low-slung belt was fastened on her hips, Serena looked at the dreaded wimple. She hated being confined, but this wasn't Hawthorne, and she needed to dress according to fashion so she didn't stand out.

"Here, let me," Claire offered.

Serena sank onto the stool as Claire brushed and braided Serena's hair. Once the wimple and veil were in place, Claire placed the deep embroidered circlet over the veil.

"How beautiful you look," Claire said as she stepped back. "Lord Drogan is a very lucky man."

Serena choked as she tried to swallow. When the coughing passed, she shook her head at Claire. "I was traveling with Lord Gerard of Hawthorne and his wife as they visited here. We became separated due to some unsavory men, and Lord Drogan and I rushed here as fast as we could."

But the light shining in Claire's eyes let Serena know she didn't believe a word. "Whatever you say, milady. I just want you to know that I think you'll make a fine match."

Serena was still gaping at Claire when Drogan entered her chamber.

"Something wrong?" he asked as Claire rushed past him out the door.

Serena nodded and rose, tugging at the hated wimple. "Aye. Claire thinks I'm to be your wife."

She expected Drogan to say something, but when he just stood there, she became alarmed. "That isn't what you're telling your people, is it?"

"Nay. People will talk, regardless of what the truth is." He leaned against the wall. "Is the idea of marrying me repulsive?"

She rolled her eyes, not believing that he would think such a thing. "You know it isn't, Drogan. I just don't like the idea of people thinking something that isn't true."

"What if we make it true?"

Her heart stopped in her chest. "What?"

He shrugged and pushed off the wall. "Just a thought." He looked her over. "I like you in yellow, though I wish I could see your hair. Why are you wearing that awful wimple and veil?"

"Because it's the fashion, and I want to fit in," she said irritably. He had thrown her off with the marriage statement, and she couldn't seem to get her heart to beat regularly now.

"If you don't wish to wear it, don't," he said as he walked toward her. "I prefer that glorious mane of yours to be seen so that I might run my fingers through its silken strands at any time."

Coherent thought deserted her. When he reached up and pulled off the circlet, she watched in wonder as it soared through the air to land on the bed. The long veil soon followed, and when his big hands gently tugged off the wimple, all she could do was sigh in pleasure.

"Much better." He was very near, his voice low and dangerous, as if he was contemplating making love to her right then.

And, Lord help her, she wanted him to.

He growled as he leaned toward her. "Don't look at me like that unless you want me to throw you on that bed right now."

"But that's what I want you to do," she admitted, her voice breathless.

He stepped back from her and ran his hand through his auburn hair. "You're going to drive me daft you tempt me so."

She smiled, for she knew exactly how he felt. "I cannot help that my body craves your touch."

Desire burned in his golden brown eyes. "You've known no other man. How can you say you like my touch?"

"I may have been an innocent, Drogan, but that doesn't mean my body doesn't know what it desires."

He squeezed his eyes shut. "I took your maidenhead."

"It was mine to give to who I pleased. Don't worry over something I haven't thought twice about." She touched his arm, hoping to ease his anguish, and waited until he looked at her before she added, "I want only two things from you."

He regarded for solemnly for a moment. "What?"

"First, help me keep Gerard, Maris, and Jocelyn alive."

He nodded. "And second?"

"Don't deny the passion between us while I'm here."

"I couldn't deny you if I tried," he said, though she saw the sadness in his eyes.

She reached up and smoothed away the frown on his forehead. "Why does that distress you so? Is it because I'm a witch?"

"Never," he said vehemently. He took hold of her shoulders. "It is because I am what I am. I've no wish to hurt you."

"I'm not asking for anything other than pleasure. I can't get hurt if I don't expect more than that."

He released her and shook his head. "I don't agree with that logic."

"I know what the curse is. I know what will happen if I conceive, and I know what the future holds for me. I will make the most of it."

"I have no will to stop you when my own body desires what you want." He sighed and gave her a half smile. "What a pair we make, aye?"

Chapter Twenty-One

rogan tried to conceal his discontent. He had no wish to hurt Serena, but what she proposed would leave him far less a man than the darkness that threatened to eat away at him.

Neither one was something he wanted to endure.

Yet, despite his options, he would much rather have time —as little as it might be—with her. She would take the sunshine with her when she left, but at least while she was with him, he could bask in its glow.

He walked her out onto the battlements and delighted in her gasp as she saw the sea for the first time. A smile formed despite his mood since he'd managed to bring her some happiness.

"Oh, Drogan," she whispered. "It's more beautiful than I ever could've imagined." She faced him, her eyes alight with excitement. "And you get to experience this every day. I envy you."

He returned her bright smile and looked at the dark blue waters of the sea. "She is rather spectacular, although she can be deadly in a storm."

"I'm sure," Serena said as she too turned to gaze at the sea. "The force of the waves and the wind would combine for certain death if one wasn't careful."

His gaze drifted back to Serena's face. "Mayhap once all this business is done, I will take you to the waters."

"Truly? I would love that."

"Then I will make certain of it."

His heart thumped in pain as he thought about her leaving. He knew better than to talk her out of it. Her way of maintaining control of the situation was to leave. And it was best because of the darkness that threatened him. He was being selfish to want her near.

She drove the darkness away, but for how long? He knew there would come a time he couldn't chase it away, couldn't force it from taking him. That day was approaching far quicker than he'd like, especially now that he'd found Serena.

The sound of a horn signaling approaching riders took his attention away from the beauty beside him. He moved to look into the bailey as the riders came through the gate.

"Who are they?" Serena asked as she stood beside him.

"My knights. I sent them last eve to return the horses to Thaddeus."

She gave his hand a squeeze. "It was sweet of you to return them to him so soon."

Drogan shrugged. "I did as I promised."

"I know you wish to talk to your knights. Go."

Drogan nodded and took the stairs to the bailey. His knights saw him as they dismounted and waited for him. He reached them as they handed the reins to the stable boy.

"Everything go as planned?" he asked them.

Thomas nodded. "Just fine, my lord, though the old man kept asking if you were Lord Drogan."

"What did you tell him?"

"At first nothing, but he overheard us talking and figured it out."

"No damage done," Drogan said. "Nice work, men. Go have some rest and food."

Drogan no longer cared if the old man knew who he was. He had a feeling Thaddeus would keep the information to himself. Drogan turned and found Serena looking down at him. He waved to her for her to join him.

As she walked down the stairs to the bailey, several of his men stopped to stare at her. He couldn't blame them. He'd done much the same thing the first time he'd glimpsed her. What disturbed him was the way some of the younger women looked at her.

"Something wrong?" Serena asked when she reached him. "Was Thaddeus not at home?"

"Nay, my men returned the horses," he said, though his eyes still watched some of the young women.

"Then what is it?"

He moved his gaze to Serena. "Nothing," he lied.

She raised one black brow. "You cannot fool me, my lord. Do you forget I'm a witch? I know something disturbs you."

He crossed his arms over his chest and gave her a half smile. "The only thing that bothers me is that we aren't in my bed making love right now."

"Shhh." She looked around to see if anyone overheard him. "Keep your voice down."

"No one heard me," he assured her.

She shook her head at him, though her laughter filled the bailey. "You're impossible."

"But you like it."

She laughed more and pushed some hair out of her face. "I do."

He'd never expected her to admit it, but now that she had, he felt almost giddy. A mighty lord and knight giddy? What was his world coming to? Not that he cared as long as Serena was around.

"It's a good thing since you're stuck with me for a while."

"You don't hear me complaining do you?" Her smile vanished, and she quickly looked away.

"Now what bothers you?" He glanced up at the sky, at the sun shining through the heavy clouds, and found himself worrying if the sun was too hot for her.

"It's awful of me," she whispered and refused to meet his eyes.

He turned her to face him. Concern welled within him,

and he silently vowed to do whatever it took to bring her smile back. "What is?"

She threw up her arms and let them fall to her side as her gaze slid to him. "Here I am flirting with you while Gerard and Maris are fighting for their lives."

"Ah," Drogan said and sighed. He grinned because he understood her dilemma. "I know what you mean, but there isn't more we can do now. To leave the shelter of these walls would be certain death for both of us. I would have left with my men last night had I not promised you I would keep Gerard and his family safe."

"I know."

"When our pursuer turned from them to come after me, it bought them time."

"But how much? We led him here, where Gerard and Maris are coming."

"True," Drogan conceded. "But the man has no idea that my knights will be with them."

Realization dawned in her blue eyes. "I see. You planned this very carefully, didn't you?"

"As much as I could. I'd hoped he would chase us rather than Gerard. I knew we could move swifter than the cart."

She nodded and rubbed her hands on her forearms as she looked at the closed gate.

He followed her gaze. "I have men stationed outside as well. They're well hidden and can send us signals if anyone approaches."

"I know," she said and leaned back against the gate. "I

cannot help but worry, and then once they arrive, the real battle begins."

Drogan nodded and looked at his men stationed on the battlements. Not only was Wolfglynn well fortified with the sea blocking two of the castle's sides, but Drogan's men knew the forest better than anyone.

His enemy would have to be as elusive as smoke to get through.

Serena hadn't wanted Drogan to leave her, but she knew he had many things to tend to after being gone. She spotted him speaking to some of the knights as he pointed to certain areas on the battlements, which she was sure had something to do with the impending arrival of the evil.

She shuddered and rubbed her hands on her forearms. A strong sense of malice had plagued her since she and Drogan had entered the bailey. She'd searched the bailey with her gaze several times but couldn't find the culprit.

At first, she hadn't known whether the malevolence was for her or Drogan, but now that Drogan was no longer nearby, she knew it was directed at her. All she had to do was find the source and deal with it. Since she could find nothing in the bailey, she entered the castle.

"Are you hungry?"

She found Claire standing at her side. ", I am."

"Come," the servant said and took her to the dais. "I'll fetch you something to break your fast."

Serena didn't have long to wait before Claire brought her food. She hated to eat alone, but there was nothing else for it. As she ate, she surveyed the great hall, for the sense of hatred had grown stronger.

Claire came into view, and Serena waved her over. "Do you know everyone in the castle?"

"I do, milady," Claire said. "Do you have need of something?"

"I was hoping you could tell me a little bit about everyone. Although I'm staying until my friends arrive, I would like to know more."

Claire seemed to accept her explanation and began talking. Serena learned of Esmee, the cook, who had come from Scotland, and of the two stable lads who had each lost their parents, and many others.

It was but an innocent remark from Claire, but Serena realized she had finally gotten some sort of clue.

"Who did you say wanted Lord Drogan as a husband?"

Claire blinked and turned a bright shade of red. "I didn't mean for that to slip, milady."

"It's all right," Serena said in an attempt to calm her. "I'm curious."

"Well, to be truthful, every woman here wants to be Lord Drogan's bride. He's a fine specimen of a man, and if I didn't have my own man, I would pine for Lord Drogan as well."

Serena smiled at Claire's wording. "It's the truth Lord

Drogan is very pleasing to the eye. But you mentioned a name."

Just as Claire opened her mouth, the castle door was flung wide, drawing Serena's attention. Drogan stood in the entrance, his eyes scanning the hall until they came to rest on her.

Serena's stomach fluttered as he strode toward her. "Hungry?"

"Famished."

From the light in his eyes, she knew he wasn't talking about food. Her body burned when she realized what he meant.

"Shall I get you something to eat, milord?" Claire asked.

He nodded to her and sat beside Serena. "What have you been doing?"

"Eating."

He chuckled and leaned back as Claire placed a trencher in front of him. "I've sent word to my uncle. He should arrive this evening or tomorrow morn. I want him here when Gerard and Maris arrive so he can get you, Maris, and Jocelyn to his castle."

"Gerard, not me," she said. "It's Gerard that needs to be kept safe."

He lowered his food. "You don't want to be here during battle, Serena."

"All right." She decided not to push now. She would get her way when the time came.

"How far away is your uncle's island? Can you see it from here?" she asked after several minutes.

"Aye." Drogan finished off his meal. "Come, I will show you."

She followed him up to one of the towers on the back of the castle. By the time they reached the top, she was breathless and gulping for much needed air. Her legs wobbled, and she feared they wouldn't hold her after the many stairs they had climbed.

Drogan, however, seemed unaffected as he sauntered to the window. After she had her breathing near regular, Serena joined him.

"There," he pointed in the distance. "Through the clouds and sea spray, you can see the top of his castle."

Serena squinted, and with a break in the clouds she caught a brief glimpse of it. "I thought he was farther away for some reason."

Drogan laughed and turned his back to the wall. "Whenever I got angry at my father, which was every day, I would come up here and scream for my uncle to come and get me. Of course, he never did since he couldn't hear me, but it helped me get through the days."

"You get on well with your uncle then?"

Drogan nodded. "He was more of a father to me than my own. I learned a great deal from him."

"You were very fortunate to have him."

"I know," he said as his gaze once more moved to look to the window.

She looked around the tower and saw another door on the opposite wall. When she crossed to it and pulled it open. She inhaled the sweet aroma of the sea and walked onto the top of the tower.

"Why do you stay inside?" she asked Drogan over her shoulder.

"I usually don't," he said as he joined her.

She leaned against the low stone wall at the edge of the tower, her hands braced on either side of her. "I can see your uncle's castle better from here."

Her words trailed off as Drogan walked up behind her and molded himself against her body. Her breath lodged in her throat when his hands came up to cup her breasts.

"I cannot seem to keep my hands off you," he whispered in her ear. "You don't know how many times I wanted to touch you in front of anyone who cared to see."

She smiled and leaned her head back against his chest. "Probably about as many times as I wanted you."

"We cannot spend every day in bed."

It took her a moment to realize he had spoken since his fingers had begun to tantalize her aching nipples. "Why not? I'm sure no one will miss us."

"Well, we're alone now," he said just before he moved her hair aside and kissed her neck.

Drogan licked her soft skin and grasped her hips to rub her against his aching rod. God, how he wanted her. His body burned for her.

She twisted in his arms and brought his mouth down for a

kiss. He moved her away from the edge until her back was to the wall.

"I need you," he said between kisses.

She ran her hand down his chest. "I'm yours."

He groaned and closed his eyes as she gripped his pulsing rod. With both hands braced on the wall on either side of Serena, he allowed her to touch him. When she opened his breeches and pulled him free, he thought he might expire on the spot.

"Drogan, please," she begged.

He opened his eyes to find her in a state of need that matched his own. He bunched her skirts at her waist until she was bared to him. Then he cupped her firm bottom to slowly lift her until her legs straddled his waist.

His rod slid into her moist sheath. They groaned in unison and clung desperately to each other. He didn't need to tell her what to do as she shifted her hips and locked her ankles together behind his back, driving him deeper.

His passion soared. With his hands supporting her, he wasn't able to fondle her ample breasts, but her seductive lips and slender neck offered plenty of places for him to kiss.

Chapter Twenty-Two

*S*erena thought she might very well die from the pleasure pulsing through her. She never knew lovemaking could be so wild and primal, and she loved it.

She clung to Drogan's wide shoulders with the last of her fading strength as her climax built. With her back propped against the wall and Drogan's strong hands holding her, she gave herself over to an explosive orgasm that ripped a scream from her throat.

Drogan's mouth claimed her lips to drown out her cries, but she didn't care. Small tremors reverberated through her spent body as Drogan spilled his seed into her.

And God help her, she hoped that seed would fill her womb.

Serena didn't want to leave the haven she and Drogan had found, but there was much he had to do. After straightening their clothes and a lingering kiss, they made their way back to the bailey.

There, she wandered the massive enclosure, getting to know the people of Wolfglynn. Every once in a while, she encountered a woman who was anything but gracious, but Serena tried not to take it to heart. Sometimes, it was hard for people to accept strangers.

She stayed at the blacksmith's for a bit to watch him repair a sword for one of Drogan's knights. She was very impressed with his skill and told him so. His smile shone brightly against the black soot that covered his face.

Her next stop was the stables. There, she examined the many horses and spoke with the stable lads. They were young boys and idolized Drogan to an extent that they thought him a god. She was hard pressed to disagree with their assessment when he had brought her to Wolfglynn without so much as a scratch.

She was headed to the castle when a sudden pain struck between her shoulder blades. The force of the hit knocked her to her hands and knees while she struggled to catch her breath from the pain. She glanced around and saw the weapon of attack, a rock that lay a few inches away.

Serena sat up and glanced between the two buildings to find a narrow passageway that could hide someone. She looked but didn't see anyone, and since she had no wish to investigate further, she rose to her feet and continued toward the castle.

The walk gave her time to contemplate what had

happened. There had been less than a heartbeat from the time she had sensed the malice until the rock had hit her. Whoever it had been had come upon her swiftly.

Serena had her suspicions about why she had been attacked, but she decided to keep it to herself. She had no wish to cause a stir within Drogan's castle when she would be leaving soon anyway. His people would discover she wasn't to be his bride, regardless of how much she wanted the position.

After climbing the castle steps, she opened the heavy door and quickly stepped inside. She tried to move her shoulders and felt her muscles ache, indicating that a bruise had formed, and a large one from what she could tell.

Hopefully, she had enough time to rub a mixture on it before Drogan saw it. She had just removed her gown and was reaching for her special mixture when Claire walked into her chamber.

"Milady," Claire gasped. "What happened?"

"I hurt myself," she lied. "Could you please rub this on me? It'll aid to diminish the discoloring."

Claire rubbed the mixture of herbs and oil in, and then helped Serena redress.

"I think I'll rest here for a while," she told Claire.

The girl nodded and left the chamber. Serena found herself drawn to her window where she looked out to see Drogan talking to a group of knights. He kept pointing to the gates, and she wished she knew what he was saying.

Her back was becoming stiff, and she needed to let the mixture soak into the skin, so she walked to the bed and lay down, intending only to rest. But, before long, she was fast asleep.

Drogan breathed deeply and leaned against the battlement walls. It had taken the rest of the afternoon, but now all of his knights were ready. He was ready. Now, once Gerard and Maris arrived, it could all begin.

And he wanted it to end. Soon.

He looked around the bailey for Serena but didn't see her. He realized she must have gone to the castle, so he quickly went to find her. When he didn't see her in the great hall, he walked to her chamber.

She didn't answer his knock, so he lifted the latch and opened the door to find her curled up on her bed asleep. He smiled, slipped inside her chamber, and closed the door behind him.

Her silken black hair spread out behind her like a fan. One arm curled under the pillow, and the other lay next to her face. She was a vision to behold while awake, but when she slept, she resembled an angel.

He ran his finger along one of her eyebrows. Her eyes opened instantly, and she gave him a sultry smile.

"Did you sleep well?" he asked.

She nodded and yawned. "I didn't even realize I was tired."

He leaned down to kiss her when a shout rose from the gatehouse.

"What is it?" Serena asked as she sat up.

Drogan got to his feet and held out his hand. "My uncle has arrived."

She scooted off the bed and began searching for something.

"What are you looking for?" he asked, eyeing the chamber door.

"My wimple and veil."

He grabbed her hand and pulled her from the chamber. "Trust me. My uncle won't care. Besides, I already told you I like your hair loose," he reminded her as they descended the stairs.

A moment after they opened the castle doors, several people walked through the massive gate. Drogan saw his uncle, and relief surged through him. With his uncle ready and able to help, Serena, Gerard, Maris, and Jocelyn would be kept safe.

Drogan walked Serena down the stairs and waited at the bottom for his uncle to approach.

"Must be a rather nasty situation you've gotten yourself into," his uncle said as he stopped in front of Drogan.

Drogan smiled at his uncle's gruff tone, which was all for show. "Uncle, I'd like to introduce you to Serena of Hawthorne."

Drogan watched his uncle's expression as his eyes moved

to Serena. His face, covered by his thick dark beard and heavily wrinkled, softened as he smiled.

"My nephew is lucky indeed to find a woman of such beauty as you. I'm Phineas."

Drogan couldn't hide his smile as Serena threw him a look.

"Hello, Lord Phineas. It is a pleasure to meet you after hearing Drogan speak so highly of you."

Phineas let out a bark of laughter. "I'll bet he had good things to say."

Drogan was amazed at how Serena handled his uncle. Few women knew what to do with him, but she seemed more than capable.

"Oh, his stories were...entertaining," she said with a wicked grin. The grin dropped, and she became serious. "However, I must tell you straight that I am here not as Drogan's intended, but on the matter that brought you to Wolfglynn."

Phineas nodded as his smile faded. "I knew as much, but an uncle can still hope, aye?"

"It'd be rather rude if you didn't," Serena replied with a grin.

She accepted his uncle's arm as they walked into the castle, leaving Drogan to stare after them. That's when he first saw the woman who had accompanied his uncle. She stood toward the back of a small group of men. Unlike Serena, she wore the traditional wimple and veil, but her demeanor caught Drogan's attention.

She seemed sad, as though she didn't want to enter the castle.

"I think my uncle forgot to introduce you," he said as she neared.

Her smile was brief and barely visible. "Nay, my lord. I asked him not to make my presence known. I had to see something first."

"And did you find what you sought?"

Her tawny eyes turned from him as she took a deep breath. "I did."

"I see it hasn't made you happy."

"On the contrary, it did," she said as her gaze slid back to him. "What saddens me is the heartache that is soon to follow."

Drogan took a step back and stared at her.

It can't be. But then again, it very well might.

He decided to put his suspicions to the test and held out his arm for her.

"Allow me to walk you into the hall," he said. "I'm Drogan."

She took his arm. "I know."

He waited for her to speak her name, but she remained silent. He would find out soon enough, so he let her keep her secret. When they reached the great hall, it was noisy and filled with people. He spotted Serena with his uncle at the dais and steered the woman toward them.

Drogan kept his eyes on Serena as they approached. They were within ten paces of the dais when Serena turned to him, but it wasn't him she looked at—it was the woman. Slowly, Serena stood, and Drogan dropped the woman's arm. The two women walked toward each other as Drogan made his way to his uncle.

"How did you know what Serena was?"

Phineas shrugged. "Francesca told me."

Drogan rolled his eyes and sank into his chair. "How long has she lived with you?"

"Several years. Before your mother died."

Drogan shifted his attention to Serena and Francesca as they began to speak.

"It is good to find another *bana-bhuidseach*," Francesca said. "I only knew of my mother and my aunt."

"You're the second I've encountered since my journey began."

"Hmm." Francesca folded her hands together. "Maybe there are more of us than I thought."

Serena shrugged, and Drogan saw her anxiety in the lines wrinkling her brow.

"I'm Francesca. I've seen you, Serena. I've seen the great evil that follows you. And I've seen your death."

Chapter Twenty-Three

*S*erena nodded to the woman and sensed the anger and fear from Drogan. "You knew I was *bana-bhuidseach*?"

"Nay. I also wasn't able to see what follows you "

That was one thing Serena hadn't been able to discover either, no matter how hard she had tried.

"No matter. We will discover who it is soon enough. You've had a long journey. Sit and enjoy the delicious food of Wolfglynn," she said and spread her arm for Francesca to sit.

It wasn't until after she had spoken that Serena felt Drogan's gaze on her. There was something making his eyes shine with happiness, and she realized she had spoken as if she were the mistress of Wolfglynn, not a visitor herself. The strange thing was she felt as if she belonged here, although she knew, no matter how much she wanted it, it would never be.

Just as she knew she would never be a mother. Her death was imminent, and nothing could prevent it.

She took the chair on Drogan's left as his uncle took the one on the right. The questions would come. She just wondered if they would wait until after the meal.

"You didn't seem surprised by her statement," Drogan said casually, though she knew he was anything but in his quest for answers.

She decided the best course of action was to lie, even if she hated to do it. "As I told you before, we see two paths."

"Did you see your death?"

"Nay." Another lie.

Drogan nodded, seemingly satisfied. "She didn't look happy to discover you, just as you don't look happy to discover her. Why is that?"

She shook her head and gave him what she hoped was a smile. "It's unusual to run into one of my kind. With what's going on around us now, the surprise and excitement gets pushed to the back in the wake of what is before us."

"I don't understand."

"My mother once tried to explain to me, but I never understood until now. Both Francesca and Adrianna sensed what was happening to me, as well as the evil chasing us. The anxiety and fear inside me overrode anything else."

"I see," he said and looked out over the great hall. "What should have been a joyous occasion has been ruined by him. Again."

Serena tensed. He spoke of the evil following them.

"Who?" she asked and tried to appear as though she didn't care if he answered.

Drogan must have caught his mistake for he shook his head. "No one. I'm talking to myself."

But Serena wasn't fooled.

The meal was a pleasant occasion with much laughter and merriment. The food was delicious as always, and the conversation remained on anything but the reason Drogan had called his uncle to Wolfglynn.

Once the meal was over, Drogan and Phineas rose and looked at the women. Serena exchanged a glance with Francesca before she followed Drogan to the solar. She took the chair on the far wall and anxiously waited.

With Drogan leaning against the wall and Phineas and Francesca sitting, Serena grew uncomfortable. All she could do was pray that Drogan didn't dig deeper into what Francesca had told her.

"So, she's how you knew I would have need of you," Drogan finally said to his uncle. "I didn't understand how you could possibly know that I would ask for your help."

"True enough," Phineas said. "You've never asked for it before, and at first, I thought Francesca might have misread things. However, she can be quite insistent."

"When it's important," Francesca said.

Drogan nodded. "How much do you know?"

Phineas shrugged. "Not much. All she could tell me was that a great evil followed you, and you would need my help. Francesca mentioned you would have a woman with you, but I knew nothing of what she saw of Serena."

Drogan waved away his last words. "That doesn't matter. Gerard and Maris are on their way."

"Gerard of Hawthorne?"

Drogan nodded. "He and his wife have a new daughter, and I was there paying my respects when there was an attempt on Gerard's life. Serena told us someone had come to kill him, and even if Maris and Jocelyn managed to escape, they wouldn't live long."

"Do you know who is after Gerard?" Phineas asked.

"It could be one of two men, and either is dangerous. Once Serena convinced Gerard, we set out under disguise, yet it didn't fool the evil."

Serena stood to stretch her legs, hoping to calm her churning stomach. "I met another *bana-bhuidseach*, a Rom, who sensed what was after us. She also sensed the evil was nearer than we expected. It was her idea for us to split up. Gerard, Maris, and Jocelyn took the cart and went with the Roma, while Drogan and I cut across country."

"When we arrived, I sent my men out looking for Gerard," Drogan said, his gaze on Serena. "They should turn up any day now."

Phineas ran a hand down his face and sighed. "Quite a mess. So you're sure you know who's after you...."

Drogan nodded. Serena held her breath, waiting for him to say the name. But she might as well have wished to fly because he didn't utter a word.

"I see," Phineas said, his eyes narrowing on his nephew. "You don't plan on telling anyone who it is."

It wasn't a question. Serena looked from Phineas to Drogan as the two men stared at each other.

"I don't. It's better for everyone involved if they don't know."

"Which tells me," Phineas said as he stood, "that it has something to do with King Henry."

Drogan didn't deny it. Chills raced up Serena's spine as she recalled the handsome horse and shiny armor of the man who had nearly caught them. Despite him lacking colors on his shield, the knight was wealthy and powerful.

"You cannot fight this man alone," she said, unable to keep quiet.

Drogan turned his golden brown gaze to her. "I can, and I will. He's no match for me."

"Then why didn't you fight him in the forest?"

Drogan leaned nonchalantly against the wall. He wasn't fooled by Serena's questions. She was after something. "I learned very early that any advantage one can gain decides the outcome of a battle."

"In other words?" she prompted, her chin raised in question.

"He wanted to find me. He had the upper hand then, but he won't have it here, although I'm going to make sure that he thinks he does."

She shook her head and began to pace. "Surely he isn't

dense enough to think he can attack this," she said with a lift of her hands, "castle by himself?"

Drogan chuckled at her growing ire. "If it's who I think it is, aye, he most definitely will."

She stopped pacing and stared hard at him. "That's the second time you've said that."

"Just what do you mean?" Phineas asked. "I thought you knew who it was."

Drogan groaned inwardly. "It could be one of two men, and I've prepared for either or both of them to attack."

Phineas looked at Serena for a moment before shifting his attention to Drogan. "I know how well defended this castle is, Drogan. You don't need my men to help defend it. Just what is it that you do need me for?"

Drogan pulled his eyes from Serena and turned to his uncle. "Take Gerard, Maris, Jocelyn, and Serena to your isle. They'll be safe there until I can retrieve them."

"Of course," Phineas said, just as Drogan had known he would.

Drogan sighed and leaned his head against the wall. "Thank you."

The night couldn't come fast enough for Drogan. All he had been able to think about was Serena. She consumed his thoughts, despite the threat that loomed above them.

He stayed on the battlements as long as he could, straining

his eyes to see into the darkness and catch a glimpse of his men leading Gerard to Wolfglynn. But, alas, there was no sign of them.

Not a sign of anything, actually, except for a lone owl that flew into the forest. He squinted at the bird, wondering if it was Serena's Nicodemus.

The silence of the wolves was telling. Whoever hunted him was out there, waiting. He was tempted to just walk out of the gates and get it over with, but he had promised Serena he would keep Gerard and Maris safe.

But, once they were inside Wolfglynn's walls, that was another matter entirely. He'd already given strict orders to his men that he was the only person allowed outside the gates. He couldn't afford to have his thoughts divided, and knowing they were all with Phineas would keep him focused.

"Do you have a moment, my lord?"

Drogan whirled around at the soft voice to his right. "Francesca?"

"Aye." She lowered her head slightly. "I'm not disturbing you?"

He shook his head. "Not at all. What can I do for you?"

She walked to the wall and looked between the merlon and crenel, her loose, dark red hair blowing in the slight breeze. She shivered and wrapped her shawl tighter around her. "You don't seem like the type of man to believe in witches."

"I'm not, but when faced with the reality of it, I adapt."

"Hmm," she murmured. "Serena is lovely, is she not?"

Drogan leaned one shoulder against the merlon and crossed his arms over his chest. "That she is. She told me of the curse."

That drew Francesca's eyes to him. "Did she? And what do you think of the curse that has haunted our people for generations?"

"I think it's awful to have to live with something like that."

"It's more difficult than you realize."

"Are you warning me away from her?"

Francesca shrugged. "That would do no good, for it's obvious she is already taken with you. Guard her carefully, Lord Drogan. I know what I saw," she said and turned to leave.

"Serena told me there are two paths that every individual can take, and that you only see one," he hurried to say.

Francesca faced him. "It's true what she speaks. I sense she rarely looks deep into a person's future, and I don't blame her. Finding death, no matter what, can leave one with a sense of...cynicism."

"True. She doesn't use that gift often. She's complained about seeing death."

Francesca lifted her face to the stars. "Though there are two paths, a good and a bad, if you will, I'm afraid with Serena it's different."

"How so?" Drogan asked and stepped toward her. Any information he could discover about Serena could only help her. Or at least he told himself it could.

"That will have to wait."

Intent on making her tell him what he needed to know, Drogan followed her as she walked into the tower, and that's when he spotted Serena. He smiled at her, despite the recent conversation, and waved goodnight to Francesca.

"I wasn't expecting you," he said.

She sighed. "I didn't want to be alone, and I knew I would find you here."

"It's one of my favorite places. I was about to come find you."

"Really?" she asked with a bright smile. "And why is that?"

Drogan chuckled and placed her hand on his bulging rod. "Need you ask?"

The laugh that came from Serena pushed at the darkness crowding him.

"I think it would be remiss of me to keep you in such a state," she said, her voice husky and low.

Excitement and desire surged through him. "Then I would suggest we hasten to your chamber."

Chapter Twenty-Four

*T*he air was so thick Drogan could have cut it with his sword. To his left, Gerard swore and shifted in the saddle as Cade whittled at some wood.

They had been waiting for near an hour for the vile Nigel to appear. He had ordered their presence at this ungodly hour, and the fact that they were in the slums of London made matters worse.

"Why here?" Gerard grumbled.

Drogan shrugged. "Can't be good, regardless."

"It is never good with Nigel," Cade said.

Drogan regarded Cade whom he'd liked instantly. Though many of the men took Cade's quiet nature as arrogance, Drogan knew better.

"You've the right of it, Cade. Now, if only he would show himself."

No sooner had the words left Drogan's mouth than the

baron rode through the thick fog with something wrapped in a dark cloak in front of him.

Unease crept along Drogan's spine. Every instinct within him urged him to run and never look back, but the knight in him refused. He would see what Nigel was up to.

Drogan woke instantly, his body covered in sweat and his breathing harsh and ragged. He wiped at his eyes and squeezed them shut.

A slender arm moved on his chest, and he pulled Serena tighter against him as he tried to calm his racing heart. Images from the awful dream refused to leave him, and the guilt and unease he'd buried began to rise.

"Everything all right?" she murmured.

"Just a bad dream. Go back to sleep."

Thankfully, she didn't ask more, and when her breathing evened into sleep, he slid out of bed and walked to the window, a hand braced on either side.

"Is it you, Cade, that they've sent?" he asked the silent night air. "Are you waiting for me even now? Once my brother, now my enemy."

No answer came, not that he expected any.

He dropped his head and blew out a breath. Mayhap Gerard had been right all those years ago that Cade kept something dark locked within himself.

And with the darkness closing in on Drogan, he could well understand it after the evil deed they'd done. He shook his head and tried to dispel the images of the nightmare from his mind, but they were lodged in place. No amount of contrition or confessing to the priests had ever changed that.

His penance had come knocking on his door, and now waited in the woods to deliver his death.

Serena watched Drogan from the bed. She wished she could help him, but she sensed that was the last thing he wanted right now.

What ate away at him she had no clue, except that it had something to do with the man hunting him and Gerard. But he and Gerard were good men. What could they have possibly done that was so awful?

Her heart ached because of the anguish that tore at his soul. She felt the darkness that surrounded him, but there was nothing she could do to dispel it. Many men succumbed to the numbing darkness until it devoured them, leaving them shells of the men they once were. She couldn't imagine that happening to Drogan, yet it seemed inevitable since she wouldn't be here to help him.

Tears stung her eyes at the thought of leaving him. Death wasn't something she wanted any longer. She'd found her place with Drogan at Wolfglynn. A tear ran down her cheek and into the pillow. Despair would get her nowhere. She wiped the tear away before climbing out of bed and padded across the floor to Drogan.

He turned and opened his arms for her. "You were supposed to be asleep."

"How can I sleep without you beside me?" she asked, pressing her face against his chest. "What troubles you?"

"Nothing."

She let him lie. Mayhap soon he would trust her enough to tell her everything.

When he scooped her up in his arms, she clung to him, knowing the passion he would wring from her would ease the troubles that clung so close to them, if only for a little while.

Drogan moved his right shoulder as he walked down the hallway to Serena's chambers. It had taken everything he had to leave her before the sun broke the horizon, but leave her he had.

He'd bathed and dressed in record time to return to her. A smile pulled at his lips. He acted like a besotted fool, but that was because he was a besotted fool. No sooner had he knocked on her door and Claire opened it than he heard a call from the gatehouse. His eyes met Serena's across her chamber.

"Go," she urged.

It was all the encouragement he needed. He turned on his heel and ran out of the castle. The gates of Wolfglynn creaked open as he entered the bailey.

"Is it Gerard?" Phineas asked.

Drogan dared not answer until he had seen for himself. He felt something on his left and looked down to find Serena beside him. Her hand found his, and he gave hers a little squeeze as the first of his men appeared.

When he saw the cart, a surge of relief swept through him. He hurried to the cart as he spotted Gerard walking beside it. He gave a wave of hello and a bright smile. It was all Drogan needed to see to know everything was all right. For the moment.

A loud wail that erupted from inside the cart brought a smile to Drogan's face and laughter from Serena, who hurried to Maris.

Drogan let her go as he waited for Gerard. They clasped hands.

"You made it." Drogan said.

"Aye, the Roma were quite adept at keeping us hidden."

"Thank God for that. No one followed?"

Gerard shook his head. "They did for a bit, but they soon changed directions. I assume they came after you and Serena?"

Drogan nodded. "We've been here for two days waiting on you."

"Thanks for sending your men," Gerard said as Maris approached.

"You knew I would."

"That he did," Maris said. "Am I ever glad to be out of that cart and safe."

Serena caught Drogan's eye, reminding him that they

needed to get Maris and Gerard out of Wolfglynn as quickly as they could. Drogan was opening his mouth to say just that when Jocelyn let out another wail.

"The ride hasn't agreed with her," Maris said.

Serena reached over and took the infant. "Come, Maris. I'll take you to my chamber."

Drogan waited until they were gone before he motioned to his uncle. "Gerard, this is my uncle, Phineas."

The two men greeted each other before Gerard turned to Drogan. "What's this about?"

"You and your family are going with my uncle. You need to be kept safe."

"You're serious?"

"Keeping you alive? Of course I am. Serena isn't the only *bana-bhuidseach* you've encountered, Gerard. She isn't making this up. You must stay alive, and to do that, you cannot stay here."

"I won't allow you to face him alone."

"Let's talk about this after they have rested," Phineas said as he stepped between the two men. "They've had a long journey, Drogan, and I'm sure they're very tired."

Drogan started to argue, but Phineas raised his hand.

"They can leave the second there's a hint of danger. Until then, give them a little respite."

Reluctantly, Drogan watched his uncle and friend stride into the castle. The impending evil was already here. Of that Drogan was sure, and the longer Gerard and Maris stayed, the more their lives were in danger.

"My lord," Grayson said, "I think you ought to know what happened."

Drogan shifted his full attention to the knight. "And what would that be?"

"I saw someone as we rode to the castle gates."

Every fiber of Drogan's body begged him to get on his horse and ride to the forest. "Where?"

"Just before we emerged from the forest, not far from the river." Grayson wiped sweat from his brow. "As we left the castle to retrieve your friends, I saw no one, but I think I was followed for some distance."

"Same man?"

Grayson shrugged. "Of that I cannot be sure, my lord."

"And this man you saw just now? He didn't move to attack?"

"He was partially hidden in the trees when I caught sight of him, but he did nothing other than watch us."

Drogan flexed his hands, wishing he held his sword, as his eyes scanned the bailey. "Interesting." His gaze returned to Grayson. "Thank you. It's good work you did. Now, go and rest."

"It'll happen soon."

Drogan halted and slowly turned to the knight. "What?"

"The attack. It'll come soon, my lord," Grayson said before walking away.

Drogan narrowed his eyes on the knight's back. Just how much did he know?

Serena was thrilled to have Maris and Jocelyn with her again. She hadn't realized how much she had missed the infant until she was able to hold her again.

"I am ever so glad to be out of that cart," Maris said on a sigh as she slipped into the hot water to soak.

Serena smiled and cooed at Jocelyn. "I know I was very happy to sleep on a bed instead of the ground."

When Maris didn't respond, Serena let her senses go and felt Maris' gaze on her, probing for something.

"What is it you wish to know, Maris?"

Maris laughed. "No matter how many times you do that, it always manages to raise bumps on my arm."

"It's because I know you so well." Serena turned to her friend. "Now, what is it?"

Maris sighed and glanced away. "You look different. Nothing I can place my finger on, but if I didn't know better, I would say you had given in to Drogan's charms."

She tried to keep eye contact, but in the end, Serena looked away. She heard Maris' sharp intake of breath and knew she was about to be bombarded with questions.

"Serena?"

She shifted her gaze back to Maris. "I know what I'm doing."

"I never questioned that," Maris said. "You know your heritage better than anyone. I'm just a concerned friend who doesn't want to see you hurt, although I can see you're happy."

Serena grinned and shrugged. "I am happy."

"Then that's all that matters. You don't have to explain or justify anything to me."

Serena couldn't believe Maris let it go at that, but she was relieved. Jocelyn began to fidget, so Serena carried her to the window while Maris completed her bath. She didn't know how long Maris and Gerard would be here, but she was sure it wouldn't be longer than a day or so.

She hugged Jocelyn to her and kissed her soft head. "I promise you'll be kept safe," she whispered to the infant. "As will your mother and father."

Chapter Twenty-Five

*I*t was nearing noon, and Drogan was training with his men when another shout rose from the gatehouse. He looked up to see his men leaning over the side, staring at something outside of the gate.

"What is it?" he called.

One of the men from the tower yelled for the gate to be opened. Drogan ran toward the stairs that would take him to the gatehouse to reprimand the guard for not answering him, but then he caught sight of the horse.

His feet slowed then stopped as the horse walked through the narrow entry, dragging one of Drogan's knights behind him.

Drogan rushed to stop the horse, but Grayson beat him to it. As Grayson held the horse, Drogan and two other men knelt and freed the knight's foot from the stirrup. Drogan leaned over and felt for breath from the knight, but there was nothing. A single arrow pierced his heart.

"So it's begun," he murmured before climbing to his feet. His gaze caught Grayson's, who gave him a nod.

The dead man was taken from the bailey, and Grayson tossed the horse's reins to a stable boy.

"What's your plan?" Grayson asked.

Drogan gripped his sword. "I want this kept quiet, at least until I can get Gerard, Maris, and Serena away from here."

"And then what?"

"And then I end this."

Serena knew something was wrong the minute Drogan entered the great hall followed by the black-haired knight who had brought Gerard and Maris to Wolfglynn. The knight was as tall as Drogan, but there was something different about him, something secretive and... She couldn't put a name to it.

His gaze came to her, and he gave her the slightest nod of his head. She returned the gesture as he and Drogan approached the dais.

"Ah, Grayson." Gerard stood and clasped the knight's arm.

"My lord," the knight mumbled.

Gerard slapped Grayson on the shoulder and smiled. "If you ever get tired of Drogan, come to Hawthorne. I'll always have a place for you."

Grayson bowed his head but said nothing.

Serena watched him closely. She loosened her senses and felt his liking of both Gerard and Drogan. She also sensed that he preferred it at Wolfglynn, and she couldn't blame him. She wanted to know more, to make sure that Grayson could be trusted, so she went a little deeper. Torment and apprehension of being discovered engulfed her.

"Serena."

She jerked her eyes away from Grayson to Drogan. "Aye?"

"I've been calling to you," Drogan said as he studied her.

Serena looked away to find Francesca watching her. She swallowed and turned back to Drogan. "Did you need something?"

A dark brow lifted as Drogan stared at her. "I was introducing you to Grayson."

"My lady," Grayson said and gave a bow.

Serena gave him a tight smile. What she had discovered could be enough to alert Drogan, but something told her what Grayson hid had nothing to do with the evil following them. However, there was only one way to find out.

She waited until they were eating before she tried her magic again. There had been a glimpse of a small boy with black hair and eyes the color of a summer's sky crying as he was pulled from a woman's arms before the image disappeared.

Her gaze snapped to Grayson to find him watching her. She blinked, unable to believe he knew that she had been prying into his mind and that he had shut her out. It was a trick her mother had showed her early on to keep other *bana-bhuidseach* from her mind. But a man?

She'd discovered something, however. Grayson wasn't helping the great evil, but there was definitely more to him than what he showed everyone.

"You've been quiet," Serena said as she approached Drogan. For an hour, he had been standing in the gatehouse, looking to the forest.

"I've much on my mind."

It would only have taken a moment for Serena to dig into his mind and discover what he kept from her, but she had no wish to do so. If Drogan didn't trust her enough to tell her, then she would leave it at that.

She was about to leave when his hand captured hers and brought her to him. She went into his waiting embrace, needing to feel his strength and closeness. He tightened his arms and his hand brushed against the fading bruise between her shoulder blades, causing her to cry out.

Immediately, Drogan released her.

"I didn't mean to hurt you," he said, a horrified expression on his face.

She was so intent on relieving his conscience, she didn't stop to think about what she was saying. "It's just a bruise."

"A bruise from what?" he asked icily.

Too late, Serena realized her mistake. "How does one usually come to have a bruise?"

"Answer me, Serena. How did you get the bruise?"

"It's nothing."

"Serena," Drogan said, his voice low.

She didn't want to lie to him, but she also didn't want to tell him the truth. That didn't leave her with many options. Finally, she decided on somewhere in the middle.

"It was a rock, I think."

"A rock?" Drogan repeated. "And where did this rock hit you?"

She shrugged, hoping to get by without answering him, but he stared at her until she responded. "In the back."

"And who threw the rock?"

"I never said someone threw the rock. I could have fallen and landed on it."

Drogan crossed his arms over his chest. "So, which is it, Serena? Did you fall, or was the rock thrown?"

Now, no matter what her answer, Drogan would be upset.

"It was thrown."

"Who threw it?" he demanded.

"I don't know. I didn't see anyone."

He sighed and wrapped an arm around her, careful not to touch the sore area of her back. "Why didn't you tell me?"

"What good has it done?" She turned her head to look at him. "I don't know who it was, and even if I did, I wouldn't want anything done to them."

"Why not? They hurt you."

"I'm a stranger, Drogan. There's talk of me becoming your wife, and I've seen the way some of the women look at you. It's jealousy."

He pursed his lips and shook his head. "It doesn't matter. I don't want my people treating guests like this."

"But it's just me, and Gerard or Maris. What does that tell you?"

He didn't answer her. Serena watched him gaze at the forest again.

"I've liked having you here e," he said all of a sudden.

Her stomach twisted at his words, for she knew what they meant. "I've enjoyed being here."

He turned to her then and held her shoulders. "It's begun."

"I assumed as much. When are we to leave?"

"During the night."

She nodded and reached for his hand. "Then we must make the most of our time."

"Serena, is there any way I can talk you into returning here?"

She wanted to cry. Not only was her time ending with Drogan, but he wanted her to return. How could she tell him that, despite her wishes, she was going to die?

Instead of the tears, she forced a smile. "Mayhap."

That one little word brightened Drogan's eyes, and a huge grin replaced the frown. "Then I shall do my best."

If only his best would be enough she thought to herself.

He had no idea how she longed to stay in this mystical castle with the sea crashing against the cliffs.

She had to be careful, though. Drogan's eyes watched her vigilantly, and she had no wish for him to know the truth of Francesca's words. If he did, his actions would undermine everything that must occur to keep Gerard, Jocelyn, and Maris alive.

"Show me the sea," Serena said.

Drogan shook his head. "It isn't safe."

She cocked a brow at him. "Are you telling me the great Lord Drogan doesn't have a route of escape to the sea?"

He chuckled and shook his head. "You know I do."

"Please," she pleaded and grasped his hand. "Just for a moment. I want to see the sea with you."

"I shouldn't." He sighed. "We cannot stay long."

Serena wanted to jump for joy. "Really?"

"Let me tell Phineas where we'll be in case of trouble."

Serena could hardly stand still as she waited for Drogan to return from his uncle. Phineas and Francesca were in the great hall, and Serena decided to remain by the door while Drogan went to them. Now, as she watched, Phineas turned his gaze to her before speaking to Drogan.

She desperately wanted to know what he said, but she wouldn't rummage through his mind to discover what it was. Despite the cloud that hovered over them, Serena refused to allow anything to spoil her time alone with Drogan.

He came to her, a smile pulling at his lips. "Are you ready?"

"Oh, aye," she said and knew her smile was huge.

"Then, come, my lady. The sea awaits," Drogan said as he held out his arm for her.

Serena took his arm and followed as Drogan led her down to what she thought was the dungeon. He veered to the left when they came to a fork in the tunnel.

The ensuing maze left her disoriented and lost, but she was too giddy to object. She heard the sounds of the waves crashing violently against the cliffs before they came to the entrance.

She stopped and closed her eyes as she listened. Beside her, Drogan took her hand and inhaled deeply.

"I love the sound of the waves. I always feel somewhat diminished to know the power they have."

She opened her eyes and looked at him. "I've never thought of it that way before, but you have a point."

"Of course I do. I'm a man."

She rolled her eyes and pulled him after her. "I don't think I can wait another moment to see the water."

Drogan pushed open the heavy wooden door, and she found herself looking at the churning waters. They were deep blue with the waves cresting to white as birds circled overhead calling out their wonderful song. One dove into the water and came up with a fish in its talons.

She gasped, eager to see much more. "What kind of bird is that?"

"A kestrel."

"They have the loveliest song."

Drogan couldn't take his eyes off Serena. Her excitement had bubbled over onto him, and though he had always loved the sea, he had never been so eager to share it.

He pulled her from the mouth of the cave and closer to the water. "The currents are swift," he said as she stopped just before a wave touched the hem of her gown. "I've seen many men swept out to sea because they didn't heed the power of the water."

"I can see some of the currents if I look close enough."

He nodded. "These waters are dangerous, but they have always called to my people."

"And to you?" she asked as her gaze lifted to meet his.

He looked into her vivid blue eyes. "Most definitely."

"Oh." She gazed over his shoulder.

Drogan smiled for he knew she was studying the castle.

"I didn't realize it was built so near the edge of the cliffs."

"My ancestors were very clever. It's a great defense." Drogan looked up at the castle far above them.

"It doesn't hurt that your uncle lives on the isle, either."

Drogan laughed. "That it doesn't."

He sat back and let her wander by herself. She squatted, reached into the sand, and came up with a shell. He smiled when she raised it up to show him. He knew he would never forget this day as long as he lived.

How ironic was it that he had finally found someone who pushed away the darkness only to lose her? Despite what she had said on the battlements, he knew she lied. She would leave Wolfglynn and never return.

Or at least that was her plan, but he had other ideas. It might take years, but he would do what he could to push away the darkness. Then he could convince her to return with him.

She belonged here as much as he did.

Chapter Twenty-Six

Their time at the water was over far too soon. He couldn't chance staying out too long, despite his longing. Serena didn't complain as they returned to the castle, but her sadness showed in her eyes.

He stopped her before they reached the door to the great hall and turned her to face him. "Once this is all over, we will spend an entire day by the water," he promised.

She nodded, but he wanted more.

"I give you my word, Serena."

"I know." Sorrow pulled at her lips.

He tilted her face to his. "Then why do I get the feeling that you don't intend to ever see the sea again?"

She ran her fingers along his lips. "No one knows what the future holds."

"Now you lie," he said before he kissed her fingers.

"I do not wish to mar this day speaking of things we know

nothing about. Let's spend what little time we have enjoying each other."

Drogan wanted to know what she hid from him, but he was wise enough to heed her words. He smiled and opened the door so she could enter the great hall. While she spoke with Maris and Francesca, he went to the bailey to check with his men.

"Grayson," Drogan called out when he spotted his commander.

The knight made his way to Drogan. "My lord."

"How do things come?"

"We are on schedule, and the men are ready."

"The men posted outside?"

Grayson glanced at the castle gates. "I have neither heard nor seen them, my lord."

"They haven't checked in?" Drogan asked, worry clouding his thoughts.

"Not as of yet."

This wasn't good. "When was the last time?"

"About half an hour before—"

Drogan held up a hand to stop him. He knew Grayson spoke of the dead knight. "Let's give it a few more hours. If you haven't heard from any of them, then it's time we went and looked ourselves."

"Aye," Grayson said, a strange light coming into his eyes then.

Drogan nodded, knowing the knight was as eager for a fight as he was. As he turned to leave, Gerard strode up, a concerned frown marking his brow.

"Everything all right?" Gerard asked.

"For now. We have a few hours before you and your family will depart with Phineas."

Gerard nodded. "Under cover of darkness."

"That was my thought. From what I can tell, the bastard came alone, which means he cannot watch both the castle and the water."

"And your plan is to make sure he's watching the castle," Gerard said with a small, knowing smile.

"Exactly."

The smile vanished, replaced by the look of a well-trained knight ready for action. "You could use another sword arm."

Drogan held up his hand and shook his head. "I don't want to hear any more talk like that. Serena and Maris would have my head if you stayed, and frankly, I like where it is. So don't think to sway me, for you won't."

"I want you to know that if anything happens to you, I will avenge you."

Drogan clenched his jaw. No one had ever said those words to him, and he was amazed he had been lucky enough to have Gerard as a friend for as long as he had. "Thank you, my friend, but I would rather you be alive to raise your daughter and have more children with Maris."

Gerard smiled sadly and looked away. "If we'd known how things would turn out, I think I would have done things differently that day."

That day. Drogan hated thinking of that day almost as

much as he detested speaking about it. "Don't," he told Gerard. "It doesn't do us any good to look back."

"The nightmares still plague me," Gerard said as if he hadn't heard Drogan. "Do you have nightmares about that day?"

Drogan wanted to lie. He tried to lie. But in the end he could only nod.

"They've gotten better over the years," Gerard continued. "Yet, still they plague me, and I think they always will."

"I know they will."

Gerard peered closely at him. Drogan tried to look away, but his friend wouldn't let him.

"The darkness is closing in."

Drogan didn't deny it. There wasn't a need. "I'll be fine."

"Nay, you won't. I've been where you are, Drogan, and I know what it feels like. It was hell."

It was much worse than that. "I won't let it overcome me."

"You won't have a choice, my friend," Gerard said sadly. "I always thought it would never claim you. I thought you were too strong for that."

Drogan shrugged. "I'm just a man, Gerard. I live with sins most men cannot comprehend. It is a wonder I've kept the darkness at bay as long as I have."

For several moments, they stood in silence, each lost in thought of that fateful day that turned the tide of their lives.

"Do you think its Cade?" Gerard asked.

Drogan ran a hand through his hair. "I'm not sure. I can't imagine Nigel coming to kill us himself."

"He would have to if he's already killed Cade and doesn't want anyone else to know what he has done."

Drogan squeezed his eyes shut, trying to block out the awful memory Gerard had dredged up. "Men don't have to know a reason if they are paid enough coin."

"True enough. I suppose we won't know until you face him."

Drogan opened his eyes. "Spend what time you have resting with your wife before your journey."

"And you? What will you do? Don't think I haven't seen the way you and Serena look at each other."

Drogan knew Gerard was digging for answers. "Serena and I have found a little happiness, and though she refuses to give me her word that she'll return to me and Wolfglynn, I plan to see that she does."

"So, you love her?"

Love. It wasn't something Drogan had thought about. "I don't know if I would call what I feel for her love. She...eases the restlessness in me, makes me forget the evil I have done."

Gerard nodded. "Maris did the same for me. I'd say that is love."

"I don't know what love is, Gerard, so I cannot claim to know, nor do I want to claim that when it may be nothing more than lust."

Gerard grinned. "Tell me, my friend, would you take Serena as your wife, as I've heard your people believe?"

Drogan groaned. "Don't listen to the rumors that abound in my castle."

"I still haven't received an answer to my question. Would you take her as your bride?"

Drogan stared at his friend. "Aye."

"Then that is love."

Gerard walked back into the castle, his words echoing in Drogan's mind. *Love.* Was that what he felt for Serena? Is that what pulled at his heart when she was close and left an empty ache inside of him when she wasn't near?

Love had never been a part of his life, and it wasn't something he could ask anyone to explain to him. He pushed the thought away and hurried into the castle to seek out Serena.

Their hours together grew short, and he wanted as much time with her as he could get.

Serena carefully laid Jocelyn in her cradle. She had spent the last half hour rocking the infant to sleep. Never before had Serena wanted a child of her own, not after experiencing her mother's fear and anger. But that was before she'd tasted Drogan's kisses and felt his caresses and heard him whisper her name as his climaxed.

"You've a special bond with the child," Francesca said as she walked up beside Serena.

"In a way." Serena sat down at the table in the great hall. She had promised Maris she'd watch over Jocelyn while Maris got some much needed rest.

Francesca joined her and folded her arms in her lap. Serena was amazed at how tranquil the *bana-bhuidseach* was despite what was going on around them.

"Why haven't you told him?" Francesca asked.

"Told who what?"

Francesca gazed at her with tawny eyes. "Lord Drogan."

"And what was I supposed to tell him?"

"That you plan on sacrificing yourself to save him and Lord Gerard."

Serena circled her thumbs around each other. "He has no need to know. He can do nothing to change it other than to get himself killed."

"You care very much for him."

"I...do, but I'd already decided upon this path before I gave myself to him."

"So you would rather die than raise the child that grows in your womb?"

Serena's hand went to her stomach. Her breath came out in a hiss, and her eyes narrowed. "Why do you tell me this? It's vital to the future of England that Gerard and his family live, just as it is imperative to Wolfglynn that Drogan remain lord."

"You've every right to be angry at me for peering into your future and telling you something you've no wish to hear, but I feel that I must."

"Stop," Serena said and made to rise, but Francesca laid a hand on her arm.

"Give me but a moment's time, and I'll bother you no more."

Serena stared into the other woman's tawny eyes, her mind warring over what to do. Part of her wanted to know more. She had been too terrified to look into her own future, yet here was one of her kin willing to do it for her. But was it what she wanted?

She resumed her seat. "Go on."

"You told Drogan that you see two paths when you look into a person's future."

"You know that's the truth. I wasn't lying."

Francesca smiled softly, sadly. "But you didn't look at your other path."

"I didn't see one that didn't involve the death of Gerard, Maris, and Jocelyn, because if there was another way I would gladly take it."

"Have you looked since you've given yourself to Drogan?"

That stopped Serena in her tracks. "Nay," she admitted in a whisper.

"Then maybe you should." Francesca rose and smiled before she walked away.

Serena almost called her back. There was no way she could look into her own future. Seeing someone else's death was hard enough, but seeing one's own was devastating, and she'd already witnessed it once.

She couldn't do it again.

Not even for Drogan or our child?

She sighed and reached into the crib to touch Jocelyn's

tiny hand curled into a fist. A child of her own. Could she really have one growing in her womb, or was Francesca playing a wicked game with her?

Either way, she knew she had only one option—tc look into her future.

Chapter Twenty-Seven

*I*t seemed like hours since Francesca had left Serena sitting in the great hall, but she knew it had been but a few moments. Her thoughts were occupied with what Francesca had said, and it left Serena doubting if she could look into her future again.

But the thought left her shuddering. She had never liked that part of her abilities, and whenever possible, she avoided it.

Yet, the thought of being with Drogan, for however long that might be, left her with a grain of hope she didn't have before, enough to make her doubt herself, something she didn't normally do.

A finger, calloused and thick, ran down her check to her neck. Drogan's scent engulfed her, and she forgot everything but him.

"Lost in thought, are you?" he asked next to her ear.

Words eluded her. She thought she nodded, but she wasn't sure. His hands caressed her skin, sending ripples of pleasure running rampant through her.

"How long are you to watch Jocelyn?"

She shrugged.

His soft laugh rumbled his chest. "It seems I'll have to take care of that."

"Take care of what?" Gerard asked while walking toward them.

Serena jerked out of her chair and hastily looked around the hall to see if anyone had seen them.

"Nothing," Drogan said.

Gerard mumbled something and reached for his daughter. "Was she any trouble, Serena?"

"She was an angel." She kissed the infant's cheek. "Did Maris get enough sleep?"

"As much as she could. She kept waking up, worrying about Jocelyn."

"Then take her to her mother," Serena said and shooed Gerard off.

"Ah," Drogan said and took a step closer. "Alone at last. What shall we do until the evening meal?" A devilish light shimmered in his eyes, one that promised untold passion.

"Do you not have duties?"

"I've taken care of everything, but I suppose I could spend the time training with my knights instead of with you." He shrugged and made to turn away.

Serena grabbed his hand, unable to conceal her laughter.

"Enough, my lord," she said as he made a mock attempt to run away from her.

Drogan stopped near the stairs. "I just needed to see if it was really me you wanted."

Serena rolled her eyes and started up the stairs when jealousy, pure and deep, assailed her. She tried to scan the hall without Drogan noticing. Whoever had hit her with the stone watched them now.

And if Serena knew anything, it was that this person would be watching again.

Drogan shut and locked Serena's door behind him. "Alone at last."

She smiled, although he could see her sadness at what was to come.

"Remember what you told me?"

"What?" she asked and cocked her head to the side.

"You said you would take whatever time we had and cherish it?"

She nodded. "Then don't think about what is to come tonight. I want nothing marring these last few hours."

She took his offered hand as he pulled her close and wrapped his arms around her. Her face tilted up to look at him, her blue eyes bright and honest.

"You are the most handsome man I've ever seen."

Her words stunned him. He had been called many things

by many people, but none had ever told him he was handsome. "Nay. Your beauty outshines that of a sunrise."

His eyes locked with hers, and the only thing he could think about was melding his body with hers. He lowered his head until their lips were breaths apart. Her mouth parted, and her chest rose and fell rapidly.

She wanted him, and that fact sent a thrill so pure and sweet through him, it nearly brought him to his knees.

He could hold back no more and touched his lips to hers. The sweet intoxication of her kiss left him weak and craving more of her flesh. His hands working quickly, he removed her gown and under things, tossing them heedlessly to the floor.

Her fingers joined his as he removed his clothing, and the more they hurried, the more their fingers bumbled. They laughed and shared kisses in between discarding his garments. As soon as he was as naked as she, he picked her up and carried her to the bed where he laid her down. He stretched out beside her, lying on his side as he ran his hand from her face to her ankle.

She was incredible, and he couldn't believe she was with him. But would she be if she knew the truth about him and his wicked past?

"Serena. I want to tell you why the man is after me and Gerard."

She raised a finger to his lips. "Shh. Later. Right now, I just want to feel you inside me. Nothing more."

Drogan hoped he had the courage to tell her later. Thoughts of his past and the ever-present darkness were soon forgotten as he marveled in her soft embrace. His body had been hard and wanting since the moment he walked into the great hall and found her sitting alone. It amazed him that he couldn't get enough of her. His mouth placed kisses along the hollow of her throat and the swell of her breasts while his hands continued to rub her hips and thighs, separating her legs. He bent over her, supporting his weight on his hands, and leaned down to take a taut nipple into his mouth.

Serena cried out and clutched at Drogan's wide shoulders as his hot mouth and tongue sent shivers of pleasure along her spine. His thick, hard cock barely touched her sex, and she moved her hips against him, but Drogan rose up away from her.

"Not yet," he murmured and moved his mouth to her other breast.

She didn't know how much more she could take. Her body needed him now, yet Drogan had other ideas. No matter how much she pressed and pulled, she couldn't get him inside of her. When he began to kiss down her stomach and pull her legs apart, she didn't think anything of it. When his fingers delved into her wetness, all she could do was sigh and take the pleasure he supplied.

But when his tongue flicked across her swollen flesh, she experienced liquid heat as her blood pounded through her. Her legs opened, allowing him more access as her hands dug into the sheets and her hips rocked against him.

She spiraled further out of control with each swipe of his tongue, and just when she thought she couldn't take anymore, the climax claimed her, sending lights popping behind her eyes.

Her body still convulsed with the powerful orgasm when he slid inside her. She wrapped her arms and legs around him. He picked her up so that she straddled him, and he leaned back against the wall.

With his hands on her hips, he guided her up and down on his rod. Serena found that if she pushed her feet together, she gained more leverage. She let her body take over as she moved her hips along Drogan's rod until his breathing became hard and uneven.

To her surprise, she felt another climax approaching and quickened her rhythm. Just as her body exploded, Drogan tensed, and he jerked her against his chest as his orgasm came.

When she was able to breathe normally again, she opened her eyes to find herself cradled against his chest. "I'm still seeing stars," he said as he brushed her hair out of her face.

She rose up and felt him still inside of her. "Me, too."

He playfully pulled on her hair, and she rubbed her breasts against his chest.

"Don't tease," he warned.

"I'm not." Her eyes widened when he began to grow inside of her.

He grinned and rolled over until he was on top of her. "I warned you not to tease," he said just before he kissed her.

"Stop it," Gerard said to his wife as she continued to pace the chamber.

"I can't help it. I worry about Serena. I think she might do something reckless."

Gerard laughed. "Serena is anything but reckless, love."

Maris rolled her eyes and then glared at him. "What do you call what she is doing with Drogan? Sensible? She knows of the curse."

"Aye." Gerard rose to comfort Maris. "She does, but Serena is a grown woman capable of making her own decisions."

"I don't want her hurt."

Gerard sighed and looked out the window. "Neither do I, but I think It is out of our hands."

"When do we leave?" Maris asked as she wiped at her tears.

"Tonight. Drogan will give us time to get away without being seen."

She crossed her arms over her chest. "I don't like this."

"Neither do I, but I know Drogan. He could take me if he wanted. He's good, Maris. Possibly the best."

Gerard didn't know if he had calmed his wife's fears, but he did know one thing. He could never leave Drogan here to face the evil alone. Gerard helped commit the hideous sin, and he would be there with Drogan to repent. There were just a few things he needed to do first.

Serena didn't want to wake up. But the reality of her life was intruding with the incessant pounding at her chamber door. Beside her, Drogan sighed and yanked the bed covers so that whoever opened the door wouldn't see him.

"I'll see who it is," Serena said as she slipped out of the bed and threw on her gown.

She cracked open the door to find Gerard standing in the hallway. The flicker of a rushlight illuminated his face as he looked over his shoulder. There were few reasons he would be here this late, and none of them comforted her. "What is it? Is Jocelyn or Maris hurt?"

"Nay," he said looked around again. "Have you seen Drogan?"

"Why?"

"I need to speak with you."

Serena didn't like the wild, determined look in his eyes. It bespoke of him doing something rash and foolish. "About what?"

"I'm not leaving tonight. I'm going to stay and help Drogan."

She gripped the door and prayed Drogan would remain hidden. She had to know everything Gerard planned. "You must go with Maris. It's important."

"Nay," he bellowed, then lowered his voice. "The evil is after me."

"You know as well as I that once it's done with you, it'll come for Drogan," she argued.

"Drogan and I committed the same sin, Serena. I cannot allow him to face it alone."

She knew there was no talking him out of it, so she had to think fast. "All right," she relented reluctantly. "I'll help you."

He relaxed and gave her a small smile. "I knew I could count on you," he said before he disappeared down the hall.

"You don't seriously plan on aiding him?"

Serena jumped when Drogan's voice sounded near her ear. She turned and found him standing beside her before she shut and barred the door.

"Of course not, but I also know there's no talking Gerard out of something when he's set his mind. He's very stubborn."

"I know," Drogan said and sighed. "I'd hoped he wouldn't try to pull anything like this, but deep down I knew he would."

"Well, he won't forgive me, but I've got a plan that will ensure he leaves with your uncle. Peacefully."

"We'll worry about forgiveness later." Drogan reached for her hand to drag her back to the bed. "Right now I've got something else in mind."

Chapter Twenty-Eight

*I*t was nearing dusk when Drogan and Serena left her chamber. Neither wanted their time to end, but time wasn't on their side.

Serena had tried to get an opportunity to look into her future, but Drogan wouldn't let her out of his sight for more than a moment or two. She ran her hand across her stomach, wishing she knew for sure whether her womb quickened with life, whether there was another path she might take.

"Do you have everything you need?" Drogan whispered as they descended the stairs to the great hall.

"Aye. Just keep Gerard occupied, and I'll take care of the rest."

When they reached the hall, Drogan left her to speak to his knights. She looked out the windows to see that darkness was already falling. Her hours here were running out like sand through her fingers.

She made her way toward the dais and took her chair before she sensed the beginnings of loathing touch her. The feeling went in and out, leaving Serena to believe that whoever it was had their attention divided from her.

Just then Claire walked near the dais, and Serena called out to her as she rose from the table. "I need your help."

"Anything, milady. What can I do?"

"There is someone here who would do anything to have Lord Drogan as a husband. Do you know of whom I speak?"

Claire glanced away and shrugged. "There aren't many women in the castle who haven't wished for Lord Drogan as their own."

"True," Serena concurred. "But there is one who would do more than wish. I need to know who she is."

Claire wrung her hands and bit her lip. "I'd hoped she would realize it was foolish."

"Who?" Serena asked as she gripped Claire's arms.

"Georgina."

Now that Serena had a name, she released Claire. "She's here now?"

The servant nodded, tears in her eyes. "She's a nice girl, milady."

"I know," Serena said, hoping to calm Claire. "Now, will you point her out to me? There is something she and I need to discuss."

She followed Claire's finger as she pointed to the servant. "Thank you," she whispered to Claire as the girl hurried away.

Serena took a deep breath and headed toward Georgina.

The servant was walking away from a table when she glanced over at the dais. Her eyes widened, and she scanned the hall.

"Looking for me?" Serena asked.

The girl swung around, and Serena found herself looking at the most beautiful creature she had ever seen. If not for the hate in the girl's light blue eyes, she would have been perfect with her tall, slender frame and glorious golden hair.

"You have a good aim," Serena said and flexed her shoulders. "My back still aches."

"It's no more than you deserve," Georgina snarled.

Serena knew it was time to put things to rest. "I didn't come here to marry Lord Drogan, Georgina. You would have discovered that had you but asked me or Claire."

"You lie."

Serena was about to lose all patience. No one liked to be called a liar. "That is something I don't do. It's true Lord Drogan is pleasing to the eye, but I am merely here with my friends. We'll be leaving soon."

Some of the hate left Georgina's eyes, and she tossed back her thick blonde braid. "Truly?"

Serena nodded. "You are a beautiful woman. I'm sure every man in Wolfglynn vies for your hand."

"Every man but Lord Drogan." She pouted.

"We cannot have all that we desire. Is that the only reason you want Lord Drogan?"

Georgina looked away, refusing to keep eye contact with Serena. "Nay."

"Now you lie," Serena said when she sensed the unease in

the servant. "It's Lord Drogan's misfortune if he doesn't see your beauty."

The servant's mouth pulled into a small grin. "I never thought of it that way."

"Then end the jealousy," Serena said. "Take your pick of the men and stop their suffering. Just look at them. None of them have taken their eyes off you all evening."

Both women glanced around to find many male eyes on Georgina. "I never realized," the servant said, awe lowering her voice.

"Then I'm glad I could help," Serena said and made her way back to the dais.

"What was that about?" Drogan asked as she took a seat beside him.

"Georgina wanted you because you hadn't noticed her."

Drogan choked on his wine. "Hadn't noticed? Serena, she all but stood naked in front of me."

"Then why didn't you take her?"

He shrugged. "I'm not sure. I just didn't want her."

It was enough that he didn't want Georgina. There was nothing she could do if some other woman turned Drogan's eye.

Their meal arrived then, giving them no more time to talk. Serena had other things on her mind than food though. She had precious little time to carry out her plan, and everything must go smoothly lest anyone suspect.

Drogan leaned over and asked, "Are you ready?"

Serena nodded, praying he didn't realize she had more than one plan in motion.

"It'll be fine," Drogan said.

She wanted to yell that it wouldn't, but found her throat wouldn't work. Instead, she nodded again and nearly cried when he squeezed her hand beneath the table.

The meal progressed without interference from Serena. She moved her food about on her trencher while people around her talked and laughed, as if the deadliest sort of evil were not approaching Wolfglynn's gates and people's lives were not at stake.

She didn't blame them though. How she wished she could laugh and joke and act as though fate hadn't delivered a very cruel blow to her.

"Ready?"

Drogan's golden brown eyes held a hint of concern for her, as well as the darkness that was always so near to him. If only she could stay to help him fight it off.

"It's now or never," she said and fixed the small vial on her palm and between two fingers on her right hand so that it wouldn't be seen.

She grabbed her goblet with her left hand and pushed her chair back to rise. Her knees wobbled, and her stomach churned, but not because she was about to betray a friend. It was because things were in motion that she had no way of stopping, no matter how she wished she could call them to a halt.

When she came to Maris and Gerard, she stopped and set her goblet as near to Gerard's as she could.

"Did you rest enough?" she asked Maris.

Maris laughed. "With an infant, there is never enough rest."

Serena forced a laugh and glanced at Gerard, who wouldn't meet her eyes. She knew he was afraid Maris would discover what he intended, and Serena wished she had been able to tell Maris of her plans.

She listened as Maris talked of inconsequential things, nodding her head and agreeing as though she were paying attention. As Maris continued to talk, Serena reached over with her right hand and went to grab Gerard's goblet.

The vial slipped and almost fell from her hand as she tried to pour its contents into the goblet. She bit the inside of her mouth and concentrated on emptying the vial.

"Whoa," Gerard said and grabbed her hand. "You nearly drank from my goblet, and I doubt my wife would approve."

Serena laughed with him and Maris as she tucked her hand behind her back. "Forgive me. I thought it mine."

She took her goblet and returned to her seat. The calm that had always been a part of her was gone, leaving her nerves raw and on edge. And she didn't like it.

Drogan leaned over and whispered, "How long?"

"It needs at least an hour." She reached down to pick an imaginary piece of lint from the hem of her gown. "If we plan it right, it should overcome him when we're at the boat."

"Perfect."

Aye, perfect. Serena straightened and closed her eyes. Her hand went to her stomach as her mind wondered. If Francesca hadn't planted that seed of doubt in her mind she would know what to do this night.

Drogan kept a watchful eye on Gerard as he finished his wine and reached to refill his goblet. Drogan let out a pent up breath and sat back to find Serena studying him. He knew what was on her mind.

"I won't fail," he said.

She shook her head. "Nay, you won't. I've seen it."

He leaned forward to place his forearms on the table. "Then what worries you? What aren't you telling me?"

"Two paths, Drogan," she murmured. "Everyone has paths to take. The choices a person makes can change the outcome."

Drogan opened his mouth to speak when Grayson approached the dais.

"My lord, a word," the knight said.

Drogan pushed back from the table and followed Grayson. He heard footsteps behind him and knew it was Gerard and Phineas. Grayson didn't stop until he had reached the bailey, well away from prying ears.

It was evident from Grayson's agitation that something was amiss.

"What is it?" Drogan asked.

"The men posted in the woods. They haven't checked in."

Drogan looked up at the sky to see it was dusk, only the barest hint of the sun could be seen as it dipped into the horizon. There wasn't time to wait now, he must begin.

He turned to the castle doors to see Serena standing there, the light from the great hall shining behind her. Their time was over. The ache in his chest was devastating, nearly sending him to his knees. But, the anger for what the evil bastard had done to disrupt his life made him eager to ride out and finish him off.

"You know what to do," Drogan said to Grayson without taking his eyes from Serena.

A hand clamped on his shoulder as Gerard came to stand beside him. "This isn't the end."

But Drogan wasn't so sure. There was something Serena wasn't telling him. He knew if it was about him, she would alert him to keep him alive. What he feared was it had something to do with her.

She had been adamant about staying behind to aid him, and once he had said she must get on the boat, she hadn't had another word to say. He wasn't a fool. He knew she had some plan working in that smart mind of hers, but there was no way he was going to allow her to stay behind. She must leave to stay safe.

"Keep an eye on her, Gerard," Drogan said.

"You have my word."

Drogan watched his friend walk to the castle doors.

Gerard stopped and said something to Serena before continuing in.

"I'll get Francesca ready to depart," Phineas said

Drogan nodded to his uncle and made his way toward Serena. The closer he got, he could tell she was fighting tears.

"I thought we would have longer than this," he said.

"What's done is done. It must end this night, Drogan." She looked down and licked her lips. "I must go and help Maris."

Drogan longed to stop her and pull her into his arms, but he was afraid that if he did he would never let go. He waited until she was out of sight before he started up the stairs to get ready.

Once in his chamber, he stared at his armor. His opponent was most assuredly wearing his, but Drogan knew he could move quicker without it. It would leave him vulnerable, but that was a risk he was willing to take.

He threw open his chest and reached inside for his padded jerkin and chain mail. He tugged off his fine red tunic, black breeches and good boots. In their place, he pulled on brown leather breeches and his favorite, well-worn boots. He put on the padded jerkin over a soft leather tunic, and then the chain mail over the jerkin.

He tied back his hair with a piece of leather to keep it out of his eyes then tugged on his gloves. He flexed his hands and strapped on his weapons.

A long, skinny dagger he placed in his boot. Another dagger, shorter and thicker, he hid beneath the padded jerkin at his back. His favorite dagger, one-half the length of his sword and slightly curved, he placed on his right hip.

A lone wolf's call echoed in the night, alerting Drogan that danger was closing in.

"No more running," Drogan said as he sheathed his sword.

Chapter Twenty-Nine

*D*rogan spotted his men waiting for him. His boots clicked on the cobbled stones of the bailey as he walked to his knights. Serena was nowhere to be found, but he thought it better this way. The thought of saying good-bye to her was too gut-wrenching to consider.

"You know what to do," he told Grayson.

"I wish you'd reconsider," the knight said as he walked with Drogan to his horse standing by the gate.

"This is for me alone. Bringing any of you out there will ensure one thing—your deaths."

Grayson snorted. "Surely one man couldn't take all of us."

"Maybe not, but I'm not willing to take the chance." Drogan adjusted the saddle, giving himself some time as he looked for Serena.

"Tell me why you're going to risk leaving the people of Wolfglynn without a lord." Grayson demanded.

Drogan slowly straightened and looked at his second in command. "Never once have I asked you about your past. I know you are no lowly knight, Grayson. You are running from something, but I didn't pry. I ask now the same from you. This is no concern of yours."

"True," Grayson admitted. "You haven't asked about my past, but you cannot think to risk your life so needlessly. Your people need you."

"Is it needless?" Drogan roared. He stepped closer to Grayson and lowered his voice. "You have no idea the sins that haunt me. I'm tired of running from them, and I will do it no more." He pointed to the gate. "There is one sin I can put right, and that's what I'm going to do."

Grayson gave a curt nod. "Fine. But know this, if I see one hint that you're in trouble, I'm riding out to join you."

"You won't see anything," Drogan promised and mounted his horse when he caught a whiff of lavender.

He found Serena standing behind Grayson. Drogan was confused by the swell of emotion raging through him, but there was one thing he couldn't deny. He loved Serena.

She walked to him and went up on her toes to place her lips against his. Drogan wrapped his arms around her and pressed her against him. He ended the kiss and put his face against her neck, inhaling her sweet scent.

"I will come for you when this is over," he promised. "Look for me."

She pulled out of his arms and smiled through the tears

that threatened to overflow her beautiful blue eyes. She tugged something over her head and held it out to him.

"What is it?" Drogan asked as he reached for her hand.

"It is all I have left of my mother," she said and dropped it into his open hand.

Drogan looked down to see a long, slender sliver medallion with strange markings on it. He raised his eyes to Serena and shook his head. "I can't take this."

"It's a gift, Drogan. I want you to have it."

He knew what she was doing—giving him something of herself so he would always remember her. Didn't she realize he couldn't forget her if he tried?

Drogan took the chain and put it over his head. He took one more look at the strange emblem before tucking it beneath his tunic and jerkin. "I'll return this to you when I get back."

She smiled sadly. "Be careful and keep your eyes open."

Her lack of response didn't go unnoticed, but he would see the medallion returned. He bent down and kissed her once more, so her taste would be with him when he left. The kiss instantly brought his body to life, and he yearned for her. With regret, he ended the contact and pulled away from her. He ran his gloved hand down the side of her face He wished he could tell her of his feelings, but they lodged in his throat.

"Serena—"

"I know," she said. "Please be careful. For me."

"I will."

"Go," she said and pushed him toward his horse. "End this tonight."

He nodded and waved for Grayson to accompany him to the gates. "Make sure she leaves with my uncle," Drogan said. "I want your word that you'll not let her do anything foolish."

"I give it." Grayson brought his right fist up to hit his heart.

Drogan mounted and was turning his horse toward the gates when Gerard came riding toward him.

"Damn," Drogan mumbled. He'd forgotten all about Gerard and the sleeping potion Serena had given him. He glanced at Serena, and he could tell by her surprised expression that, she too, had forgotten.

"You aren't leaving without me," Gerard said. "We were both part of this, my friend, and we'll both end it."

Drogan watched him. Gerard kept blinking his eyes and shaking his head. "Everything all right?" Drogan asked.

"I'm fine and ready for battle."

Out of the corner of his eye, Drogan saw Serena grab Grayson and lead him next to Gerard's mount. Drogan heard Gerard swear just before he fell sideways out of the saddle and was caught by Grayson.

"What happened?" Maris screamed as she rushed to her husband.

"Serena saved him," Drogan said. "His plan was to come with me while you and Jocelyn went with my uncle."

"He wouldn't dare," Maris ground out, hands on hips as

she looked at her sleeping husband being held on his feet by Grayson. "He gave me his word."

Drogan shrugged. "Serena took care of it. It's time for you to get to the water and leave."

He waited until Grayson, carrying Gerard over his shoulder, Maris, Serena, and Phineas were out of sight before he turned to the gates and his destiny.

"Open the gate," he called out.

Serena carried Jocelyn as Phineas helped Maris carry her and Gerard's belongings to the boat. Gerard hung limply over Grayson's wide shoulder as they traversed the maze of tunnels that lead from the castle to the sea.

Serena struggled to think of anything but the time she'd spent with Drogan in these same tunnels. Their time together had passed quickly, as if a dream. Longing ripped through her heart as she emerged from the tunnel and the sea sprayed her with a fine mist. She closed her eyes and held Jocelyn a little tighter.

She still hadn't decided what to do. She knew she needed to stay and help Drogan so that he would live, but to do so would mean the death of the child growing in her womb. Time hadn't permitted her to look to her future, but she *knew* life grew within her. She didn't need to look to her future to discern that.

"Serena?"

She found Maris watching her. Serena walked to the boat and handed Jocelyn into Maris' waiting arms after her friend had climbed into the boat.

"What aren't you telling me?" Maris asked.

Serena let the first of her tears fall. "I don't know what to do."

"What do you mean?" Maris asked, her forehead creased in a deep frown. "You're coming with us. Aren't you?"

"If I do, Drogan will die."

Maris inhaled sharply. "What? Why didn't you let Gerard go with him then?"

"Because if he did, then all of you would die as well."

For several moments Maris stared at her as the boat rocked gently in the waves. "You knew from the very beginning," Maris said. "That's why you insisted on coming with us."

Serena nodded. "I just didn't count on giving my heart away."

"That changed everything, didn't it?"

"More than you could possibly know," Serena said. "But you must go, and keep Gerard there until Drogan can return for you."

"And you?" Maris asked.

Serena didn't want to tell her that she was going to die. Instead, she put a bright smile on her face and hugged her friend close. "I'll see you soon."

Maris relaxed and sat down, Jocelyn close to her heart. "You had me worried there for a moment."

Serena didn't let the smile drop until she turned away from the boat to find Grayson and Phineas blocking her path.

"I cannot allow you to go anywhere but that boat, my lady," Grayson said. "I gave my word to Lord Drogan."

Serena took a deep breath and stepped closer to the men. "If I don't stay, then Drogan will die."

"Francesca said you would say that," Phineas said.

Serena's eyes jerked to Drogan's uncle. "Did she? What else did she say?"

Phineas rubbed his bald head. "She told me not to stop you."

Serena stomach knotted. So, her fate was set, despite her hope that she might somehow come out of this alive. "Then, let me pass."

"Nay," Grayson said and sidestepped to stop her.

"Grayson, please," Serena begged.

"Why?" Grayson asked.

Serena frowned. "Why? Because I love him. Because I can't bear the thought of Wolfglynn being without him. Because his people need him, and because of so many more reasons I won't state here now because it's wasting time."

"The first one was enough," Grayson murmured. He sighed and stood straight. "I've never broken my oath before. Lord Drogan made me swear I wouldn't let you do anything foolish."

"This isn't foolish."

Grayson snorted and shook his head. "Call it what you will, my lady, but Lord Drogan will have my head for this."

"I'll see that he doesn't, lad," Phineas said. "I must be off now."

To her surprise, Serena found herself engulfed in Phineas' arms. "I have faith in you, lass. Keep my nephew safe and stay alive." He turned away and strode to the boat.

Serena watched him as he and a knight rowed out to sea. She wrapped her arms around herself for warmth in the harsh sea wind. It was then she realized someone was missing. Francesca.

Drogan walked his mount into the woods. The eerie quiet would have unsettled most men, but it calmed him. He knew what awaited him, and he was ready to face it.

No more running. No more hiding.

His horse snorted and sidestepped. Drogan reached down and patted the animal on the neck to calm him. "I feel the evil, too," he whispered as he fingered the long dagger at his right hip. "Where are you?" He looked around the quiet forest.

Leaves rustled off to Drogan's right, and he found a wolf staring at him. For long moments, he and the wolf watched each other. Drogan had seen wolves in the forest, but none had ever ventured this close to him before. Its gray coat was thick, and its eyes were a vibrant yellow as it gazed without blinking. Drogan could have sworn the wolf was trying to warn him, but clearly he was wrong.

His hands gripped the reins tighter as he closed his eyes and listened to the forest. Instinct told him to turn left and check on the knight who should have been keeping watch nearby. When Drogan opened his eyes, the wolf was gone, making him wonder if he had seen the animal or not. Surely, his horse would have reacted to having a predator so near.

He clicked to his mount and moved off the trail into the thicker foliage. His ears were tuned to pick up any sound that wasn't part of the forest, but he heard nothing. And that's what worried him.

A forest in silence was a forest with evil.

As he pushed aside the large bush growing beside a willow, he found his knight. Drogan hung his head and clenched his teeth. The knight hung lifeless by a rope strung on the very branch from which he had kept watch.

Drogan didn't need to check the other five posts to know his knights were dead.

Guilt hung heavy around his neck, but he would make sure the bastard paid for this. And now he knew exactly who he was up against...Cade.

Chapter Thirty

Serena wrapped her arms around herself and shivered. The sea became more turbulent the longer she watched, and she shook from the cold wind slicing through her. She feared Maris and Gerard might not make it to Phineas' isle.

"I've seen him row that boat in stronger weather than this," Grayson said from beside her. "And I made him take one of my knights since Gerard wouldn't be able to row."

"I'm sure you're right," she said and made herself turn away.

She walked to the opening of the tunnel and tried to yank on the heavy wooden door, but it wouldn't budge.

"Let me," Grayson said and easily pulled it open.

They walked into the tunnel, the few torches lighting the way as they wound their way back into the castle. Grayson stopped her just short of reaching the door that would take them into the great hall.

"What's your plan?"

She shrugged and swiped the damp hair out of her face. "I don't know."

He swore and fisted his hand. "I knew I should have made you leave with Lord Phineas."

"I wouldn't have gone, and you know it. I had a plan," she said and looked away. "I just need a new one."

"And what was your old plan?"

She raised her eyes to his black ones. "To save Drogan of course. That hasn't changed. I just need to figure out how to stay alive."

"What?" Grayson's eyes narrowed on her, and his mouth flattened into a thin line. "Are you telling me your original plan was to sacrifice yourself for Drogan?"

She nodded. "Is that so hard to believe?"

"You love him that much?"

"Aye," she answered without wavering. She didn't care who knew her true feelings. Soon it wouldn't matter anyway.

He nodded stiffly and reached to grab the handle of the door. "I understand you wanting to help, but I cannot allow you to go out of the gates."

Panic twisted in her stomach. "Nay," she said and took hold of his arm. "Don't you understand? I've seen his death. I know how to prevent it."

"Then tell me," he said as he leaned close. "War is the

making of men, my lady. You have no business in the middle of it."

She shook her head and stepped back. "You won't be able to save him."

Serena didn't know how to tell Grayson that it would be Drogan's concern for her safety that saved him and killed her. She blinked back more tears, hating herself for the weakness that caused them.

"I will save him," she vowed as she swung open the door. "With or without your aid."

Serena strode into the great hall to find it all but deserted. She walked to the hearth and tried to catch her breath and calm her racing nerves. A new plan was required, and she needed to think fast.

"I'm going to regret this," Grayson said as he came to stand beside her. "I'll help you."

She smiled and started to thank him, but he held up a hand.

"But you aren't going alone. I'll be there, as will other knights."

She nodded, not caring who came as long as she was there. It was her destiny to save Drogan, just as she had saved Maris, Jocelyn, and Gerard.

"And do you have a plan?" she asked the knight.

He raised one dark brow. "A knight always has a plan."

The moon gave little light through the thick clouds, but Drogan knew these woods like he knew his castle. There wasn't a place Cade could hide that Drogan wouldn't find him.

Thunder rumbled in the distance, and the wind blew in spurts. A fitting scene for such a battle that was to come. Drogan slid from his horse. He slung his bow and arrows over his shoulder and hooked his shield onto this left arm.

"It's better if I go this alone," he whispered to his mount.

The stallion watched him for a moment before lowering his head to munch on the sweet grass. Drogan knew the horse wouldn't move until he was called or someone came to get him.

Drogan adjusted his shield and started out through the woods. He hadn't gotten far when the wind whipped through the trees and more thunder boomed in the sky. His skin prickled and the sense of being watched assaulted him.

Cade.

Drogan pulled his sword from its sheath and whirled around only to find a tree tilting in the wind. He narrowed his eyes and stared at the spot, waiting for some sign that Cade had been hiding, yet there was nothing.

With an inward groan, Drogan turned back and proceeded deeper into the forest. It wasn't a good sign that his senses were off kilter. If they didn't align, he was as good as dead. The thought of leaving this earth didn't frighten him, but not being with Serena did.

Despair wrapped around him, setting her tendrils deep in

his body as the darkness crept closer. It would be so easy to give in and let it overtake him. Fighting it all these years had taken a lot out of him, and he had been ready to give up when he had found Serena.

Serena.

The only brightness in his sin-soaked life. He shrugged off the despair and pushed away the ever-present darkness. It moved away. For now. But he knew it would be watching, waiting for the chance to overpower him and snare him in its clutches, devouring his soul and marking a place for him in hell.

Lightning ripped across the sky, and for a brief moment the forest was lit as though it was day. And in that instant, Drogan saw him.

Serena shivered and pulled the cloak tighter around her as the wind howled and the thunder rolled. The storm was going to be fierce and violent. She could smell it on the wind. Even the animals were restless and trying to seek shelter.

She looked down at the bailey from the battlements to see a handful of knights without armor, but laden with weapons. Grayson was taking no chances, she could see. Not that she could blame him. She would ride out with an army of ten thousand if she could.

Grayson gave her a nod. It was time. She wrapped the cloak around her and started down the steps. Ever since

Grayson had said he would help her, she'd been atop the battlements, hoping to see something of Drogan or the evil that had chased them to Wolfglynn, but there had been nothing except the movement of the trees as they swayed in the growing wind. A glance above her showed thick, black clouds waiting to release a torrent of rain.

"You're going to need a weapon," Grayson said as she approached him. He held in his hand a dirk with a small handle and a blade narrow and long.

She shook her head. "A weapon will do me no good."

He stared at her and continued to hold the dirk. Serena sighed and took the weapon. If it would make him feel better, she would carry it.

"Thank you, my lady," he said and whistled. A gray gelding trotted to Grayson and nudged the knight with his huge head. Any other time Serena would have wanted to inspect such a magnificent creature. Her eyes blurred with unshed tears, and her hand went once again to her stomach.

In the time Grayson had taken to ready the men, Serena had sought out solitude to view her future. Aye, Francesca had been correct, there were two paths. And neither one Serena wished to take.

One was with her child, back in Hawthorne, with Drogan dying this night. The other she saw Drogan standing on the battlements of Wolfglynn looking out at the sea she loved so much, but she wasn't with him.

It hadn't taken her long to discover that either way, they would never be together. Either she lived and had their child, or he lived. Never before had Serena thought fate so cruel. And it just wasn't in her to decide if she and their child or Drogan should live. That, she was also leaving up to fate.

"My lady?" Grayson asked, a concerned frown marking his brow. "Are you sure? It isn't too late for you to reach the isle."

Serena took a deep breath and nodded. "I've never been more sure of anything in my life."

"I wish you would come with me," he said as he walked with her to the postern door in the side of the giant curtain wall.

"I wish I could also, but we would accomplish nothing if we all went as a group." She touched his arm as he turned to walk away. "The knights who were on guard. They're dead."

"I know," he said after a moment's hesitation.

"Be careful. The evil out there is greater than anything you've ever experienced before. Drogan doesn't realize it yet, and he won't until it's too late."

"Is that why you didn't try to talk him out of it?"

She shook her head. "Drogan must kill the evil. Gerard didn't stand a chance against it, and..." She broke off and shuddered.

"What?"

She couldn't tell Grayson about the darkness that was so near to Drogan. Drogan had fought that battle alone for years, and he must continue to do so. Only Drogan could send it away, but Serena worried that it might be too late. The darkness had grown and nearly consumed him, and if it did, the evil would win and Drogan would die.

"Just make sure you and your men stay alive. I don't want any of you attacking the evil. None of you will be able to stand against it."

Grayson snorted. "You speak as though it isn't a man."

"It isn't," she said. "He sold his soul long ago. All that remains is the hollow shape of the man, and inside is nothing but wickedness."

Grayson frowned and took a step back. "I don't believe in such as you say."

"Believe or not," she said. "Just heed my words. I pray otherwise, but I fear you'll see much more tonight than anyone should."

Just then lightning streaked across the sky. For a brief moment, there was silence before the thunder boomed around them and the sky opened, sending sheets of rain.

Serena reached for the handle of the postern door and looked once more to Grayson through the rain. "Heed my words well, Grayson. Your very future depends upon it."

Grayson watched her go, unable to suppress the shiver that ran down his spine. If what she said was true, then no amount of weapons would aid him or the men. He scanned the large bailey of Wolfglynn, the only place he had felt he belonged. His eyes came to rest on the church and a thought took root.

He ran to the doors and threw them open to find the priest inside.

"My son?" the old priest said. "Can I help you with something?"

"More than you could possibly know," Grayson said as he stepped inside the church for the first time in years and shut the doors behind him.

Serena wrapped her already soaked cloak tighter around her and sprinted toward the forest. She felt naked and vulnerable as she ran from the shadows of the castle to the foreboding trees several hundred yards away. When she reached the forest, she leaned back against a tree and looked to the castle. Her breath came in great gulps, and her heart pounded in her ears, but she had made it. Her palms were wet, not from the rain, but from fear. She rubbed them together to warm them as she took her first steps into the woods. Thankfully, the many trees afforded her some shelter from the pounding rain.

She'd seen this so many times in her dreams that she knew where to go. She followed the line of pines as they curved around a gnarled oak, and it was there she found the dead knight and Drogan's horse.

The horse raised his head as she approached, and she reached out to pet him. "Not a fit night for man nor beast, eh my beauty? Stay close. Drogan will need you soon."

She focused her gaze in front of her where she thought she heard something over the din of the pouring rain. The clang of swords, perhaps?

She crept closer to the edge of the forest and spotted Grayson and the knights leaving one by one from the castle. Again she heard something, this time behind her. She turned toward the sound, but found nothing but the shadows of the trees. Fear rooted her to the spot. Something stood just ahead of her, although she didn't know what, or who, it was. If she thought she could outrun it, she might try.

Nay, she was alone.

She focused her senses toward the trees and tried to feel if it was the evil. Her body jerked painfully when she felt the deep, unfathomable darkness that surrounded this person, the same darkness that had all but overtaken Drogan.

Her hands reached behind her, and she took hold of a tree. The rain caused her hand to slip, and the bark left several small cuts. It was enough to break her from her terror. She picked up her skirts and ran as fast as she could, never looking back. She had to find Drogan before it was too late.

The great evil wasn't alone.

Chapter Thirty-One

*T*he evil that had haunted Drogan for years stood not thirty paces from him in full armor, sword drawn and ready. The hair on Drogan's body stood on end as another flash of lightning zigzagged across the sky. He dropped his bow and arrow at his feet and gripped his sword and shield tighter.

Rain fell so hard and fast he had to shake his head to clear his vision of the water. But his gaze never wavered from the man in front of him. Not one to wait on anything, Drogan took a step toward his foe. Without a sound, his enemy raised his sword and charged. But Drogan was ready. He easily sidestepped the armored man and whirled around, ready for another charge.

A hiss sounded from his enemy, bringing a small grin to Drogan.

They circled each other. Drogan lunged forward and

slashed his sword toward his opponent, only to have the knight bring his shield up to block it. Before Drogan could attack again, he had to jerk his shield up to protect his neck from the savage thrust of his foe's sword. Drogan ducked and twisted, coming up behind his opponent.

"You won't win this, Cade," he yelled over the roar of the rain.

He didn't know what he had expected, but it wasn't the hollow laugh that followed.

"Remove your helmet, or are you afraid to look me in the eye?" Drogan taunted.

In the past, it would have taken the slightest insult to bring out Cade's response, but not now. Time changed everyone, but it seemed that time had changed Cade most of all.

Drogan tamped down his regret at having to kill someone he had once considered a brother. He bent his knees, ready for another attack. He didn't have long to wait.

The knight held his sword over his right shoulder and brought it down in an arc toward Drogan's head. He had a heartbeat to respond. Drogan rolled forward, dropping his shield, and reaching for his dagger, as came up on his knees just in time to block a thrust aimed at his back.

His opponent had a better angle than he did, but Drogan was a superior fighter. With his left hand he slashed backwards and heard a grunt, telling him he had hit Cade's leg with his dagger.

Instantly, the pressure on his sword was gone, and Drogan

gained his feet, ready for more. He looked down to find there was no blood on his dagger. His eyes narrowed as they rose to gaze at the knight.

How was that possible? He had felt the dagger pierce the skin between two of the armor plates on the calf, heard the howl that followed. There should be blood on the blade.

There wasn't time to think more about it as his foe charged. The clang of swords was deafening as they fought. Each jab and thrust met with a parry or a shield. Drogan didn't miss his shield, in truth, he fought better without it. He had his dagger in his left hand, giving him an added advantage if he could get close enough to stick it in his foe's neck between his helmet and his chest armor.

But the chance never came.

Each time Drogan got close enough, the knight increased his swings, causing Drogan to step back to keep his balance. His chest rose and fell rapidly as he gulped in air, but his opponent didn't look winded at all. Drogan tamped down the anger rising within him, knowing it wouldn't help him win the battle. With skill honed from many hours training and more battles than he liked to admit, Drogan worked his way closer to his enemy.

He saw the sword rise, ready to fall downward where he would need to block it with his sword, and it was all the time he needed. With his dagger still in his left hand, he raised it and punched his foe in the face with the dagger's hilt.

Drogan watched, satisfied, as Cade stumbled backwards, his hand to his helmet. Just as Drogan had hoped, he had smashed the helmet inwards, just below the eyes. If his opponent wanted to continue the fight, he would have to remove his helmet.

He waited, feet braced apart, to see the face of his once good friend now come to kill him.

What he didn't expect was for the helmet to repair itself and the knight to charge.

Serena didn't know how long she ran. When she stopped beside an ash tree, she noticed she had run farther into the forest than she had ever intended. She cursed for the first time in her life and brushed away the hair that clung annoyingly to her face. Her fear had ruled her, and she couldn't allow that to happen again. Everything depended on her.

After a few deep breaths to stop her racing heart, she started back the way she came. Again she heard the unmistakable clang of swords in the distance.

"Drogan," she whispered and whirled toward the sound.

She had taken five steps when the man stepped in front of her. A gasp tore from her throat as she took a step back.

"You cannot go to him," the man said.

She wished for lightning so she could see his face, but she knew without a doubt it was the same person she had encountered earlier in the forest. The darkness surrounding him was thick and suffocating. She didn't know how he bore it.

"Who are you?" she asked.

"That doesn't matter. If you wish to live, return to the castle."

She stopped retreating and straightened her shoulders. She would fight whoever or whatever she needed to ensure Drogan's life. "Nay."

"If you don't, you'll die."

"I know."

Even in the shadows she saw him cock his head to the side. "You're only a woman. You cannot save him."

"I can try," she said and started toward him.

But the closer she got, the more the darkness surrounded her. She stopped and leaned against the tree. The darkness took away everything but despair and a great empty void.

She heard footsteps and raised her gaze to see him step back.

"What are you?" he asked, confusion filling his voice.

She shook her head and pushed off from the tree, once again herself now that the darkness had abated with his retreat. "It doesn't matter."

"Halt," he said again as she took a step toward him.

Serena shook her head. "The only way you can stop me from aiding Drogan is by killing me, and if you must, then get it over with quickly."

For several moments she waited, eyes closed, yet nothing happened. She opened her eyes and scanned the area. He was gone. She hadn't expected that. There was something strange about the man, as if the evil darkness surrounding him didn't belong.

She took a deep breath and listened for the sound of swords so she would know where to go, but there was nothing. And that silence terrified her like nothing before.

Drogan stared at the helmet, not believing what his eyes beheld, but there was no denying it.

"I'll kill you," the knight said as he took a step toward Drogan. "Then I'll find Gerard and kill him and his pitiful little family."

The voice was muffled, deep, angry and…something else. Almost as if what he fought wasn't quite human. And if Drogan had learned anything in the time he had spent with Serena, it was to believe that many things do exist.

"Are you Cade?" he asked, desperately needing to know.

The wind howled, causing the rain to come down in a slant, right into Drogan's eyes. He lifted his left arm to shield his vision, but still he could barely make out anything, much less his opponent.

The jab came out of nowhere, landing squarely in his stomach. Drogan doubled over and almost dropped his weapons, hanging onto them by sheer force of will. As he gasped for breath and tried to rise, an armored knee came toward his face. Drogan jerked away just in time to avoid it slamming into his nose, but his jaw took the brunt of the blow, leaving his ears ringing as he lay on his back with the rain blinding him.

"You're no match for me," the knight said and jerked Drogan up by the collar of his tunic until his feet were once more beneath him.

Drogan shook his head and blinked as he planted his feet and readied his sword. He caught sight of his enemy and lunged at him, only to find himself propelled backwards. His back landed hard against a tree, knocking the breath from him and his weapons from his hands. He fell forward, landing on his hands and knees as breath finally filled his lungs. The quick rush of air had him seeing bright spots before his eyes. He blinked and shook his head to clear his vision.

Drogan searched through the pine needles and grass for his sword and dagger but came up empty-handed. He glanced up to see the knight striding toward him. Just before the knight's foot could connect with his face, Drogan rolled to the side and came up on his feet.

He rushed his enemy, grabbing him about the waist and shoving him against a tree. Drogan heard the knight grunt a moment before a fist hit him in the side. Vicious pain lanced savagely through his body.

Before he could take a breath, a fist came at his face, connecting with his chin and driving him backwards to once more land on his back. With a moan, he rolled over and found steel, not grass, under his hand. He gripped the pommel of his sword tight as he came to his feet.

He wiped away the blood that trickled from the corner of his mouth and did his best to ignore his aches and pains as he came to his feet with the aid of a tree.

"You never did know when to quit," the knight said as he circled Drogan.

Drogan spit out the blood that had pooled in his mouth. "Apparently not," he said as he kept his eyes on the knight. "Why come after me now, after all these years?"

"Wouldn't you like to know," the knight mocked.

Serena rushed through the forest, desperately trying to find Drogan or any of his knights, yet she found only rain and trees.

Tears of frustration coursed down her face. She stumbled on a root and fell to the ground to find herself land on a dead body. She screamed and rolled off, but became tangled in vines that seemed to have come alive. The vines seemed as though they were reaching for her, causing fear to pulse through her and turn her blood to ice.

Until she remembered the dirk.

She palmed the weapon and chopped at the vines until she was free. She stepped back to get herself under control and glanced at the body. It was one of Drogan's knights. His mouth was open in a silent scream as his eyes looked heavenward. A gaping hole in his chest told her he had been run through.

She shivered and continued on her way. The rain became lighter, allowing her to see. The lightning wasn't frequent, but the thunder seemed as though it was right on top of Wolfglynn. When lightning flashed, she was able to see an opening through the trees and she headed in that direction. As she came closer, she could hear something.

She crept toward the clearing and saw the knight dressed in full armor with his back to her. Her gaze darted around the clearing for Drogan who must be near.

Just then the knight moved, and she spotted Drogan.

Chapter Thirty-Two

The pain abated enough so that Drogan could push away from the tree. "If you wanted to kill me, you've had plenty of chances to do it."

"True. I wish for you to suffer, as you made me suffer."

Drogan grimaced. Cade could be referring to Drogan's failure to stop Nigel that day. Cade knew, just as Drogan did, that the only one of them who could have prevented the sins of that day was Drogan. Yet, he hadn't. Fear had impeded him.

Now, he would pay for it.

"Then let us be done with this," Drogan said and raised his sword.

The knight swung his sword in an arc, and Drogan could hear the smile in his voice. "I've been waiting for this for years."

They charged, coming together in a violent display of swordsmanship. Sparks flew from their swords as they clashed together. Drogan, already weak from the beating, could feel his strength ebb with each swing of his enemy's sword, yet he refused to give up. He'd given his word to Gerard and Serena.

"Nay," Drogan bellowed and slashed and thrust his sword like a man possessed, for that was exactly how he felt.

He gripped his sword with both hands and continued his assault, driving his opponent back into a tree. But Drogan didn't stop then.

With his left hand, he reached up and grabbed the knight by the neck, squeezing as hard as he could. With his right arm, he ran his sword through the opening of the armor on the side. His sword sank into Cade's flesh.

Drogan released his opponent's neck and pulled his sword out as he stepped back. He closed his eyes and hung his head. He never saw the fist come at him to land in his chest. The impact was so powerful that Drogan stumbled, barely staying on his feet.

He didn't have time to take a steadying breath before the sword came at him. Drogan jumped away, but not in time.

The swing was so powerful that it cut through his chain mail. The only thing that saved his life was his quick thinking. Even so, he landed heavily on his back.

"You cannot kill me," the knight said as he stood over Drogan.

Drogan blinked at the knight through the rain that landed on his face. This was it.

He had failed.

Serena had seen enough. She ran from the trees, screaming Drogan's name, screaming for him to get up.

When the knight turned his head toward her, she knew what true evil felt like. Coldness gripped her soul as the knight walked toward her. She glanced at Drogan, but he could barely move, much less help her, and there was no use calling for Grayson. He would never hear her in the rain.

So Fate had chosen who would die. She squared her shoulders and faced the great evil.

"I know what you are," she said as she walked closer.

"And I know what you are. Your kind is burned alive," he taunted.

"And your kind is sent back to Hell."

She felt more than saw his eyes narrow on her. "You think you're powerful enough to try?"

Serena stood trembling in the rain. She was cold and wet, her blood frozen in her veins, but she wouldn't cower. She kept her gaze on the knight, afraid if she looked down at Drogan she would lose what little control she had. Out of the corner of her eye, she saw that Drogan hadn't moved other than to shift his head toward her.

"I do," she answered, willing Drogan to gain his feet while she had the knight's attention.

The knight laughed maliciously. "You? A mere woman? I think not."

Serena didn't have time to react before the knight raised his sword over Drogan and plunged it into his chest. She fell to her knees, her arms stretched toward the man she had given her heart to as a scream ripped from her throat.

All sound came to a halt, even the rain ceased to be heard. For a heartbeat, the earth stood still before blinding light erupted around them.

Serena felt something whiz by her arm leaving nothing but a searing pain. She tried to open her eyes, but the light was everywhere, enveloping everything.

She stayed on her knees, her head down while her left hand held her throbbing arm. With a final boom, the light was gone. Slowly, she opened her eyes to see Drogan trying to sit up. Elation erupted through her. She didn't know how he had survived, but it was enough that he had.

Her gaze went to her arm, and she saw blood ooze from between her fingers. The herbs she needed to tend this had been lost when she had fallen into the river. Without them she was as good as dead.

The last thought that raced through her mind before she passed out was that she had at least saved Drogan.

Drogan was slow to move. His eyes burned from the blinding light, and for a brief moment, he feared he had lost his sight. His hand went to his chest where the sword had struck him, but all he felt was the amulet Serena had given him.

He looked down and found a massive indentation in the middle of it. Drogan's eyes looked around the clearing. It didn't take him long to spot his enemy lying against a tree. Whether he was knocked unconscious or dead, Drogan didn't know. Yet.

It was just as well the knight couldn't fight him, Drogan thought. He couldn't have lifted his sword now if he tried. The blows he had received had been ferocious and near inhuman.

His head swam as he pushed himself into a sitting position. He took deep breaths to calm his churning stomach. When the world ceased to spin, he opened his eyes and spotted Grayson stumbling into the clearing with a bottle in his hand.

"What are you doing here?" Drogan bellowed.

Grayson brought a hand up to his head and winced. "Saving your arse," he said and cast aside the bottle.

"What was that?"

"Holy water," Grayson mumbled. "I thought to use it on the man since Serena said he was evil, but I see it isn't needed now."

Drogan somehow managed to climb to his feet. Pieces of the knight's sword were scattered all over the clearing. "What happened?"

"I'm not sure," Grayson said as he walked next to Drogan. "I saw Serena—"

"Serena." Drogan's whispered word cut off Grayson. Panic seized Drogan. "Serena," he shouted as he searched for his beloved.

"There," Grayson said pointing.

Drogan turned to where Grayson directed. He shook his head, disbelieving his eyes. "Nay," he croaked as he stumbled toward her. He fell to his knees and gathered her limp body into his arms. "Serena. Serena, don't leave me." He rocked her next to his heart. "I cannot live without you."

"We must stop the bleeding," Grayson said, urgency tumbling his words.

Drogan raised his eyes to the gaping wound on Serena's upper arm where blood flowed freely. He shifted so that Grayson could reach her arm, but it didn't matter how tight they tied the cloth, the blood continued to pour.

He raised his eyes to Grayson. "I cannot lose her."

"And you won't, my lord," said a feminine voice.

Drogan and Grayson lifted their heads to find Francesca standing just inside the clearing.

"We must get her to the castle immediately," Francesca said. "I can save her, but we cannot waste time."

Drogan didn't argue. He lifted Serena in his arms and got to his feet. He would walk through Hell itself if it meant saving her.

Emotion, strong and clear, clogged his throat as he looked

down to see the life slowly draining from his beautiful Serena. "Stay with me," he said and continued to repeat it to her as they raced to the castle.

Just as he reached the gates of Wolfglynn, something stopped him, and he turned toward the forest. A lone man stood against the mighty trees.

Drogan would have known that face anywhere. "Cade."

"My lord."

Francesca's urgent voice rushed to his ears. He followed her through the gates and into the castle, Grayson on his heels.

By the time Drogan laid Serena in his bed, he feared she was already dead, but Francesca pushed him out of the way.

"Either help me or leave, but do not get in my way," she ordered as she rushed around the chamber.

"I'll help," Drogan managed past the lump in his throat.

Francesca raised her tawny eyes to him. "There are herbs I need."

"I'll find them."

"As will I," Grayson said as he stepped forward.

Francesca listed the herbs and plants as Claire rushed in with a bowl of water.

Drogan committed the herbs to memory and left his chamber. He wanted nothing more than to climb in that bed with Serena and hold her. But she needed him now. Without the special herbs, she'd die.

He immediately thought of the bag she had carried with

her from Hawthorne and rushed to get it. When he ran back into his chamber he found that Francesca had cut away Serena's sleeve to get better access to the wound.

"She brought herbs with her," he said as he handed Francesca the bag.

She took it and rummaged through it. "There are a few things I can use. I cannot believe she didn't bring more."

"She did. They would probably still be in there if she hadn't fallen into the river," he explained.

Francesca nodded. "You can find what I need in the forests, Drogan."

"Tell me."

"They're small white flowers with five petals surrounded by dark green foliage. They grow in clumps on the ground that also have long, thick briars. Don't delay," she shouted as he rushed from the chamber.

As if he would. Exhausted though he was after the beating, he could have run to the stars and back to save Serena. His feet flew down the stairs, across the bailey, through the gatehouse and back into the woods.

He heard movement and spotted Grayson not far ahead of him as he dug through the foliage to find what Francesca had described. His fingers, numb with grief and pain, seemed to have a life of their own. He couldn't get them to grab hold of the little white flower that Francesca had explained in detail. Drogan cursed and tried again, but once again he was unable to pick through the briars to the precious flower. He tilted back his head and roared, frustration gripping his heart painfully.

When he looked back down, he wasn't alone. Cade was beside him, leaning over picking the white flowers without so much as a scratch on his hands from the briars.

He handed the flowers to Drogan, his light blue eyes holding no emotion.

"Cade," Drogan said as he took the flowers.

"She needs you," Cade said as he rose to his feet. "Go now. You don't have much time."

Drogan didn't argue. He found the two other herbs he needed and raced to the castle. As he entered the bailey, he saw Grayson stepping through the castle door with his hands full of herbs.

Yet Drogan didn't slow until he reached his chamber. He found Francesca leaning over Serena with her mouth pressed in a firm line. She raised her eyes to Drogan, and he knew real fear.

"Nay," he said and shoved the herbs at her. "We got what you needed. You cannot let her die!"

Francesca glanced down at her hands that now held the herbs. "I'll do what I can."

Drogan went to the other side of the bed to hold Serena's hand. Her skin was cold and drained of any color. Even her lips were turning blue. Though it had been years since he had prayed for anything, he bowed his head and began to send up his prayers to anyone who would listen.

He had no idea how many minutes or hours passed until

Francesca touched his shoulder. His eyes rose to her face to see tears in her tawny eyes.

"I'm sorry."

Those two words were so simple, yet the world around him crumbled at his feet.

"Nay," he roared and pulled Serena against his chest.

Chapter Thirty-Three

Serena didn't want to go to the light that beckoned her. She wanted Drogan, but there wasn't much she could do now. Death, it seemed, had chosen her and her unborn babe. All of her dreams of a family and Drogan had vanished in a puff of smoke. She wanted to scream and curse, and instead only found tears available.

Then she heard it, the ever so distant call. It was her name! She recognized Drogan's voice then, and started to turn back from the light. Drogan's voice became more insistent, calling her, screaming at her to return to him. Tears coursed down her face as she heard his plea.

Yet the light wouldn't release her. It tugged and pulled her toward its center. Serena almost gave in until she thought of the babe in her womb.

"Nay," she said between clenched teeth and raced toward Drogan's voice.

"Serena!"

She took a deep breath and felt the pain throughout her body.

"She's breathing," Serena heard someone say, the voice female.

Francesca?

"Come back to me," Drogan said near her ear.

She wanted to tell him she had, but her lips wouldn't open. Slowly, she was able to open her eyes to see the most beautiful sight she had ever beheld.

Drogan.

Her head rested against his chest as he stared down at her with a bright smile, his eyes shining and wet auburn hair clinging to his head. "You came back."

Serena nodded, but it was difficult to keep her eyes open. There was so much she wanted to say, to ask, but Drogan placed a finger over her lips.

"I'll be right here," he promised. "Rest."

Her eyes closed, and she let the healing sleep take her then.

Drogan lowered her to the pillows and stood on shaking knees. When he was able to tear his gaze from his beloved Serena, he found Francesca and Grayson staring at him.

"How did you do that?" Francesca asked. "She was dead, Drogan."

Drogan raised one shoulder. "I...I don't know."

He was weary and tried to walk to the stool, but his legs gave out on him. Grayson caught him as he fell. Now that

Serena was all right, Drogan found himself barely able to keep his eyes open.

"You gave me your word," he mumbled to Grayson.

Grayson had the good graces to look ashamed. "Berate me later, my lord. Right now, we must tend to you."

"Nay," Drogan said when he saw they would carry him from Serena. "I promised her I wouldn't leave."

Thankfully, after they removed his bloody clothes, they laid him next to her on his bed. He reached over and took her hand in his as he felt Francesca's gentle hands wash the blood from his face.

"You let this happen," Cade bellowed.

Drogan made himself look away from the dead body. Aye, he was to blame. He could have stopped it easily enough, and he should have. As leader of their group, he should have made sure if anyone was to kill, it would be him.

"I'm sorry."

Cade backed away, shaking his head at Drogan's apology.

"We'll get through this," Gerard said as he tried to move toward Cade.

But Cade was too quick. He stepped away and jumped on his horse.

"It's too late," he said. "It has taken me."

"Cade," Drogan bellowed as his friend and brother rode off. The only sound that remained was that of Nigel's laughter.

Drogan opened his eyes to see the stars shining in the sky. He had no idea how long he had slept, but he felt better than he had in years.

Something stirred next to him, and he turned his head to find Serena on her side lying beside him, their hands still entwined. He reached over and ran his finger down her fair face, her skin glowing and healthy once more.

Her wet gown was gone, replaced by a dry one, and Drogan noticed that he, too, wore dry clothes. He smiled, wondering how Francesca had managed that without help.

He still couldn't believe he had called Serena back because Francesca had been right. Serena's life had gone from her body, yet somehow she was with him now. He had been given a second chance with her, and he was going to grasp it with both hands and not look back.

But the darkness hung next to him, calling him to its bittersweet depths. Cade had fallen to it, just as Drogan had nearly done.

He mourned his lost friend. Cade's lifeless eyes were the first evidence that the darkness had taken hold of him. *Cade*. His dear friend, the little brother Drogan had never had. It had been his duty to look after Cade, to keep him away from the horrors Drogan so often found himself in, but he'd failed.

Miserably.

A soft sigh passed through Serena's sweet lips, and Drogan

watched as her beautiful vivid blue eyes opened to stare at him.

"Hello."

She smiled. "Hello."

"How do you feel?"

She took a deep breath. "Much better. You look better than the last time I saw you. Cleaner."

He chuckled, thinking of the mud and rain and blood on him after his battle with...

"What is it?" Serena asked, her brow puckered in a frown.

"I thought it was Cade I was fighting."

"Cade?"

Drogan nodded. "Cade was with me and Gerard as we did the king's bidding. But it wasn't him."

"Are you sure?"

"Very. I saw Cade when I went to search for the herbs Francesca needed to heal you. He helped me."

"Then who was it you fought?"

That left only one man. "Nigel."

"At least he's dead," she said, a small shudder moving through her. "Who was this Nigel?"

It was time to tell her. Drogan had put it off long enough. "A powerful lord and close friend of the king's. Everyone in court thought him magnificent and kind, but only a few of us knew the truth."

Serena's small hand touched his arm. "Drogan, you don't have to."

"I know," he said and gave her a small smile. "I need to."

She nodded and Drogan took a deep breath.

"Since Nigel was so close to the king, we often took orders from him. Only the best swordsmen were called for special assignments."

"You and Gerard?"

"And Cade," Drogan said sadly. "Cade was younger than Gerard and I, but he was just as good with a sword. God blessed him with a talent, and Nigel used it to his advantage."

"As he did you. What kind of assignments were you sent on? Escorting royalty?"

Drogan laughed dryly. "Nay, that duty was left to the lesser swordsmen ironically. Gerard, Cade, and I were sent in the dead of night to take care of things that weren't getting resolved in court."

He waited for Serena to realize just what he was saying. She gasped, her eyes wide. "The king sent you to kill people?"

"Nay. Nigel sent us to get rid of traitors. None of us could commit murder, so we would issue challenges to at least give the person a fighting chance."

Serena leaned over and kissed his shoulder. "That was good of you."

Drogan looked up at the canopy, afraid to gaze into Serena's eyes when she heard what was coming next. "That was nothing compared to the day that changed all of us."

"What did Nigel come after you about?" she whispered.

Drogan nodded. "We were awakened in the middle of the night and ordered to meet Nigel in the heart of the slums of

London." He turned his head and asked, "Have you ever been to London?"

"Nay."

He looked away. "Some of it is magnificent. A city that is always growing, but there is a part of it that is awful. People so poor they are starving to death. The stench of rotting food and bodies is unimaginable and unbearable."

His voice died as he relived his nightmare. But he needed to continue. He swallowed and started again.

"Gerard, Cade, and I got there long before Nigel arrived. There had been no word of what he needed us for, but our assignments were becoming more and more evil. Cade wanted out. Even then the darkness was with him, we just didn't know it."

"You can't blame yourself for that, Drogan. You had no idea what to look for."

"Maybe, but I do blame myself. I could have stopped it all that day. Nigel had threatened all sorts of things to keep us in line, but we were ready to go to the gallows rather than continue as we were. Yet, when Nigel arrived with a small boy in tow, we did nothing but stare."

"What happened?" she asked after several moments.

"Nigel ordered us to kill him. He was a bastard of the king's, and Nigel didn't want the boy threatening the crown. Already the mother of the boy had been killed for mentioning to Nigel that she wanted to tell the king of his son."

"Nigel killed her?"

Drogan nodded. "He boasted of it."

"That poor woman."

He silently agreed with Serena. "At first, we refused to kill the boy. He was so little and scared. He looked at me with his wide, dark eyes, wordlessly begging me for help."

Drogan could still see him in his dreams, his little body shaking with fear as tears coursed down his face. The silence in the chamber was deafening. Drogan was afraid to look at Serena, to see her repulsion of him. He had come this far, though, so he would finish with the telling.

"Gerard refused to kill the boy. Nigel threatened to have Hawthorne taken from him, but Gerard didn't care. And Gerard, being Gerard, didn't leave. He stayed by Cade and me.

"Sometime during our many escapades, I had become the leader of our trio, and Nigel knew this. He looked to me then, taunting me with tales he would tell the king to have me killed for treason and threats to have Phineas executed."

"Phineas?" Serena repeated.

"Aye. It is what he always used against me. Phineas was all the family I had left, and I did many things to keep him alive. I didn't want to lose Wolfglynn, but I would have given it up, and Nigel knew it. That's why he used Phineas."

"By the saints," she whispered.

"As much sin as I had committed, I couldn't add the murder of a child to my list. I knew I could outride anyone and reach Phineas in time to warn him if need be, but I wasn't going to kill that boy. Cade was another story. Nigel had something on Cade, something that made him do anything Nigel asked for. And when Gerard and I passed, Nigel looked to Cade."

Drogan sat up and put his head in his hands. "Cade asked me to stop it, but I knew all Cade had to do was refuse, and we could all walk away. I'd take the boy, if need be, but whatever Nigel had was powerful enough to push Cade.

"Nigel didn't even have to say anything. He just smiled at Cade. Gerard and I didn't understand why Cade didn't refuse or why he hadn't shared with us what Nigel knew. And before we could blink, Cade pulled his sword and killed the boy."

"Oh, my God."

"I could have stopped it. I should have stopped it. All I had to do was yank the boy away from Nigel and ride away. Wolfglynn is impenetrable. Nigel wouldn't have stood a chance. And I should've seen what Cade was going through. We were the best of friends, we three. As close as brothers."

Slender arms came around him as Serena laid her head on his back. "It's easy to look back now and think about what you should have done or could have done, yet it doesn't erase the fact that something horrible happened. You didn't do it. Cade did. Cade has to live with that."

"The darkness claimed him that day, Serena," Drogan said as he turned to face her. "Gerard and I ended all ties with Nigel after that. We had been in service to the king long enough, and we walked away. But we couldn't find Cade. It was the last time I saw him until today."

"How long ago was that?"

"Nearly six years."

She sighed. "Thank you for telling me. You've kept this with you all these years despite the fact Cade was a grown man able to make his own decisions?"

"I should've seen it coming."

"You aren't all-seeing, Drogan," she argued. "It is in the past, and the past is now dead."

Drogan no longer wished to speak of the past. He wanted to think of the future. With his hands wrapped around her waist, he pulled Serena to him until she lay atop his chest.

"Do you ever think of anything else?" she teased him.

"Not when you're around," he answered honestly and claimed her lips.

The passion between them soared. Their lovemaking was slow, unhurried as they explored each other, kissing every inch of skin and savoring their second chance. Drogan was careful around her injured arm as he raised her up and slid her down on top of his aching rod. He buried himself deep within her and felt her expanding to accommodate him.

She sighed and dropped her head back. The feel of her silken black locks against his thighs was heavenly and arousing. Drogan moved his hips and heard her moan his name. It wasn't long before she took over. She circled her hips then rose up and lowered herself back down on his staff. Pleasure consumed him, and he knew he wouldn't be able to last much longer, but he didn't want to go without her.

His thumb found her soft nub between her silken curls as his other hand cupped her breasts and pinched a taut nipple. Her sighs came faster, the moans catching in her throat, and

Drogan knew she was close, very close. He moved his thumb so that he barely touched her, but he increased the pressure on her nipple, and she cried out as her body jerked.

He felt her spasms around his rod, and the sensation sent him over the edge. His climax was swift and so intense, he forgot time and place as he grabbed her hips and buried himself deep within her.

She fell on top of him, her breathing ragged. He pushed the damp tendrils from her face as he raised her face to look at him.

"I love you."

Her eyes widened, and a single tear fell down her cheek. "And I love you."

It was enough for now Drogan told himself as he pulled the covers over them. They would talk more tomorrow.

But tomorrow wasn't better.

The day dawned bright and beautiful, as it often did after a vicious storm.

The chamber door opened, and Francesca sashayed into the chamber. "Are you ever going to climb out of that bed?"

Drogan reached over to make sure Serena was covered only to find her gone. "Where is she?"

"At the water."

Drogan jumped out of bed, not caring that he was nude and Francesca was in the chamber. He heard her mutter something under her breath as she slammed the door behind her. He flung open the lid of his chest and grabbed the first thing he saw to put on. He slid his boots onto his feet as an afterthought before he raced from the chamber.

People called to him as he sprinted down the stairs to the doorway that would take him to the secret tunnel. Terror had taken root in his heart when he had found Serena gone. He burst through the doorway of the tunnel and was blinded by the sun.

His arm came up to shield his eyes as he looked for Serena. He found her some ways down the beach walking very near the waves, but never letting the water touch her feet.

He calmed a bit once he found her, but he knew by the way she held her hands in front of her and twirled her thumbs that something was wrong. He sighed. It was time to get it all out in the open now.

She continued to walk with her back to him, but it didn't take him long to catch up since she was walking so slowly.

"Serena."

She whirled around to him, a small smile pulling at her lips. He held onto the fact that she smiled at seeing him. That said something, didn't it? "You should have woken me."

She shrugged and looked at the waves rolling in. "I wanted some time to think."

"About what?" he asked and came to stand beside her as he watched the water.

"You."

He figured as much. He looked at her. "What worries you? The curse?"

She rolled her eyes. "Of course, the curse, Drogan. After everything you've seen, you still don't believe it?"

"I believe it."

"Then what don't you understand?" she asked and threw her hands up in frustration.

"Why don't you fight it?"

"My people have. Every woman who has ever given her heart to a man has fought this curse, yet it always wins. I cannot bear it."

He took her hand and ran his thumb over her knuckles. "We don't have to worry about that until you get with child. There are ways we can go about making love without you conceiving."

Serena winced. "I wish we would have thought of that before."

His nostrils flared, and his eyes widened before a huge smile broke across his face. "Are you carrying my child?" he asked, hope shining bright in his eyes.

Serena would be happy, too, if she didn't know she was going to lose him once the child was born. She nodded when her throat closed and wouldn't allow her to talk.

Drogan wrapped his arms around her and picked her up. He twirled around, shouting joyously. By the time he set her down, she was laughing.

She stepped back. "It doesn't change anything."

"I'm not leaving you," he vowed before taking her lips in a kiss that ignited an inner flame for him alone.

She ended the kiss and took another step away from him. "I know you will."

"Fine," he said and reached for her hand. "Marry me."

She laughed. "Nay."

"Admit that you love it here, that Wolfglynn is in your soul."

"I admit it freely. I love this place."

"As do I," he said. "It's my home, Serena. I would never leave it, nor would I ever send you away."

She wanted to believe him, but she knew better. Many men had promised all sorts of things to her kind, yet they always left in one way or another.

"Don't take away the joy I've found," he begged as he took her shoulders. "You brought me back from the darkness."

How could she say nay to that? It was hard to deny the happiness within her when she was with Drogan, and though she knew she should leave, she wanted Drogan to know his child. If he chose to abandon her or send her away some day, then so be it. She nodded and allowed him to lead her back to the castle.

His joy had spread to her as they walked into the great hall. She decided then that she would stay as long as he wanted her. It would break her heart when the day came that he asked her to leave, but there was no way she could leave now. She loved him too desperately.

Their laughter died, however, when they entered the hall and found Grayson waiting for them.

"What is it?" Drogan asked.

"We've collected the bodies of all the knights who were killed."

"Good," Drogan said. "We'll bury them immediately."

Grayson glanced away and shifted feet.

"Out with it," Drogan said and gave her a smile.

But Serena couldn't return the smile. She knew what troubled Grayson.

"You didn't find him, did you?" she asked the knight.

Grayson shook his head.

"What are you talking about?" Drogan asked.

Serena faced him. "Nigel. He's not in the forest."

Chapter Thirty-Four

*T*he smile vanished from Drogan's face as he stormed from the castle. Serena had to run to keep up with him. When they reached the forest, she was out of breath and her wound ached from running.

She was thankful when Drogan stopped and looked around as if listening for something. She leaned against a tree and gulped in much needed air as Drogan circled the small area in which she and Grayson stood.

"My lord?" Grayson said. "What is it you see?"

Drogan held up a hand and stood as still as a statue for several moments before he sighed. "I thought...I thought someone was near."

Grayson pulled his sword out. "Who?"

"You won't need that," Drogan said.

Serena straightened and turned toward the castle as she heard a horn. "What is that?"

"Phineas," Drogan replied. "He's returning with Gerard and Maris."

Serena wished they hadn't returned so soon, at least not until things were settled.

"It'll be all right," Drogan said and took her hand.

She followed behind him as he began the walk to the clearing. Grayson was behind her, his sword still in his hand. They soon came to the clearing, and she heard Drogan mumble a curse as he walked from the trees. Serena bent down and picked up a silver fragment. "What is this?"

"A piece of his sword," Drogan said as he turned toward her. "It's what cut your arm."

She raised her gaze to him. "How did you manage to shatter his sword?"

His smile melted her heart. "It wasn't I, my Serena, but you that did it."

"Me?" She was stunned by his words.

He withdrew the amulet she had given him. The beautiful long, narrow pendant now had a large dent in the center. "

"I don't understand," she said as she fingered the amulet.

"When he plunged his sword, he hit the amulet and not me."

She shook her head, confused how a simple amulet had saved Drogan.

"It's because it was blessed in the church."

Serena and Drogan lifted their heads to find a man stepping from the woods, his golden blond hair well past his shoulders. She knew him. It was the same man she had seen in the woods.

"I don't know if it was blessed or not," she said.

His golden head lowered just a bit. "It's the only explanation, since it's the one thing that could have stopped Nigel."

Drogan stared at his friend, not recognizing the man that stood before him. The shell was Cade, but inside...inside was something dark, dangerous, and fearsome.

"Why are you here?" Drogan asked.

Cade lifted on shoulder in a shrug. "I knew his plans, and I knew you wouldn't listen to me, so I went to Hawthorne and waited."

"For what?" Serena asked. "Are you the one that attacked Gerard?"

"Nay," Cade answered as he shifted his gaze to her. "I knew you would leave, and I followed to keep you safe."

Drogan narrowed his eyes and recalled the many times of having the feeling that someone watched him. "It was you I saw at the river with the wolves."

Cade barely nodded his head. "I managed to keep him away from Gerard and Maris, but he picked up your trail before I could do anything."

"Thank you," Drogan said. "For then and last night. I wish you'd let me know you were here. I thought I was fighting you."

To Drogan's surprise, Cade said not a word. Serena crept closer to Drogan, and he put his arm around her.

"Why did you take Nigel's body?" Drogan asked.

Cade shook his head. "I didn't."

Drogan wiped a hand down his face. "Cade, don't lie. There's no need. I just want this over with."

"But it's not," Serena said. "Far from it, Drogan."

Drogan looked from Serena to Cade. "What is going on?"

"I know how well you fight," Cade said. "Years ago, you could have taken him easily. Don't you wonder why you had such a hard time of it last night?"

Drogan shrugged. "He landed some good punches, though I never knew him to be that strong."

"Because he isn't," Serena said. "That thing you fought wasn't human."

There was a groan behind him, and Drogan saw Grayson leaning against a tree with his arms crossed over his chest.

"Groan all you want, Grayson," Serena said, "but there will come a time that you will have to believe."

"Doubtful," Grayson said.

"I used to not believe either," Drogan said. "Not until I met my first witch."

Grayson pushed away from the tree. "Witch? There aren't any witches."

Drogan decided to let that go for now. "All right. Then what was he?"

"He sold his soul."

Drogan glanced at Serena to see her nodding her head in agreement.

"To Satan," she confirmed. "How could you not realize it when you were fighting him?"

Drogan shrugged and had the urge to roll his eyes. "It isn't something I normally look for."

"At any rate, he's gone," Cade said and turned to go back into the forest.

"Wait," Drogan called, stopping him. "What do you mean gone?"

"He's not dead," Cade explained. "He'll wait for another opportunity to strike, except this time it'll be without warning."

"And Gerard and Maris?"

Cade looked to the castle. "He'll come for you and me first. He thinks Gerard will be an easy target and will save him for last."

"How do you know this?"

Cade took a deep breath and turned his ice blue eyes to Drogan. "You don't want to know the answer to that."

Maybe he didn't, Drogan decided after seeing the look in Cade's eyes. "Now that you are here, come back to Wolfglynn. It's been a long time since I've seen you, too long in fact."

Cade once again looked to the castle. "I can't," was the only thing he said before he walked into the trees.

Drogan hurried after him, but like the shadow he always was, Cade seemed to disappear in the thick foliage.

"You'll see him again," Serena said as she walked up to him and took his hand.

"He's changed."

"Everyone changes," Grayson said as he joined them.

Drogan nodded, and they walked toward the castle. Just before they left the woods, Drogan heard something off to his right and turned to see a wolf trotting with him. He smiled and nodded to the wolf, but when they reached the edge of the forest, the wolf stayed.

When he faced the castle, he found Serena watching him with a smile on her face.

"Are you staying?"

She was quiet so long, he was afraid she wouldn't answer.

Then she said, "I don't think I could leave if I wanted to." She stopped and turned to him. "I gave my heart to you, Drogan, when I swore I wouldn't."

He cupped her face and kissed her. "Will you stay as my wife?"

"I don't think I could bear that," she said and backed away, but he held onto her.

"Why? Because of the curse?"

She nodded.

"What if I swear I won't ever leave you?"

Serena shook her head and gazed at Wolfglynn, the sun shining high overhead. She loved it here and never wished to leave, but she knew all things had to come to an end. The only way she would ever be content was to realize from the beginning that she would lose him one day.

"Swearing will do no good," she answered. "There isn't anything you can do that will appease me."

"So there isn't any way I can make you my wife?"

She mulled that over a moment. She didn't want their child to grow up a bastard. If she would stay and bear his child, why not have it all, even for the briefest of time? Being his wife in the eyes of God and the church would not make the pain hurt more or less?

She answered her call to love. Her decision made, she leaned up on her toes and kissed him. "Aye, Drogan, I'll be your wife."

Epilogue

"*A*re you sure?" Gerard asked Serena for the hundredth time as they stood on the steps of the church.

She smiled and nodded. "I've never been more sure of anything in my life. No matter how long it lasts, it's everything I dreamed of."

"You know you'll always have a place at Hawthorne."

"I know, and I thank you for that."

"All right then," Gerard said and held out his arm. "Your future husband awaits, my lady."

Serena held her breath as the church doors were opened, and she saw Drogan standing with the priest. She couldn't help but smile to see Grayson inside the church. Drogan's commander looked anything but comfortable.

The wedding was over so fast Serena barely recalled it, but it didn't matter. She was Drogan's now.

They walked from the church arm in arm to the great hall where a feast had been prepared. After much congratulating, Drogan pulled her aside for a moment of peace.

He walked her onto the battlements as the sun was setting over the water. She nestled in his arms, a sigh on her sweet lips.

"Happy?" he asked.

"Very much so."

"And you still don't believe that I'll stay?"

She groaned and pulled out of his arms. "It doesn't matter. Please, let it rest."

Drogan wasn't about to let it drop. He would ask her every day for the rest of their lives if he had to, but he would make her understand that he wasn't going to leave.

"They're calling us," Serena said. "We must return."

Drogan followed her back into the castle when he turned to the woods. There, a man stood staring at Wolfglynn.

"Are you sure, my love?"

Serena wanted to bash his head in. "I'm the one carrying the babe. I think I know when I'm about to give birth!" she yelled.

"All right," Drogan said and threw up his hands. "What do you need?"

"She needs me," Francesca said as she strolled into the great hall.

Serena was relieved to see her. When she spotted Drogan rolling his eyes, she kicked him under the table. No sooner had she done that than a contraction hit her, doubling her over. She bit back a groan and struggled to breathe.

"We must get her to a chamber," Francesca said. "The babe will come any moment."

Out of the corner of her eye, she saw Drogan shake his head. "These things take time, Francesca. It'll be hours before our child comes."

Serena giggled then. She didn't know what had come over her. Terrible mood swings had hit her over the past couple of weeks, and Drogan had been so patient, so kind to her when she knew he wanted to throttle her.

"What's so funny?" Drogan asked as he helped her up the stairs.

"I've been in labor all day."

"What?" he thundered.

Serena shrugged. "I didn't wish to sit in the bed for hours, at least not until it was time."

Drogan mumbled something under his breath, but she couldn't pay attention. The contractions were coming faster and harder. She didn't know when she made it to the bed; she just knew she opened her eyes and she was there.

Tears were flowing down her face and everyone thought it was because of the pain, but that wasn't it at all. It was because she knew the dream she had been living for the past nine months was now over.

"Push, Serena," Francesca yelled at her.

Serena bit down and pushed, the contraction so fierce she cried out from it. Holding her hand was Drogan, urging her on and wiping her head all the while.

"I see the head," Francesca said.

Serena fell back against the pillows before another contraction hit.

"I love you," Drogan said. "Remember that. Always."

She opened her mouth to reply when the contraction came. Moments later, Francesca gave a shout and held up the infant.

Serena smiled as Drogan held their baby and the infant wailed, his little arms quivering. To her surprise, Drogan cleaned him and wrapped him in a blanket before he handed her the infant.

She smiled down into her son's face. Her heart swelled with joy. Life was wonderful. At least for a moment in time.

"He's perfect," Drogan said and leaned down to kiss her. "Thank you."

"Thank you," she said.

"Well, what is his name?" Francesca asked.

She and Drogan exchanged looks, for they had talked at length about this.

"Conrad."

One year later...

"Will you ever believe me?" Drogan asked. "The spell is broken."

Serena smiled and watched their young son take his first steps around the bailey. As far as she knew, none of her brethren had kept a husband for longer than a month after a child had been born.

"Maybe so," she agreed.

Drogan turned her to face him. "You're my life, Serena."

"And you're mine," she said.

They watched Grayson help Conrad back on his little feet.

"There you go, little one," Grayson said to Conrad before walking to Serena and Drogan. "I'm leaving."

"Leaving?" Drogan repeated. "To go where?"

"I'm not sure. I've waited long enough though. It's time."

"Thank you for everything." Serena tried to peek into his future, but he blocked her easily. "You'll be missed."

Grayson looked around. "And I'll miss Wolfglynn and its people." His gaze came to rest on Drogan. "Thank you for allowing me to train here."

"I did nothing but realize what a great asset you would be to my knights." Drogan held out his arm to Grayson. "You're welcome to return anytime."

Grayson clasped arms with Drogan. "I'll return. Someday."

After a brief nod to Serena, Grayson mounted his horse and rode out of Wolfglynn's gates.

"I'm going to miss him," Drogan said as Grayson rode away.

Serena turned her gaze toward the isle—Phineas' isle—and thought about Francesca and the other *bana-bhuidseach*.

Aye, the curse was broken.

For her.

THE END

* * *

Thank you for reading SHADOW MAGIC.
I hope you loved the story as much as I loved writing it. Next in the Sisters of Magic trilogy is ECHOES OF MAGIC.

BUY ECHOES OF MAGIC NOW
at www.DonnaGrant.com

* * *

To find out when new books release
SIGN UP FOR MY NEWSLETTER today at
https://www.tinyurl.com/DonnaGrantNews

Join my Facebook group, Donna Grant Groupies, for exclusive giveaways and sneak peeks of future books.
https://www.facebook.com/groups/DGGroupies

* * *

Keep reading for an peek of ECHOES OF MAGIC...

SISTERS OF MAGIC

Echoes
of
Magic

DONNA GRANT

NEW YORK TIMES BESTSELLING AUTHOR

ECHOES OF MAGIC

SISTERS OF MAGIC, BOOK 2

Hiding a secret so awful that his only hope for survival is to remain hidden, Grayson has lived most of his life pretending to be someone he isn't. After years serving as a commander to his lord and friend, Grayson can no longer hold back the past. He leaves in search of answers only to find evil awaits him. Until he discovers an achingly beautiful woman who stirs his deepest passions and all-consuming need.

Adrianna knows what her future holds for her as a witch - loneliness and heartache. She has accepted that. Until she discovers Grayson near death in the forest. Saving him is her only choice, and even as she falls deeper into the attraction surrounding them, can her magic be enough to stop Fate or the evil that awaits them.

An Excerpt of the next Sisters of Magic Book

ECHOES OF MAGIC

Summer 1127
Western England, near the coast

*A*drianna stretched her neck and flexed hands that had gripped the reins for far too long. When the Roma she'd traveled with for the past three years halted for a rest, she gladly hopped down from the seat of her wagon.

The stretch of road they'd journeyed was narrow and surrounded by woods. She loved wandering with the Roma but, for the past week, she couldn't shake the feeling something was wrong. Or was about to go wrong.

No amount of magic had given her a clue, either.

As a *bana-bhuidseach*, a witch, she had spent her time trying to decipher just what was out of alignment. Each *bana-bhuidseach* had a special gift, and hers was seeing the future.

Adrianna was many things, but she wasn't courageous

enough to look into her own future. Not when her kind was cursed and slowly fading into legend. As far as she knew, there was only one other *bana-bhuidseach*. Where once they covered all of Britain, soon no more would see the beautiful land.

The *bana-bhuidseach* had been around for so long that none remembered their true origins, though some texts claimed they hailed from an ancient land of sand and sun.

Adrianna pushed a stray hair behind her ear and moved into the forest. She leaned against a tree and let the beauty and nature of the area soak into her. The need to be alone had driven her into the trees, but it would also help to calm her and the constant fear that something...evil...was about to descend.

The other *bana-bhuidseach* she had met, Serena, had been followed by a man drenched in evil. Ever since, Adrianna had sensed a growing malevolence throughout the land.

Her hands traveled down the elm tree, the bark scratching her palms. She sighed and began to turn back to her wagon when she caught a glimpse of something in the underbrush. Adrianna leaned down and peered through the ferns to find a bloodied hand.

With her heart hammering in her chest, she pushed aside the underbrush and discovered a man lying on his side. His long black hair covered his face and was matted with leaves, blood, and mud. By the look of the fine material of his tunic, he was a nobleman who had been ambushed most likely by a roving band of outlaws.

She sighed at the loss of life and began to rise to her feet when a moan stopped her.

"By the saints," she murmured and gently pushed his hair from his face.

With her finger beneath his nose she felt his slow, shallow breathing. If she hurried, and his injuries weren't too extensive, she might be able to save him.

"Milosh! Yoska," she called.

As tenderly she could, she turned the man onto his back. Blood had pooled beneath him and stained his light blue tunic. She saw no weapons, no jewelry.

"Drina!" Milosh shouted.

Adrianna lifted her head when she heard the Roma leader call out the pet name he had given her. "Over here."

When the tall Romanian burst through the trees, his brother, Yoska, was right behind him. The men had the same black hair, dark eyes, and tall, rangy build. They had welcomed her into their family when she found them, never asking questions of her past. For that, she would be forever grateful.

Yoska said something in Romanian that made Milosh nod absently.

"Please help me get him back to my cart," Adrianna said. "He's wounded, but alive."

"And soon to die," Milosh said.

"Please. I cannot just leave him."

The two brothers glanced at each other before they bent down and carried the man toward her cart. He groaned as soon as they lifted him, his head lolling to the side. Adrianna winced and hurried ahead of the brothers to make room for her new patient.

She quickly moved things out of the way and cleared the bed. Then she began to tear one of her old gowns to use as bandages.

"Strip his tunic," she ordered the brothers as she dug through her herbs.

All *bana-bhuidseach* were able to heal, but only a few had the true gift and were able to heal others without the addition of herbs or magic.

She turned just as Milosh lowered the man, now bare-chested, to the bed. For a moment, Adrianna couldn't move. The man was a giant, most likely larger than even Milosh. His body was corded with muscles, and even unconscious he emanated power and stealth.

Danger.

"Drina?"

She jerked and tore her gaze from the man. "Thank you," she murmured.

"You're going to need help," the leader said as he glanced at the warrior. "He's a big man and, even wounded, he'll be strong."

Yoska stepped near her. "I'll stay."

Milosh nodded and jumped from the cart. "I'll have one of the other men drive you."

Adrianna raised her hand to let him know she'd heard, but

her attention was on her patient. "Yoska, can you roll him to his side?"

The big Romanian pushed the warrior toward the side of the cart, exposing his back and the wound to Adrianna. She cursed under her breath and hurriedly wiped away the dried blood. "It's an arrow."

"It's in deep. By the looks of it, the arrow was cut off."

Adrianna paused. "He couldn't have done that. Not where the arrow penetrated him."

"Nay. Most likely one of his attackers sliced it off while taking a swing at him."

"However it happened matters little now. We need to get it out. Already a fever has taken root."

Yoska's lips flattened at her words. "Hold him."

She crawled onto the bed and gripped the man's arms in a vain effort to keep him down. With one swing of his thick arm, he could send her flying off the bed. She found herself gazing into a face that, even covered in dirt, couldn't hide the ruggedly handsome hallowed cheeks, strong jaw and chin, and wide mouth.

He murmured something when Yoska gripped the edge of the arrow.

"Make it quick," she told the Romanian. The last thing she wanted was to try and take the arrow out while traveling over the rough roads.

Yoska shook his head. "I don't like where it's at, Drina. We could do more damage by removing it."

"We don't have a choice. I cannot heal him unless it's gone. Please, Yoska."

The big man gave a single nod of his head to prepare her before he reached down and jerked the arrow out. The warrior stiffened before he bellowed in pain, his hands painfully gripping her arms. When Adrianna looked down, she saw eyes the color of silver winged with thick, black lashes staring at her a moment before he fell back unconscious.

For a moment, she couldn't move, couldn't think beyond the man she held.

"I don't think it was mere thieves after him, Drina."

She turned to Yoska and the arrowhead he held up for her view. The arrowhead was unlike anything she had seen before. The tip was thin, the sides jagged, causing it to go deep and tear flesh, bone, and organs when it was removed. She was amazed they had managed to get it out of the warrior, but it explained his immense pain when they did.

"Hold him," she bade Yoska as she scooted from the bed to examine the arrowhead herself.

The metal was different, thinner, almost as if it were made of magic. It oozed evil, making her skin crawl. She touched the tip of the arrow, and blood instantly beaded on her finger.

"Careful, Drina." Yoska's voice was low and filled with trepidation.

She set aside the arrow and licked her lips. She wanted to toss the arrow from her cart, but decided against it as her wagon lurched into motion. There might be a need for it later.

For the next few hours, she cleaned and bandaged the warrior's wound, trying to ignore the hard body and warm skin beneath her fingers. Each time she glanced at his face, she expected his unusual silver gaze to be on her and, when it wasn't, she found herself disappointed.

When she was done, she sighed and motioned Yoska to lower the man gently to his back. Adrianna wrung out another strip of bandages from the bowl and wiped the dirt and blood from the man's face.

"I've a bad feeling," Yoska murmured. "This man was supposed to die. That much is clear. Whoever is after him will return to finish the job."

She glanced at her friend over her shoulder. "I also have a bad feeling, but I refuse to leave a man to die when I can save him."

"This has to do with the group we met last year, doesn't it? The one that had the woman like you, the witch?"

"Serena. Aye, I believe it does. The arrow smells of the same evil that followed Serena and Drogan."

"Was this man with Lady Serena's group?"

"Nay."

"You're sure?"

She was positive. There was no way she could have missed a man so imposing and powerful...and good-looking. "I'm sure."

"I'll report to Milosh. He'll want to know how the man fares."

Before she could respond, the Romanian was gone from

the slow-moving cart. Now that she was alone, she could look her fill at her patient. It had been quite awhile since a man had caught her attention. Though she wasn't sure if it was because he was wounded or because she sensed something else in him, something powerful yet to be unleashed, she found she couldn't keep her hands from him.

She smoothed her hand down his sculpted chest and over the ridges and valleys of his abdomen corded with sinew. It had been a long time since she'd given her body to someone, and she had never thought to find another who would tempt her so, not when the curse had already touched her.

The man stirred, mumbling in his sleep and tossing his head. The fever's hold on him was strong.

"Shh," she whispered near his ear while stroking his face. "Rest easy. You're safe."

Her words soothed him after a moment, and he settled once more into a deep, even sleep. As imposing as he was in sleep, she couldn't imagine the warrior he was awake. And she could hardly wait to find out.

It gave her pause, her sudden and unstoppable interest in her patient. It was almost enough to make her throw caution to the wind and give into the desires awakening in her body just by looking at him. But with the longing came the reminder of what she was, of what kept her from happiness.

The curse.

While he dreamed, Adrianna's thoughts turned to the curse and her people.

Every *bana-bhuidseach* was destined to feel the curse.

Since only women held the gifts of their people, it was the women who were fated to fall in love with a man who would leave them as soon as a child was born.

Many *bana-bhuidseach* let the anger and resentment turn their gifts to hate, souring everything around them until finally death took them, their magic lost to the wind.

The women were all cautioned to accept their fate if they gave in to the desires of men for, once you gave in, there was no turning back.

Adrianna hadn't wanted to live her life alone, never having a child or knowing any kind of joy. She thought it would be worth the pain, worth being alone for the rest of her days.

Until she lost both her lover and her child.

ABOUT THE AUTHOR

New York Times and *USA Today* bestselling author Donna Grant® has been praised for her "totally addictive" and "unique and sensual" stories.

She's written more than one hundred novels spanning multiple genres of romance including the bestselling Dragon Kings® series that features a thrilling combination of Druids, Fae, and immortal Highlanders who are dark, dangerous, and irresistible. She lives in Texas with her dog and a cat.

www.DonnaGrant.com
www.MotherofDragonsBooks.com

facebook.com/AuthorDonnaGrant
instagram.com/dgauthor
bookbub.com/authors/donna-grant
goodreads.com/donna_grant
pinterest.com/donnagrant1